The ANCIENT'S GIFT

HUGH A. FLOWERS

Cover Design – C.A. Simonson

Publishing Coordinator – Sharon Kizziah-Holmes

Paperback-Press
an imprint of A & S Publishing
A & S Holmes, Inc.

ISBN -13: 978-1-945669-76-7

CHAPTER 1

Lieutenant Junior Grade (jg) Adam Lundberg Bloodworth awoke to the Battle Stations klaxons blaring sound. His engrained reaction was to hurriedly don his ship suit and shoes and run to his duty station in the Weapons Section. Upon his arrival at Laser Cannon Starboard/6 he quickly surveyed the situation and noted that the posted status screen showed that there were 160 incoming missiles heading toward their fleet of one Battleship and eighteen Heavy Battle Cruisers.

The last two of his crew, Petty Officer's Stewart Linski and Nicole Hedrick, soon joined him at his duty station. He understood PO Hedrick's arrival time because her quarters were the furthest from her duty station; however, PO Linski was always one of the last crewmen to arrive at his station even though his quarters is the closest.

"PO Linski what's your excuse this time?"

"Sorry Sir! I couldn't find my shoes. Somebody must have moved them."

"Never mind that for now, the status screen shows eighty bogies incoming from the Starboard side and another eighty are attacking the majority of the Fleet on the Hulk's Port side. In about twenty minutes they'll be in range of our Lasers! PO Hedrick your practice test scores are the team's best, so get in the hot seat, and PO Linski you'll act as her spotter. You other two make sure the LC doesn't overheat, so keep it cool!"

Adam continued watching the scan screen as the bright pips came ever closer toward the Hulk. Finally, the pips turned red as they crossed the 50,000-mile range of the Laser Cannons and he ordered, "Fire, fire, fire!"

The screen showed the short bright laser trail as it left the ship and hit a missile, then another hit, too fast to even acknowledge as the gunner shifted from target to target, and sometimes the explosion of the incoming missile took out more of its kin. There were seven other laser positions on the Starboard side and together they eliminated all the missiles before they were within 10,000 miles of their ship. The screen showed that the Port side was clear of enemy missiles as well.

Lieutenant Bloodworth read the scan from the machine and smiled slightly, "PO Hedrick you got twelve of the missiles. Well done! The best the other Starboard Lasers gunners killed was eight; your beer tonight is free, paid for by the other starboard gunners."

The smile on Nicole's face was more from the release of tension, than from her winning free beer. However, when her crew crowded around her slapping her on the back she got into the celebration.

Later after shift, Bloodworth showed up at the crews bar to make sure everyone got into the spirit of the celebration before leaving and checking in at the Ship's hospital. Doctor Lucy Lundberg Hendricks looked up at her nephew when he arrived.

"What's up Adam?"

"Just checking in, did we have any casualties from that ambush?"

"No, but one of our Battle Cruisers on the Port side took a hit - three dead and eight injured. We will get their injured when things settle."

"How is Hope doing? This is her second week as your assistant nurse and Mom's afraid she's too young at sixteen to do this kind of work."

"The Captain is overprotective of her youngest. You remember how she was with you? Now look at you, a Lieutenant (jg) at only twenty."

"Yeah, but my goal is to get a position on the Bridge. That's where I can see the big picture, not down in the Laser Section. How's your husband, Lt. Commander Hendricks getting along since he took over as Assistant Weapons Officer? I hear Commander Alice Beeker is a bear to work under."

"Poor Kory's putting in a lot of hours since he took over the position, but it's starting to get better. I think I've talked him into starting our own family soon and I've got my fingers crossed."

* * *

Fleet Admiral Eric Bloodworth and his wife, Captain Hanna Bloodworth, were in his Flag office aboard the (United Earth Ship) UES Hulk drinking coffee and talking about their last engagement with their alien enemy, the Xones. "Hanna, the Xones are starting to get more innovative. I wonder who's calling the shots for them now?"

"I know what you mean Eric. Placing standalone missile launchers 180,000 miles inside a warp gate is definitely new. Our first indication was their launch of missiles! I wonder how the platforms knew when to fire?"

"They must have had a small crew aboard, we were too far away for an automated proximity alert to work. Whatever pushed their fire button actually worked to our advantage. If the fleet had been closer when they fired we would have suffered much more damage."

Hanna nodded her head in agreement, "I checked with the Assistant DH of the Laser Section and Adam's team destroyed more missiles than any of the other Starboard gunners. He apparently started a competition among the Starboard laser gunners for free beer to the one with the most kills, paid for by the losing gunners."

Eric chuckled, "Who won?"

"PO3 Nicole Hedrick and apparently it was her first time as a gunner. Do you think we should give her some special recognition, like a step-up promotion?"

"Why not ask Adam? He knows the situation better than anyone."

Hanna nodded her head, "Comm to Lieutenant Bloodworth, report to the Captain in the Flag Admirals Office ASAP."

Fifteen minutes later a breathless Adam arrived, "Ma'am, Lieutenant Bloodworth reporting as ordered."

Hanna Bloodworth looked at her son with a smile before saying, "As you were. Come sit with us as we have a question about one of your crew you could help us with."

After they were all settled, she looked at her oldest child with love and respect at how quickly he was progressing through the ranks. Coming to the point of their meeting she asked, "The top Laser Cannon scorer was from your section. PO Hedrick's kill score was exceptional and I want your opinion if this justifies an action from me, such as a promotion or something less?"

"She was just promoted to PO3 and I've already made a notation in her performance file that she has performed exceptionally in her new duties as a Laser Gunner. Her fellow gunners on the starboard side have honored her for having the highest scores. Anything more at this time does not appear to be warranted."

"Very good, I'll leave it in your hands then. Another matter has come up; the Heavy Cruiser that suffered damage is Captain Fieldspire's ship, Aqua's Flagship the Trojan Horse. She requested a review of her ships laser training methods, and since your team scored highest, I think the proper political move would be to send a low ranking officer from the Hulk to check it out."

"What if I find something bad over there?"

"Check with me before reporting to Captain Fieldspire."

"When do I leave and do I go alone?"

"Do you think taking a member from your team will provide any benefit?"

"I've got a team member that needs a little encouragement that I might be able to provide on an alien ship."

Hanna looked at her son questioningly, but seeing the gleam in his eyes she knew he had a plan. "Very well, take whomever of your crew and pack for a three-day stay leaving from Shuttle Bay One at 10:00 hours."

After Adam left, his father asked, "What do you think he's planning?"

Hanna gave her husband a crooked smile, "I'd say he's going to use a little blackmail to get better performance out of one of his crew."

* * *

Adam returned to his duty station and pulled PO Stewart Linski aside. "PO you're going with me to one of the Aqua Battle Cruisers to check out their training methods for their Laser Cannons. Pack for three days and we leave from Shuttle Bay One at 10:00 hours."

At Adams announcement, Linski's face turned white, but he responded, "Yes Sir. I'll meet you there."

Not knowing what to expect from the food served aboard the Aqua ship Adam hurried to the Officers Mess for breakfast, and then to his quarters to pack. Two hours later he was waiting in Shuttle Bay One for Linski's arrival. Two minutes before 10:00 hours he arrived at a dead run and stopped next to Adam, who gave him the evil eye.

The flight to the Trojan Horse took twenty minutes and Adam asked the shuttle pilot to circle the Cruiser looking for the extent of the damage caused by the enemy missile. The Xones missile missed the Cruisers missile tubes and hit high in the port bow section.

After landing in the Trojan Horses' shuttle bay, the two were met by a female Lieutenant, who they saluted before she escorted them inside the ship. "My name is Lieutenant Karrie Fieldspire Becker and I'm the Assistant DH for the Laser Section. Mother is busting my ass for the missile hit on her ship. However, if you find anything we haven't been doing correctly please let me know. Now, who are you Lieutenant?"

He had been feeling uneasy from the moment of his meeting with Lt. Becker and as he shook her hand it was almost like touching an electrical circuit as his body stiffened. He recovered enough to reply, "My name is Adam Lundberg Bloodworth and I was sent by my mother as a political move to not cause any waves, if possible. This rating is Petty Officer Stewart Linski who is part of my crew on Laser Cannon Starboard6."

When Adam withdrew his hand from hers he immediately felt a sense of loss.

* * *

Karrie had a similar experience, but it was overpowered by her knowledge of who he was. Her eyes got big as he began speaking, but then she started smiling as the humor of the situation became evident. "Adam, I've heard about you and your sister…Hope?"

At his nod, she continued, "We all need to get together and plot our revenge against our parents for putting us through this torture."

Adam asked, "Are you an only child?"

"Yes, I think that makes it worse for me. At least you have your sister, I'm all alone."

Adam wanted to change the conversation away from family as he said, "Karrie, you have four lasers on each side of the Battle Cruiser to protect against missiles. Were you overwhelmed?"

"Yes, but it was mostly because we lost one of our lasers due to a malfunction."

"What happened?"

"The laser that failed recently was shut down to replace a part, which I think failed after its first shot during the attack."

"You've had the part tested?"

"Yes, but I can't find anything wrong with it."

Adam turned to Linski. "PO Linski, didn't you have a similar problem last month?"

"Sir, yes sir. One of the connecters had gunk on it. I used some solvent on it and it worked fine after that."

"Karrie, take us to the broken laser and have someone bring the suspect part to us."

Ten minutes later they were standing next to the laser, waiting on the part to arrive. Lieutenant Becker touched Adam's arm, "It's odd we're both working the Laser Section. It's almost like fate."

Adam looked at her with a raised eyebrow, "Perhaps, but I feel the tender fingers of our mothers in my being here now."

She looked at him in surprise for a moment before inhaling a deep breath, "Crap! You're right. But, what's their purpose?"

He smiled at her and winked, "Well, we're both attractive and unmated, maybe that's it?"

She returned his look with wide surprised eyes, "Noo! She wouldn't do that…yes she would if she thought my options here on the Trojan were lacking. What about you? Do you have a girlfriend?"

He grinned at her question. "Yes, but it's not serious, I think she's more interested in my potential than me as a mate. How about you? You're a beautiful woman, much like your mother. Dad told me that when your mother and father met it was love at first sight for both of them."

Karrie smiled slightly, "Yes, they still love each other very much, it's a little embarrassing sometimes when they stare at each other across a room with such love in their eyes."

They were interrupted when a rating arrived with the part in hand. Lieutenant Becker took the part and handed it to PO Linski, who turned it over in his hands checking each connection.

"Sir, this looks just like the one we had."

"Okay, show it to Lieutenant Becker and then clean it. I'm curious if this is all that's wrong with the Laser."

The officers watched as the ratings showed others what the problem was and then supervised as they reinstalled the part. Becker then ran tests to ensure the laser was in working order before giving Adam a crooked smile. "Well, that seems to have taken care of that problem. What are we going to do about the other?"

Adam winked at Karrie. "Why don't you have one of your ratings escort mine to lunch while we discuss it at your Officers Mess?"

She turned to one of her female ratings. "PO Cercea, escort PO Linski to the Crew Mess and then show him around until we page him."

"Yes ma'am, PO Linski follow me and we'll get something to eat."

When they were alone Karrie smiled at Adam. "Well, that takes care of him, have you eaten Aqua food before?"

"Every time we re-provision at Aqua."

"Oh, that's the raw food. We cook it different than your cooks do. Who knows, you might like it."

When they were seated, he asked, "Do you have anything like a beef steak?"

She gave him a blank look. "Do you mean animal flesh like from what you call a cow?"

He started to smile, but then pretended to be disappointed when she made a motion like gagging. "We don't eat animal flesh. Let's try something else. I'll order you a sampling of the foods I enjoy and you can try them to see if you like any of them."

When Karrie's meal arrived she looked at it with relish. She pointed at one of the foods, "This is called candied swordtail."

He took a small portion and gingerly placed it in his mouth, happily savoring its sweet taste. "Hey, that's good! What's next?"

They continued this procedure until he had four different dishes he liked, which he then ordered. Later, after they finished the meal they sat and stared at each other memorizing the details of the others face, body, and movements. Adam eventually realized what he was doing and grabbed her hand while saying anxiously, "Karrie, I don't know what's come over me? I have this attraction toward you that has been growing since I first met you and now I suddenly ache to be with you and I feel this need to touch you!" He said while squeezing her hand.

Karrie's body jerked slightly as if her body felt a connection when he touched her hand. She shuddered while grasping his hand as if it was a lifeline and nodded her head. "I feel the same way as you. I can't believe it! We seem to be affected the same way my parents were when they first met. I'll comm Mother and ask to talk with her ASAP."

Taking out her handheld she spoke, "Comm to Captain Becker from Lieutenant Becker. I need a personal meeting with you ASAP."

Thirty seconds later came a reply; "Meet me in my quarters at 13:00 hours."

Adam raised his eyebrows at her. "That was fast! You have twenty minutes to get there."

"Like hell, you're coming with me. Let's go!"

They had three minutes to spare when they arrived at the Captains Stateroom. Karrie straightened her uniform and took a deep breath before pushing the buzzer. The Captain opened the door and appeared to be surprised when she caught sight of Adam standing close while holding her daughters hand. Captain Becker stared at Adam for a moment before giving him a slow smile.

"Come in Karrie and Adam. What can I do for you?"

After they each found a seat, Karrie spoke. "Lieutenant

Bloodworth came over this morning to determine what was wrong with the laser that failed. He and the rating he brought with him fixed the problem and I've left instructions to check all our spare laser parts for similar problems. During this short time we have developed feelings for each other and want to be assigned on the same ship so we can determine how serious these feelings are."

Captain Becker turned her attention to Adam. "This was quick, even quicker than with her father and I. Adam, are you as emotionally aroused as my daughter appears to be?"

"We both have an emotional connection that's impossible to ignore. I look at her and become lost in her eyes, and she appears to have the same response to me."

"What you haven't said is that you both hurt when you are separated from each other. Is this true?"

Karrie looked at her Mother and smiled. "This is how you feel about Dad?"

"Yes, and how he feels about me. This is now twice this has happened between our races. I have a feeling we will see it occurring again as our two races interact with each other. I'll contact Captain Bloodworth and we'll arrange something for you two. I feel both happy and sorry for you two as you begin your relationship."

CHAPTER 2

Captain Hanna Lundberg Bloodworth handed the comm she just received from Captain Becker to her husband, Fleet Admiral Eric Bloodworth, who took a surprised intake of breath as he read the comm. He frowned as he asked, "Honey, you know how close the Becker's are to each other. If Adam and Karrie are like them, then they need to stay together! Where do you want them, here or on the Trojan Horse?"

"Here of course! We have a bigger ship and have more opportunities for each of them. Oh, my heart aches for them. I wanted this relationship to happen, but not to the extent it's become. I guess the best place for her is the port side Laser Section. That way they have separation of duties, yet are close to each other."

"What about Hope? It seems both our children are about to leave their nest. She wants to be a doctor like your sister, Lucy."

"When we return to Earth she will have to leave the ship to finish college and begin Medical School on Star Fleet's dime, like Lucy did."

"Have the two of you settled on which schools she's going to attend?" Eric said.

"Lucy went to the Medical College in Berlin, but Hope is

leaning toward the Johns Hopkins School of Medicine in Baltimore, Maryland. She wants to concentrate her training in the treatment of traumatic injuries and limb replacement; however, she still doesn't know which University to attend to finish her pre-med degree."

"Well, she has at least another year before we're back in Earth orbit and the last I heard she was in her third year of college computer courses. I wonder if John Hopkins will allow her to test out to enter their medical school?"

Hanna looked thoughtful before saying, "Honey, that's something I'll look into when we get back to Earth. Now, I better contact Mae and get Karrie transferred to the Hulk."

* * *

Ten hours later Lieutenants Adam Bloodworth and Karrie Becker were aboard a shuttle headed towards the First Fleets Flagship, the Battleship UES Hulk. At Karrie's feet was her kit containing all her possessions. She was still a little dazed and confused by the fact that she was making this change in her life without any second guesses; however, she wasn't harboring any misgivings about following Adam back to his family's Flagship.

Her mother was a hero from Aqua, but the Bloodworths were the ones who brought word of the Xones alien race that was threatening to destroy everything in their path. Her mother helped convince her world to accept the Katz' help in bringing their world into the fight. She hadn't yet met any of the alien Katz, who were thought to be an ancient race that no longer had the stomach for a pro-longed fight with the Xones. They instead tried to find aggressive races to fight their battles. At this time it was Earth and Aquas against the Xones hoard.

* * *

The Aqua Lieutenant returning to the Hulk with them confused PO Linski as he hadn't previously heard of any Aqua personnel serving aboard Earth starships, so he asked, "Lieutenant Becker, if you don't mind me asking, are you coming aboard the Hulk for training?"

Karrie and Adam shared a smile. "No, I'm actually transferring to the Hulk to work in the Laser Section."

That answer only brought several more questions to mind that he had no desire to ask.

When the shuttle was secured inside Shuttle Bay One, they walked toward the waiting Captain Bloodworth.

* * *

After their shuttle arrived aboard the Hulk, they each saluted the flag and asked for and received permission to board from the DO (Duty Officer). Afterward, all but PO Linski followed Captain Bloodworth to her Bridge office.

Captain Bloodworth looked at the two young officers with compassion, "Karrie, I've talked to your mother about your similar emotional situations and understand your need to be near each other. Unless you can think of something better, I'm having you assigned to Port side lasers while Adam is at Starboard side lasers, giving each of you a separation of duties yet close proximity to each other. I'll gladly arrange your wedding when you feel it's appropriate, as it will simplify your room arrangement. Any thoughts or questions?"

Adam's face colored with embarrassment as he spoke, "Mother, we haven't had any alone time and this is hard for both of us, having this strong draw toward each other and unfamiliar need to be near each other. Yet, even without intimate physical contact I know she is my chosen one. Karrie, do you feel this way too?"

She got up from her chair and sat in his lap, giving him a long passionate kiss. When she straightened up he used a finger to wipe a tear from her cheek. Then she hugged him tightly, "Does that answer your question Adam?"

Karrie looked at Hanna and smiled, "Whether we're married or not, we've already given our hearts to the other. We need to share quarters if we're to function properly."

Watching the two together, Hanna's eyes were bright with unshed tears. "Very well, I'll call a Chaplin and you'll be married as soon as your parents get here. Is that satisfactory?"

At their nod, she started making preparations for a wedding.

Three hours later the couple were standing before the ship's

Chaplin saying their vows with their ship families standing with them. Afterward, the newlyweds appeared shaken as if they were not in control of their destiny, but when each side of their families came together to congratulate them they held hands and looked forward to a new beginning.

Captain Bloodworth gave them a three-day pass to move to new married quarters, make the necessary changes at Personnel, and have Karrie draw new uniforms from the Quartermaster. Their first night as a married couple was a passionate discovery for both of them. After their first coupling they realized they were now a shared identity; they were no longer separate individuals, but instead were now a couple. Later, while each was doing separate tasks, they both knew where the other was at all times. The knowledge of each other was always there at a subconscious level.

Lieutenant Karrie Becker Bloodworth was assigned to supervise Laser Cannon Port8. The previous supervisor was routinely transferred to another Duty Section. Karrie reviewed her new crews performance reports and all were experienced except for one new transfer.

After she reviewed her crew in action during a drill, she took each rating aside and reviewed their observed performance. The last rating reviewed was PO Lorie Graham, "You are a recent transfer from Supply, why the change?"

"Ma'am, Supply is boring. I thought manning a laser would make my life more exciting."

"Yes, exciting it is. But it also requires people who are responsible for their actions. The Laser Section directly protects this ship and indirectly the Fleet as a whole. You need to learn not only your position, but also all the others around you in case of battle casualties. If one of your crew is disabled and his duty station is more critical than yours, then you must pull your crewmate aside and keep the laser firing. Do you understand me?"

"Ma'am, yes ma'am!" Graham said as her face lost all of its color."

"Do you still want to transfer to this duty station?"

"No ma'am, Supply is where I belong."

"Very well, return to your previous duty assignment."

She watched Graham leave with a little shake of her head. PO1 Woodruff spoke from behind her, "Ma'am, you did the right thing, she didn't belong here."

Karrie raised an eyebrow at the older rating, "Yes Mr. Woodruff, she might have come around but why waste our time training someone who obviously doesn't fit. The rest of this crew looks good, how did they fare at the last dust off?"

"We came in second for the Port side. Your husband's team came in first on the Starboard side. I think we should start a contest like them, where the gunner with the most kills gets free beer paid by the other gunners."

"I like the idea, it's not so much an incentive, but a way to blow off steam afterwards. I'll check with the other supervisors and try to get it started on the Port side."

CHAPTER 3

Fleet Admiral Bloodworth was taking stock of this voyage since leaving Earth ten months ago. Before he started this voyage he expected to be gone a year Ship Time, or about two years Earth Time. Warp travel time is slower by half as those who are left behind on a planet. This is the reason ship personnel bring their families with them, otherwise, ship personnel would lose years of their children's lives and marriages would fail. Shipboard marriages seemed only logical for those who travel aboard a warp ship.

This voyage has resulted in three pitched battles with the Xones and now this ambush where they have suffered casualties, but all First Fleets ships were still able to travel together. The next gate would take the fleet into their eighth system since leaving Earth and he estimated that they destroyed approximately 280 Xones Cruisers at this point in their cruise. The enemy was increasingly finding and using different tactics in their efforts to slow or end Humanities' advance.

Earth's Second Fleet is advancing on a second front, but is currently in Earth orbit while First Fleet is attacking from the Aqua sector. The Home Fleets of Aqua and Earth are strong, but still the fear of a strong sneak attack against either home worlds keeps one battle fleet at home while the other is attacking.

Two more months should place them into the tenth system, the furthest they have traveled inward on their arm of the Milky Way Galaxy Spiral to date. What they find there will determine future Fleet plans.

He was interrupted in his musing by a comm from his wife, Captain Bloodworth, asking about lunch. He replied, "I'll meet you in our stateroom in twenty minutes, go ahead and order for us."

When he arrived, their Stewart, Jason Mao, greeted him. Their previous Stewart, Yue He, retired after their last cruise and by now they were all used to each other's habits. Eric removed his jacket and Mao helped him into a silk-like robe before joining his wife at the dinning table. He never got tired of gazing at his beautiful wife, even after almost twenty-five ship years together.

Before taking his seat he came over and gave her a kiss, causing her to smile up at him. "What was that for Dear?"

"Because I love you and you look especially beautiful today. Any news on how Adam and Karrie are coping?"

"She appears to be settling in and he's ready to be promoted and reassigned. Where do you think he should go next?"

Eric considered for a moment, "I think he should stay in weapons, say the Missile Section, for another six months before coming to the ships Bridge."

Hanna nodded her head in agreement. "I'll bring Karrie along behind him. Together, they'd make a good team when they're both here with me."

The next day the ship was at Battle Stations as the fleet approached the next warp gate. Three Battle Cruisers cleared out the expected minefield before the gate and a probe was sent through the gate to check what was waiting for them on the other side.

The probes return message torpedo reported that there was a great deal of enemy activity in the tenth solar system. There was a minefield beginning 2,000 miles from the gate, and then two enemy formations of thirty ships each 80,000 miles from the gate and 20,000 miles apart. In addition, there were another two formations of the same size 300,000 miles from the gate and 30,000 miles apart.

Fleet Admiral Bloodworth ordered two Cruisers to clear the

minefield with two salvos of missiles launched through the warp gate, and then stand aside to make way for the Hulk to transit the gate. When the Battleship cleared the gate into the tenth system it immediately orientated itself so that its port side broadside was facing the closest two enemy formations and fired a salvo of forty missiles at the left formation, quickly followed by another salvo at the right formation after spinning the ship to engage the starboard side. It then repeated salvos until 120 missiles were heading toward each enemy formation in three waves.

The Hulk's Laser Cannon crews were watching the approach of three salvos of enemy missiles totaling 900 missiles, which quickly passed the Hulk's Laser Cannons range of 50,000 miles. Suddenly, the space between the Hulk and the two enemy formations became a boiling infernal as the defending lasers hot fire found its targets and the resulting explosions killed other nearby missiles, killing all the first wave. There was a short break and then the next wave of 300 missiles entered the fray and the Laser Cannon fire again turned space into a blazing infernal until those were also destroyed. The Starboard Laser Cannons were becoming overheated, so the Hulk quickly rotated putting its fresh Port side Laser Cannons on the target.

Before the third salvo of 300 missiles was in range of the Hulk's Laser Cannons, its own missiles reached the enemy formations with devastating results. While the Hulks missiles were not as numerous as the Xones, the enemy didn't have the same ability to kill the Hulk's missiles whose first wave of missiles killed ten ships causing mayhem in its defensive formations. The Hulk's second wave killed another forty ships, and the third wave left nothing but debris.

The Hulk's fresh Laser Cannons quickly laid waste to the Xones' third wave of missiles, leaving Fleet Admiral Bloodworth facing the next formations of enemy ships who launched three salvos, totaling 900 missiles toward the Hulk. Since they were 300,000 miles from the gate, both sides had other options than just slugging it out with each other. After launching their missiles, the two enemy formations started moving toward the next gate at 3 gravities (g's), the fastest they were capable.

Both sides were now cutting off the missile thrust before reaching their limit of 100,000 miles. The object was to give the missiles the ability to maneuver by turning the missiles back on when they were approaching their target. Admiral Bloodworth was waiting for the enemy missiles to turn themselves off before he made his countermove.

His science officer said, "Sir, the first wave has turned itself off."

"Very good, now let me know when the third wave does the same."

"Sir, the second wave and now the third wave have shut down their thrusters."

"Thank you Commander, Comm to Captain, initiate Plan X-ray 1."

"Captain to Fleet Admiral, initiating Plan X-ray 1."

The Hulk moved 200,000 miles to the right of its former position. "Comm to Captain, when you are ready after calculating the intercept position of the enemy fleet, please fire three salvos at each group of ships. Also send a message torpedo through the gate to have the fleet join me after those pesky missiles have left the area."

"Captain to Admiral, time of enemy missile arrival is three hours, fifteen minutes. Time to our missile fire is... five minutes. Counting down now... firing missiles now."

After the sixth salvo was on the way, a message torpedo was sent back through the gate recalling the remainder of the fleet after the incoming missiles passed. Four hours later all the fleet were in formation behind the UES Hulk as they headed toward the next gate at a sedate 2g's.

Six hours later they passed the debris field of the second enemy fleet where none of the enemy ships survived their encounter with the Hulk's missiles. Admiral Bloodworth elected to refuel the fleet's reaction mass from a nearby Gas Giant before checking out the eleventh system.

Later, after finding no active ships from their scan of the next system, Fleet Admiral Bloodworth informed the fleet that they were returning to Aqua and then Earth. Ten months later they were back in orbit around Aqua, where they found Second Fleet waiting on them.

Fleet Admiral Bloodworth called for a Dinning conference between heads of First and Second Fleet and the Aqua Navy onboard the UES Hulk at 18:00 hours, in about three hours. The first thing Admiral Bloodworth noted when First Fleet made orbit was the presence of two Battleships, Aqua's Navy must have finally received its promised Battleship.

When everyone arrived they held an informal gathering exchanging family news before sitting down for dinner, which passed quickly as they were all anxious to get to the war news. Admiral Vlad Pavlova of the Second Fleet was given the floor as he had just arrived from Earth.

"Ladies and Gentlemen, the war against the Xones is progressing well from Earth. Since we last met about two years ago, Second Fleet has met the enemy in nine battles resulting in enemy losses of 620 ships, and only small battle damage and six casualties for Second Fleet. Earth's Home Fleet has been increased to one Battleship, ten Heavy Battle Cruisers, and twenty Cruisers; Star Fleet Headquarters now considers Earths Solar System sufficiently protected save an all-out Xones attack. In addition, we have brought Aqua a Battleship to add to its Battle Fleet."

Captain Mae Fieldspire stood, "I want to thank Admiral Pavlova and Earth for the gift of our first Battleship. I checked with our shipyards before this meeting and our first home constructed Battleship will be ready in about three months. I intend to use it as defense rather than offense and will add it to our Home Fleet. Once it has been fully crewed and trained our Home World will finally be adequately protected."

Fleet Admiral Bloodworth stood and smiled at the officers gathered, "We have become more than just fellow officers, many are now related by marriage which brings its own problems and joy. Our son, Adam Lundberg Bloodworth, and Admiral Becker and Captain Fieldspire's daughter Karrie Fieldspire Becker, are now married and serving aboard the Hulk. We have endured five battles with the Xones and destroyed about 400 ships. Recently, we were ambushed by two standalone missile arrays where we lost three crewmen and suffered some damage to one ship. This is a new tactic that will be hard to guard against; our first warning was the launch of missiles against the fleet. We were lucky they didn't launch when we were closer to their arrays."

Before the First Fleet departed Aqua orbit, Karrie visited with her parents knowing that it would be about two years before she returned to Aqua, and when she left the Trojan Horse there were tears shed by mother and daughter.

Almost four months later the First Fleet was back in Earth orbit after more than two years ship time – four years Earth time. The Bloodworth family was anxious to spend time on Earth visiting relatives and after so long a time they felt a need to mingle with other Earth bound humans to reconnect with their home world.

Hanna contacted the Johns Hopkins School of Medicine and asked if a family member of Fleet Admiral Eric Bloodworth could test out for admission to its medical school. She soon received a comm from the schools Admission Director, Dr. Jessica Burns.

"Captain Bloodworth, what pre-med school has your daughter attended?"

"Hope Lundberg Bloodworths entire education has been through computer classes. She's earned sufficient credits to graduate from any four-year college with a pre-med major."

"I see…how old is she?"

"Dr. Burns are you familiar with the warp time effect on aging for starship humans?"

"No, could you explain?"

"While aboard a starship we go by ship time, which is different from the time on Earth. While in orbit we age at the rate as those on the ground; however, once we go through a warp gate we age at a slower rate. If we spend the majority of our time in warp space while on a voyage, when we return to Earth we will have aged only about half as much as those on the ground. Getting back to how old Hope is – she is seventeen years old by ship time and about thirty-two by Earth time. When you see and talk to her she appears to be a typical seventeen year old girl."

"I believe I see a problem looming for all applicants from starships. I'll discuss this with the Board and get back with you soon."

"Think you Doctor, I hope to hear from you soon."

Two days later, Captain Bloodworth received a return comm from Dr. Burns, "Captain Bloodworth, after consultation with the Board we came to the conclusion that out of fairness any applicant from a starship be allowed to test out rather than attend classes at a pre-med school. The next term for freshman students is in three months. She may come here within the next two months to take her tests."

"Dr. Burns, I have another question, my daughter will be coming as a uniformed officer of Star Fleet when she attends classes. Is this going to be a problem?"

"No, we have had uniformed officers before. There should be no problem."

"Very well, I would like to make an appointment for her tests at this time. We have been away from Earth for two years and would very much like to visit relatives."

"Very well, let me check my calendar; how about two weeks from tomorrow. That would be Monday, March 15; say Nine A.M. at our campus in Baltimore, Maryland?"

"That would be fine, how long will the test take?"

"Three days, plus one day for lab."

"What does lab consist of?"

"Just the preliminary lab work she should have encountered while attending college."

"Doctor, remember she has never been exposed to that doing computer classes."

"Yes, I realize that but it doesn't count high in the final grade."

"Very well, we will be there at the appointed time. Do you mind if we bring the press with us? It would be great PR for Star Fleet and your school."

There was silence for a few moments before she responded, "Yes, I agree, we look forward to seeing you."

Captain Bloodworth thought about the lab portion of the test before calling her sister, "Comm to Dr. Lucy Lundberg Hendricks."

"Yes ma'am, this is Dr. Hendricks."

"Lucy, what do you remember about any lab work you did while attending pre-med college?"

"I don't remember doing any lab work. We did cover that in some cases blood should be sent to a lab to be tested for certain deceases."

"I just talked to the Dean of Admissions for Johns Hopkins School of Medicine who said testing would take three days plus one for Lab. I questioned her on the Lab portion, as Hope had not been exposed to any Lab work. Her response was that portion did not carry much weight overall in the test results. Does this seem odd?"

"Yes, should I call them back and make a pest of myself?"

"Yes please! Maybe they are looking for a way to deny Hope's application."

After giving Lucy the necessary contact information, she moved on to other matters at hand. However, two hours later she received a comm from her sister, "Hanna, I talked to your Dr. Burns and she told me that upon further consideration that the test would not contain anything regarding Lab work and she hopes that she will see you and Hope at the scheduled time. This still seems a little squirrelly to me about the Lab part of the test."

"Okay, thanks for your help Lucy. It looks like you're eventually going to get an intern when she graduates."

CHAPTER 4

Captain Hanna Lundberg Bloodworth escorted her daughter, Hope, to the Dean of Admissions Office to begin her testing for admission to the Johns Hopkins School of Medicine. They were met outside the Admissions building by the press to publicize the youngest daughter of Fleet Admiral Bloodworths entry into medical school. After a short interview with Hanna and her daughter, pictures were taken and then they made their way into the building.

Inside, they were met and escorted into Dr. Jessica Burns' office where introductions were made. Dr. Burns sat back into her chair and studied the young applicant who actually looked like a seventeen year-old getting ready for college and not medical school. However, Dr. Burns remembered other youngsters entering medical school and most thrived. This one should be no different.

"Hope, this entrance testing is to ensure that you're mentally ready to begin studies at our school. The test is in three parts, each with a six-hour time limit. After completion of the last part you will be notified of the results within three business days. If you are successful an entrance packet will be mailed to your ship. Are there any questions? None, very well, please follow the young lady outside to your testing room. There will be a one hour lunch break at noon."

After Hope left the room, Dr. Burns turned to Captain Bloodworth saying, "I'm sure Hope will do well in her tests, after all she is used to using computers and it should be second nature for her. The Board wishes to acknowledge their thanks that Hope selected our school to obtain her medical knowledge."

Hanna smiled at her, "My sister, Dr. Lucy Lundberg Hendricks obtained her medical degree from the Berlin Medical School and interned on my ship; assuming Hope passes her tests and graduates, she will also intern on my ship. We need her medical experience because the Xones are becoming desperate and have caused increasing casualties among our fleets. Should I check back here for her noon lunch break?"

Dr. Burns nodded her head, "Yes, there is a dining hall nearby you can use."

* * *

Hope L. Bloodworth was with her parents at Grandmother Alice's home in Hamburg, Germany. When they first arrived her Grandmother hugged her tightly and kissed her cheeks while tears glistened on her cheeks, "Honey, it's been almost five years and you've hardly changed."

"I know Granna, it's just the way it works in warp space. How are you? Are you feeling well? Still taking your medications?"

Alice turned to her daughter, "Hanna, she talks like a doctor already. Just like Lucy when she came home."

"Well, they are like minded. Hope starts med school soon in America; maybe you'll see more of her while we're on another voyage."

"Oh honey, this is going to be the first time you'll be separated. How can you stand it?"

Hope put her arm around the shoulders of her Granna, "Oh, she will finally get some peace with both of her kids out of the cabin. Feel sorry for me, I'll be all by myself out there on a planet with no overhead and the weather elements conspiring against me. Mom, how did you and Dad ever get used to that?"

Hanna smiled at her daughter, "We were used to living on Earth, it took us a long time to get over the sterile smells of a ship when we remembered the smell of a spring rain, flowers in bloom, and other smells that make up our Earth. You have a lot to learn about living on Earth, our mother planet."

"Well, it's going to be at least four years before I graduate, so I'll probably be sorry to leave when you come back for me. By the way, I've learned the names of my two roommates, Joey Willoughby and Olivia Langley. I wonder where they are from?"

"Wherever they come from it won't be further than where you were born," Hanna said with smile.

"Yeah, there is that, I guess I'm almost an alien. Mom, I need to buy myself some school clothes."

"You won't need much since you'll be in uniform most of your time there."

"I know, but I'll need nightgowns, slippers, underwear. I know, I'll copy what my roommates wear off campus."

Alice took Hanna's hand, "I know what you're thinking, it's the same as me when you left for the first time. It's not going to get easier, but you'll find pride in their accomplishments."

After a week, they travelled to Springfield, Missouri to visit Grandma Bloodworth. She was different than Mom's mother; her only child was my Father, who grew up to become the Fleet Admiral of two planets. Sarah now had two grandkids, and she was the only one here to receive all her love, especially since her husband died last year. When Hope first got out of the car in her driveway, Grandma just stood there with her hands outstretched toward her until she was drawn into her arms with tears of joy.

Sarah wasn't as tall as Hope, but she hugged her granddaughter tightly while softly asking, "How long do I have?"

"Mom and Dad are here a week, but I'm staying until I start med school in twelve days."

Grandma gave her a quick hard hug before releasing her and welcoming her parents. Hope started unloading the car and it wasn't long before they were all inside talking over each other as they carried the bags upstairs.

Later, Sarah served her tart lemonade and all was well with Hope, *She didn't realize how much she had missed her Grandparents; however, both sets now looked noticeably older than they had at her last visit. Well it's been over four years!* "Grandma, can we visit Grandpa's grave while I'm here?"

"Yes dear, we'll all go tomorrow. Adam would have been happy to see that everyone was well and you had made it back safely."

Hope asked, "How have you been keeping busy?"

"Oh, the same ole things. I have my monthly Bridge Club meeting to catch up on the gossip, and now that you've arrived I'll have them all asking about your visit. I did see you and Hanna at that press conference not long ago and I almost didn't recognize you. You've grown up into a beautiful young woman."

"Ah Grandma, don't say that; however I have started to fill out my clothes better. I'm a little anxious about meeting my fellow students and I'm going to stand out from the others by wearing my Star Fleet uniform."

Hanna smiled at her comment, "Hope, remember your Aunt Lucy wore her uniform while she attended Med School and I thank she enjoyed the attention it gave her."

"Mom, Aunt Lucy and I have different personalities. She is so much more outgoing than I am. I'm even worrying about my roommates liking me."

Hanna smiled at her as she replied, "Yes, you're spoiled rotten, they are bound to think you have a swollen head."

"MOM! That's not true at all, and you know it! Oh crap, you got me again. How come I'm so easy a mark for everyone?"

"You're too trusting of any new person you meet, especially boys. Don't take everything they say as the complete truth. The boys will attempt to inflate your ego, telling you how pretty you are, that you have a great personality, all with the goal of getting something from you, such as, a kiss or a favor. Studying together may be a ploy to get closer to you. You might want to stick with your roommates until you are wiser about the mating habits of your male classmates."

Hope looked at her mother with wide eyes. "Mom! How come you're giving me the facts of life now?"

"Because aboard ship, you're male shipmates were scared of you because of your parents. Down here you're on your own! You're a beautiful woman and that uniform isn't going to deter very many, so beware. The marines have taught you self-defense, so if a man gets too personal first tell him to back off, and if that doesn't work, get physical."

Hope looked at her mother with wide eyes, "I assume you're talking about your own experiences. How do I know if the guy is the right sort and won't try to take advantage of me?"

"Usually you'll know right away, and sometimes they try to fool you, but eventually you'll know their true selves."

Eric hugged his daughter, "The first time I met your mother we had a connection, but then it was impossible for us to get personal because of Navy Regulations. Eventually, that changed and your brother and you were born. Remember, if you have a relationship with an Earther it will be doomed to fail when you return to Space."

* * *

Twelve days later Hope entered Wolman Hall, the Freshman Dorm at Johns Hopkins School of Medicine. Her dorm room was on the third floor and when she entered she found her luggage sitting inside, along with that of her roommates. The room had a bed and study desk for each student, but they shared a bathroom, mini-kitchen, and TV area. She decided to claim the center personal space for herself and started unpacking her luggage.

About an hour later she heard a tentative knock on her apartment door and she yelled, "Enter!"

A young woman stuck her head into the room and asked, "Am I in the right room? I'm supposed to room with Bloodworth and Willoughby."

Hope walked up to her and shook her hand, "I'm Hope Bloodworth, so come on in. Do you have any other luggage?"

"No, just this handbag. I see some of our stuff has already been delivered. By the way, my name is Olivia Langley. I see you picked the center, so I'll have my choice of either end."

Hope pointed at the restroom, "The heads there if it makes a difference to you."

"Yes it does. You must be a Navy military brat by your use of the word Head. I am too, my Dad was a marine before he died."

"Mine's the Fleet Admiral of Space Fleet, and my mother is his captain."

She looked at Hope with wide eyes for a moment before taking a seat with tears running down her cheeks. Hope quickly sat with her and asked, "What's the problem?"

"My brother is a marine aboard the UES Hulk."

"What's his name, I might know him although it's not likely."

"Lance Corporal Jason Langley. He's been aboard for about four years."

She grinned at Olivia, "I helped treat him for a second degree burn about a year ago. He didn't mention anything about his family."

"My mother forbid him joining the marines after Dad died, but he did anyway and all we've heard since was that he was aboard the Hulk. You worked at the hospital?"

"Yes, my Aunt was the Doctor and she let me work on simple things with supervision. Did you know she was the first Doctor to Intern aboard a Starship?"

Just then the door flew open and a tall woman wearing a Bush Jacket and jeans strode inside. She looked at us on the couch and asked, "You two Bloodworth and Langley?"

Hope got off the couch and held out her hand, "I'm Hope Bloodworth and you must be Joey Willoughby?"

"That's right. Is any of this luggage mine?"

"Check it out. I've got the center bed, Olivia has the one next to the head, and so you get what's left."

Joey looked at Olivia uncertainly, "What's with the tears?"

Olivia got up from the couch to shake Joey's hand. "Oh, I just found out she knew my brother who's a marine aboard the UES Hulk."

Joey looked at Hope uncertainly for a moment, "Bloodworth! You're the daughter of Fleet Admiral Bloodworth and Captain Bloodworth, Wow! That's royalty in our family. I've got three relatives in Star Fleet, but none on the Flag Ship. Did you say my bunks on the left? I'm getting hungry, anybody know where the chow hall is?"

Hope said, "I'm getting hungry too. I took my entrance tests near here where there was a dining hall, how about it Olivia, you ready to eat?"

Fifteen minutes later they were standing in line for a cafeteria-style meal. After they finished their meal, they looked around at their fellow students. Hope was easily the youngest looking in the room, while most appeared to be in their early twenties. It seemed that for now the students were sitting at tables of the same gender.

CHAPTER 5

Lieutenant's Adam and Karrie Bloodworth were visiting his Grandmother in Springfield, Missouri and found that they missed the rest of the Bloodworth family by a week, with Hope just leaving a few days ago to med school.

When Sarah first answered the door, she was at first taken aback by the tall handsome man in Space Fleet uniform, but then it clicked who this must be. "Adam! You're here."

Then seeing the beautiful dark-haired woman beside him, she gushed, "Oh my gosh this is your wife, Karrie! Come in, the both of you."

Sarah with much excitement in her voice said, "Your father told me of your marriage, but very little else. Adam how in the world did you talk this lovely woman into marrying you?"

Karrie, a little overwhelmed by Sarah's excitement, replied, "It was almost a mutual proposal at the time."

Adam said, "Karrie is from Aqua and for some unknown reason when we first met a bond between us was established that we both immediately felt. Karrie's mother felt it when she first met Commander Becker at first contact with Aqua. They couldn't stand being separated for very long and were eventually married. For some reason, this bond is even stronger for us and within hours of meeting we were married."

Sarah looked at the two with concern, "Are you happy being married to each other?"

They looked at each other and smiled before Adam said, "This bond is more than just lust, we really love each other with all our hearts. We each know where the other is without a conscious thought and it's comforting to know your mate is well at all times."

Sarah replied, "This sounds like you two are beginning to merge your minds together"

"We have already came to the same conclusion, but since we can't do anything about it we live for today and let tomorrow happen as it will."

Sarah looked at the beautiful pair and felt a tear make its way down her cheek, "I assume your children will have this same bond when they meet their mates?"

"We don't know. We guess the female carries the gene, but does it get stronger or weaker after each new child is born, we don't know?"

Sarah looked at them uncertainly, "To me it's obvious that it's getting stronger; however, looking at you two I don't see a downside besides what might happen if one of you dies."

She put those thoughts aside and concentrated on learning how Adam and his new wife were adjusting to married life aboard a Starship.

* * *

Fleet Admiral Bloodworth was on Earth at Star Fleet Headquarters located near Phoenix, Arizona, to meet with Admiral James Cochran. He replaced Admiral James Randall who retired three years ago and previously had a background in Earth's wet Navy, much like Bloodworth.

After the welcoming pleasantries were over they sat together drinking coffee and discussing each other's family. Cochran was very interested in how the fleet was handling extended tours with their families aboard with them. After finding that the on-board divorce rate was less than ten percent of the wet Navy's and morale was at an all-time high, it was obvious that Star Fleet was on the right track.

After discussing ship construction and manpower allocations, Admiral Cochran asked about Bloodworths long-term plans against the Xones threat, who replied, "Sir, we are still pushing against the Xones on two fronts with all the ships we have in our Battle Fleets. It would be helpful if we could find and enlist the help of another friendly race. A third front would greatly help in pushing the Xones back toward their home world, wherever that might be."

Cochran nodded his head in agreement, "So far, our explorations further out into our Spiral Arm have been fruitless. We have found intelligent life, but none beyond our own stone age. Based upon what the Katz own experiences have been, this is consistent with what they have found. However, it's possible we will find a planet overlooked by the Xones on our inward push."

Bloodworth nodded his head, "Possible, but not likely. They would have been missed by both the Katz and the Xones for that to happen. When was your last contact with the Katz?"

"Shortly after your tour in Aqua began. They seemed happy with our progress against the Xones, and Admiral Gamma Killa sends her regards and hopes to meet you again shortly. What is your take on her personally?"

"She's an unusual person; when we first met she came on to both my wife and me, but didn't take offense when we didn't respond favorably. She couldn't fathom some of our society's norms, but passed along their knowledge on what long-term absences did to family relationships. That was the basis of my recommendations to change regulations pertaining to relationships within chain of command and eventually bringing families aboard our Starships."

"So your history would be favorable with her."

"Yes sir. I just wish they would contribute their ships in a meaningful way to our mutual fight."

"Yes, but they did provide us with ships and the knowledge to fight them. It's well we are an aggressive and innovative race and we were able to made their first designs into much better fighting machines. When do you plan of leaving?"

"We've been here about three months and our ships are about 80% re-provisioned. We should be ready to leave in another forty to sixty days after all our crews have returned from leaves. I'm planning on being gone about two years your time. The new Battleship and four Battle Cruisers will be helpful, especially after I formulate a new Battle Plan for their usage."

When he got back to the Hulk he called a meeting for all captains and XO's of First Fleet at the UES Hulk tomorrow for a working breakfast at 07:30 hours. He also invited Admiral Cochran to attend if he was available.

That evening Eric was eating dinner with Hanna in their Stateroom and asked, "Have you heard from Hope since she's started school?"

"Yes, she appears to have made strong friends with both her roommates and so far classroom lectures are more interesting than her computer courses. She also said we have a brother of Olivia Langley in our marines, a Lance Corporal Jason Langley, who's estranged from her family but she wishes to contact him."

"What do you think we should do, if anything?"

"I'm going to meet with him and see if he's interested in corresponding with his sister before we leave Earth for another two years. Apparently Hope's roommate was pretty broken up when she found out Hope was from the Hulk."

"Okay, I don't think me doing that would work. Thanks for taking care of it."

Hanna asked, "Do you want me to do anything for tomorrow's meeting?"

"Check to make sure the XO's get all the answers to their questions."

"Okay, I'll get my XO, Commander Betty Conner to solicit their questions."

The following morning Fleet Admiral Bloodworth and his Flag Captain Hanna Bloodworth greeted the Captains and their XOs as they entered the conference room. One of the first to arrive was Captain Samantha Lopez and her XO Alex Keller of the Battleship UES Madrid; Erik told her captain to remain after the meeting for discussions.

The last officer to arrive was Admiral Cochran and his aide. Admiral Bloodworth escorted Admiral Cochran to a separate table facing the others where the two sat with his Flag Captain, Hanna Bloodworth, while Bloodworths Chief of Staff sat with Cochran's aide.

After everyone was seated Eric tapped his water glass to get attention, "Ladies and gentlemen, captains and executive officers of the First Fleet, we are graced with the presence of Star Fleet Admiral James Cochran. He's here to observe how we do business and perhaps answer your questions after the meeting. First we eat and then we work, bring on the food."

Later, after the dishes were pushed aside they got to business when Fleet Admiral Bloodworth stood. Everyone went silent as the Admiral looked over his command, "Officers, we now have two Battleships and fourteen Heavy Battle Cruisers. That's a lot of firepower and I'm going to experiment in how best to use it. In some instances I intend to split this force into two equal attacking forces; however, on our trip toward hostile territory we are going to train until we act as if we were one unit."

"Now, I'm going to open this meeting for questions – give me your name, title, and ship, who's going to be first?"

"Sir, Captain Tara Cederblom of the Heavy Battle Cruiser Crusher. I'm one of your new ships and do I get a list of past codes for ship patterns?"

"The short answer is yes, but I generally update these at the beginning of each cruise. Next?"

This continued for forty minutes, until Bloodworth said, "Does anyone have questions for Admiral Cochran?"

There was one hand in the air, which Bloodworth acknowledged.

"Sir, Captain Ryan Cox, Heavy Battle Cruiser El Rod. Do we have anything new in the works to help us in the field?"

"Captain Cox, are you with one of the new Cruisers?"

"Yes Sir!"

"Well, beginning with the next Cruiser built, it will contain better Laser Cannons that boasts its range from 10,000 miles to 20,000 miles. Better yet, when you have your next Earth layover, you can be retrofitted."

At that news, there was a loud murmur followed by a general clapping of approval.

There were no further questions for Admiral Cochran, but he continued to stand before them gathering his thoughts. "Fellow warriors, before you go out again to face our enemy, remember that it's Earth you're protecting from this evil scourge that has infected our Galaxy. We must fight them until they're no longer a threat, no matter how long it takes."

Fleet Admiral Bloodworth stood followed by the others as they all clapped their approval.

* * *

Lieutenant (jg) Hope L. Bloodworth finished her first years study at Johns Hopkins School of Medicine and was feeling homesick for life aboard the UES Hulk. She knew her ship was probably just now approaching the war zone of past battles and was feeling concern for her parents and brother, but rather than dwell on that she decided to take summer courses that started in two weeks. She packed her bag for a week's stay and headed to the airport for a flight to Springfield, Missouri. Her grandma was ecstatic about her coming for a short visit.

All the airlines were offering free flights to uniformed Star Fleet members, so that was helpful to her pocketbook. That evening she arrived at her Grandmother's home by taxi and Sarah was in tears when she saw her Granddaughter in uniform and immediately hugged the tall form. They were in tears when they broke apart.

Hope found that she needed this dose of family love her grandma brought to her. They stayed up late that night going over what her first year of class work entailed, but eventually after the long day for her and her grandma's age, they turned in for the night.

She wasn't surprised that when she awoke at 06:00 hours, that she heard noises from the kitchen. Putting on her robe, she went downstairs with the intention of helping her Grandma with breakfast. However, she was told to get her own coffee while Sarah did her thing in the kitchen. Hope got herself coffee and they made conversation until Sarah brought a plate of ham and eggs for her.

Sarah drank her coffee while watching her Granddaughter eat breakfast. Hope looked up from her meal and asked, "How about you Grandma, don't you eat?"

"I ate my toast and jam before I started yours. I love to cook for others, but can't take all that grease you and your brother like."

Hope spent her time with her Grandma soaking up all her love before returning to her dorm in Baltimore. Both of her roommates had returned to their homes for the summer, so she had the room to herself. She found that many of the students were taking summer courses to shorten their time in med school.

At her first day of classes she found herself following a good-looking man from her dorm to the same classroom she was attending. She followed him inside and took a seat next to him and gave him a tentative smile when he looked at her as she sat down. He gave a little start as he took in her uniform, but returned her smile.

During a break between classes they both headed toward Norton Hall, the schools study/break area. After getting herself coffee she headed toward a table to prepare herself for her next class. She was a little surprised when the same man came to her table and asked, "Hi, my name is Jeff Fellows, may I sit with you?"

Hope smiled and nodded her head while pushing out a chair with her foot. When he was seated, she said, "My name is Hope Bloodworth."

"You're more than just a med student, you're wearing the uniform of a Star Fleet Officer."

"Yes, my parents are both officers as well. I was commissioned and placed on temporary duty to attend school."

"You look a little young to start med school, where did you go for pre-med?"

She gave him a small smile; "I didn't attend any classes before arriving here. I was born in Space and got all my education from computer courses."

He looked at her in surprise for a few moments digesting what she had just revealed. "That's amazing! How did you do for your first year of classes?"

"I'm not sure, my class position is fifteenth. Is that good or bad?"

His eyes got big and he rolled his eyes, "Believe me, that's good. You placed fifteenth in a class of 265 students and you've never taken classes before. I'd say you've done very well."

"My roommates did well too if that's the case. Their class positions were eighteen and twenty-one."

"I assume you study together on the same classes?"

"Of course, why do you ask?"

Because my class position is thirty-one and I want to improve my position. Please study with me when we take the same classes this summer?"

"What other classes are you taking this summer?"

He smiled at her as he replied, "Anatomy II and Infectious Deceases."

She smiled at him, "Three for three. That gives us Tuesday and Thursday to study together. Let's meet here at 08:00 hours. Agreed?"

"Is that eight a.m.?"

She raised her eyebrow at him, "Of course. Oh, you're not knowledgeable about military time, is the time okay?"

"Sure, I'll buy the coffee and sweets."

"Coffee – no sweets! I have a hard enough time keeping my shape without having that to burn off."

"You exercise too?"

"Yes, I run every morning at 06:15 hours – that's 6:15 a.m."

"Okay, downstairs dorm main entrance at 6:15 a.m. God, I hope you don't kill me the first day."

The next morning when he arrived she was still stretching her muscles, so he copied her routine until she stood and started off slowly for his benefit. They ran down the sidewalks, which were empty at this hour except for a few other runners. At thirty minutes she stopped so he could get his wind. Gasping for air he asked, "How long do you run?"

"Usually an hour, but I don't think you can do that yet. Why not walk back to the dorm and we'll meet at Norton Hall at 08:00 hours."

He nodded his head and she took off at her regular pace leaving him still gasping for air. Later, while showering in her room she smiled at his obvious out of shape self, trying to keep up with her.

After the summer class session ended, Hope and Jeff compared their grades. Her grade average had improved to fourteen, while his was now twenty-nine. They improved their averages, but the real deal was when all the students were back for the fall session. Hope was in the dorm room when her roommates came in together with their luggage.

Joey yelled at her, "Hope don't just stand there, help us bring this crap inside!"

Smiling, Hope hurried to help them get their belongings inside, and afterwards they all collapsed on their couch sighing in relief. Olivia asked, "Hope, how did the summer session go?"

"I did well, and I met a nice man."

"What!!" They both said with wide eyes of surprise.

"Yes, his name is Jeff Fellows and we studied and jogged together."

Joey got up and dropped to her knees in front of Hope, "Tell me everything about him."

Hope knew her roommates thought she was clueless about men, so she went along with Joey.

"Well, he's older than me."

"Ha! Everyone is older than you. How much older?"

"About your age. When he found out my grade average he asked me to study with him as he needed to bring up his average."

"He admitted that up front?"

"Yes, I think we actually helped each other as both our averages increased after the summer session."

"Is he a hunk?"

"Define hunk?"

"Oh come on! You know what I mean."

"At first he was a little soft around the waist, but after running with me I'd say he was a hunk."

Olivia spoke up, "Hope, let's invite him over for a little party. We need to check this guy out, especially if we're going to study together."

"Okay, but no booze! Remember I'm jail bait."

They both looked at her and then the pillow fight was on.

CHAPTER 6

Lieutenant Adam Bloodworth was inspecting the Port upper launch tubes when he received the comm to report to his Department Head (DH) in her office. After reaching her office he came to attention before her desk and greeted her, "Ma'am, Lieutenant Bloodworth reporting as ordered."

Beeker has been the DH of the Weapons Section since Bloodworths father captained his first starship. She and the Admiral fought many battles together and standing before her was another Bloodworth learning the ropes as he advanced toward his first captaincy.

"Lieutenant, how do you like working in weapons?"

"Ma'am, it's all a learning experience; however, I preferred working in lasers as I can get immediate feedback from my efforts against the enemy."

"Yes, I can sympathize with you on wanting to shoot directly at the enemy; however, as you advance in the ranks you get further away from your direct involvement in firing against the enemy. You become a planner on different ways to use your weapons against the enemy's ships, where you can overwhelm his defenses and kill him with the least exposure to yourself. Your wife,

Lieutenant Karrie Becker Bloodworth is also working on missiles, but she's assigned duty on the Starboard side tubes. The two of you have both been fast tracked where you'll next be assigned Bridge duties. Is there any area you think you or she needs additional exposure?"

"Ma'am, no ma'am, the two of us are equal to any task assigned us. Bridge duty would be welcome at this point as it's our hope to eventually be placed in command of a Starship."

"Very well, expect to receive orders for transfers to Bridge duties in the near future. You are dismissed."

Bloodworth saluted, did an about face and left her office. Walking back to his duty station he mentally sent glad tidings to Karrie.

* * *

Fleet Admiral Bloodworths First Fleet was approaching the fourth gate from Earth under Battle Stations when he had a sudden thought, *what if he used a different speed at this gate?* "Comm to captain, instead of transiting the gate at our normal speed of 2g's, we send the probe across at 1g. Program the probe to scan and return here, and if this doesn't get a result, try 2.5g's and then 3g's."

"Captain to Admiral. Aye sir, try different transit speeds until we fail or get results. I will send the first probe in twenty minutes. Recommend disbursal of fleet in standard pattern."

"Comm to Fleet, stop and use standard disbursal 20,000 miles from gate. Sending first and perhaps other probes in twenty minutes."

The first probe at 1g was sent through the gate. "Captain to Admiral, the probe is due to return in thirty-five minutes."

The senior officers were taking a coffee break together when the probe returned and broadcast that it detected that there were several individual readings near the second and third planet of the system, but no concentrations that would indicate fleet activity.

Admiral Bloodworth thought a moment before saying to his Flag Captain, "Before we do anything we need to send the probe back through at the normal 2g's to ascertain what's waiting for us there."

"Captain to Bridge, Send a probe at the normal 2g's to check for any activity."

"Comm to Captain; aye ma'am, reprograming probe to send at 2g's speed."

Twenty minutes later a message torpedo returned showing no activity within the next system.

Commander Dana Williams, the Admirals Chief of Staff, joined the Bloodworths in discussion. "What can of worms did we turn over here?"

Admiral Bloodworth replied, "Remember, we have another alien race four jumps out from Earth. I had a hunch here and it seems to have worked. I think we should check it out, but slowly. We don't know what they have, but they are apparently more advanced than we were when the Katz showed up on Earth, what do you two think?"

Hanna considered for a moment, "I don't think we should approach their home world with all our force, but instead let's keep half our force back at the gate in case someone follows us through while the other half makes contact."

"Dana, your thoughts?"

"Yes, that's prudent, one Battleship and seven Heavy Battle Cruisers make the initial contact. That's more than a factor of ten for what's shown itself here so far."

Eric responded, "I agree with both of you. I'll contact the fleet and tell them what we plan on doing, and let's hope these people are friendly and willing to help."

After Fleet Admiral Bloodworth informed the First Fleet about their plans, they made their transit through the warp gate and split the formation in half as they had practiced. The UES Hulk led its seven escorts inward toward the two planets with activity at a sedate 2g's acceleration.

It would take them seven hours to reach the nearest planet and as they approached they were trying to catch anything locally being transmitted from the various ships and planets. After two hours they were fairly certain the third planet was their home world, and best of all it was another water world. One hour from the planet the First Fleet started broadcasting across the band to anyone listening.

The first thing they checked for was orbiting space stations and defensive platforms. They found three space stations, but they found no apparent defensive devises. Admiral Bloodworth thought parking in orbit near their largest space station might work best in getting people to talk to them. Three hours after achieving orbit a small shuttle departed the station heading for the Hulk, their largest ship.

When the shuttle approached the Hulk, a shuttle bay was opened for them. They stopped short of the bay looking it over, but when a crewman from the Hulk motioned them to come inside, they slowly approached and were secured, while the bay doors closed behind them.

Nothing happened for ten minutes while they apparently discussed their next move, then the shuttle's door opened and a person in a spacesuit stepped outside. The Officer on Deck stepped forward and showed the alien an electronic tablet that showed stick figures moving inside to a room divided by a glass wall, where both parties could talk safely without wearing a suit.

The person nodded its head and followed him inside a short distance to the room depicted, who then looked around the room noting the translation machine and a chair, and then walked to the Glass Wall and shrugged its shoulders. The OD placed the screen of the tablet against the transparent wall and pointed at it. It showed the person removing its spacesuit, which the person started doing until an obvious woman was down to a skintight body suit.

The OD held up a finger to her and left the room, but another person immediately replaced him. Doctor Lucy Hendricks walked up to the wall and held her arms wide before removing her white lab coat, showing the woman she was also a female and not armed. She picked up the tablet and placed it against the wall and motioned for her to come closer. Intrigued, the alien stepped closer and watched the stick figure climb into the machine and then after a period of time step back out and conversed with our stick figure.

The alien woman turned and walked over and examined the machine. She frowned and turned, mimicking shooting herself in the head; whereupon, Lucy violently shook her head no. The alien woman smiled at her and climbed into the machine and pushed the green button depicted on the tablet. The machine quickly closed and started giving her the Universal language.

Three hours later, the machine opened and Lucy helped her out of the machine and gave her some distilled water to drink.

"How do you feel? Any discomfort anywhere?"

"You are not afraid of germs from me?"

"No, we checked your spacesuit and found nothing to be concerned about. The machine also took a blood sample from you and apparently we have similar DNA. We've found another race similar to us about four warp gates in the opposite direction from our home planet."

She gave Lucy an uncertain smile, "My name is Gwen Spicer and I work at the habitat nearby over our home planet we call Green."

"My name is Lucy Hendricks and I'm the medical doctor for this ship. You are aboard the Battleship UES Hulk and we are fighting a vicious enemy across all this Spiral Arm of our Galaxy. We call them the Xones and they destroy all they encounter whether a threat or not. Perhaps you can arrange a meeting with a ranking member of your military so that a treaty can be arranged. This tablet recorded our conversation and to turn it on you press this button, see...and turn it off by pressing it again. Your spacesuit is by the door, but you won't need it to return to your shuttle. Maybe we'll see one another again when a world representative is chosen to come here."

Gwen smiled at Lucy and picked up her spacesuit before following her out of the room toward the shuttle bay containing her ride back home. Fifteen minutes later the Green shuttle was on its way back to the habitat.

Captain Bloodworth stood next to her sister as they watched it leave, "Lucy, you did well. Gwen Spicer remained relatively calm and she now knows the Universal language. I think we did well for our first contact. I wonder how long it's going to take Green to find and send us a planet representative. It took us almost two weeks when the Katz arrived above Earth."

Ten days later a ship from Green arrived at the Habitat and an hour later a shuttle left heading towards the Hulk. There was no hesitation this time as the shuttle headed toward the same open Shuttle Bay as before. The shuttle approached and settled into position as if it had done this many times before.

Captain Bloodworth waited until three people stepped down from the shuttle, then she and her sister, Lucy, walked toward them. They both wore their military uniforms and one of the three they were meeting also wore some kind of uniform. As they grew closer they recognized Gwen Spicer as one of the trio, so they had an interpreter.

They stopped about ten feet apart and the man in uniform gave them a smart salute, which they returned. Captain Bloodworth said, "Welcome to the Battleship UES Hulk. We have arranged a small conference room to begin our talks. How long are you prepared to stay with us?"

Gwen immediately repeated what Hanna said, and then waited a few minutes while the other two conferred. The two men finally nodded to each other and spoke to Gwen, who then turned and said, "As long as it takes to come to an understanding."

"Very well, my name and rank is Captain Hanna Bloodworth and this my sister Commander Lucy Hendricks. She is the ship Medical Doctor in case any of us becomes ill."

Gwen repeated what was said, and the men nodded their heads in understanding.

"Very well, let's proceed to the meeting room. Please follow me."

When they nodded their understanding, the two Earth women led the way until they entered the conference room some fifteen minutes later. They took seats at opposite sides of a long narrow table. "If you are not familiar with my rank, the Captain commands the ship. In this case the UES Hulk is the Flag Ship of First Fleet commanded by Fleet Admiral Bloodworth, my husband."

When the translation was complete the man in uniform gave her a surprised look. He then made a short comment to the other man, and then spoke to her. Gwen translated, "You must command a family ship?"

Hanna smiled, "I don't think it's a family ship as you mean it. Travel in warp space distorts time in that it passes slower than normal time. We find that for our voyages of one year for us is about two years for people on our home planet."

After translation, they nodded their heads and the uniformed man twirled his hand impatiently wanting more information.

"For that reason marriages where one of the party is land bound cannot survive long. We now mate or marry people on the same ship. Both my sister and I have married men aboard this ship, I have two children born aboard while I commanded this ship."

After this translation, the three looked at each other in wonder. The uniformed man spoke and the translation was, "This procedure is much too slow, can we both receive this Universal language?"

"Yes, but it will require a separate machine for each person. It takes about three hours." She then pointed at the clock on the wall.

After the translation, Hanna got up and walked to the clock pointing at the small hand, then down three numbers.

All three nodded their heads in agreement and the uniformed man stood and spoke. The translation was, "I will look forward to talking with you directly and not through a translator."

Lucy escorted the two men and the interpreter to where the learning machines were located. She explained how the machine worked and asked each of the men to remove their jackets. After this was done, they each stepped into separate machines and settled themselves. Lucy pushed the start buttons and the machines closed up.

She then explained to Gwen that a crewman would monitor the operation and would let us know when they were finished. Gwen nodded her head and they returned to the conference room.

When they arrived back she asked Gwen Spicer if she would like some refreshments while they waited after pointing at a table that held coffee and sweet rolls. The Interpreter proclaimed the coffee was too bitter by the way she reacted after the first sip, Lucy said, "Try the distilled water in the white pitcher."

After hearing this she immediately went for the water. The sweet rolls were a hit and she asked what it was called. After hearing the translation she smiled and wrote its name on a pad of paper.

Lucy asked Hanna, "Should we offer a fruit drink?"

Hanna asked Gwen if they had fruit trees on Green, and after she nodded yes, Hanna used her tablet to display the different fruits from Earth, Gwen slowly scrolled through them until she pointed at a pineapple and said, "Everyone likes its juice."

Hanna then ordered a thermos of chilled pineapple juice for their guests, while Gwen searched for other common fruits. Eventually, they also found apple and oranges growing on Green; however, pineapple was their favorite fruit juice.

Their discussions eventually revealed that the uniformed man's name was Jorge Hinderman and held the equivalent rank of a Major General in their Army. The Ambassadors name is Wil Pardon and was from their world government headquarters located on the larger of the planets two continents, in a city called Valley Center, named after the long valley in which it resided. The second planet where spacecraft were noticed was called Raylee, named after an early explorer. It has a much warmer climate where some crops are grown and minerals excavated for use on Green. The total population within this system is about one billion, compared to 7.5 billion on Earth in 2017.

The Ambassador and the General eventually returned from the Learning machine escorted by Lucy. When they entered the conference room Hanna asked if they were hungry. The General nodded his head, "I think I could eat about anything."

"Maybe, but let's try our food a little at a time. I'm going to order a variety of foods that I like and have you each try a small portion of several to see if you like its taste and that it agrees with your system, okay?"

When the food arrived, the first sampled was a small portion of beefsteak, cooked medium rare. They looked at it suspiciously, smelled it, and finally cut a very small slice and put it into their mouths savoring its taste. They then smiled before chewing and swallowing it. Jorge asked, "What was that?"

Hanna replied, "We call it beef from a large animal raised for food."

"So it was animal flesh we ate. We have something similar, but this tasted much better."

"What kind of vegetables do you grow for food? We have two different samples here – a potato and carrots. Each of you try a little of one different from what the other selects and then switch."

Gwen placed a spoon full of white mashed potatoes on her plate, while the two men tried the orange colored sliced carrots. She asked, "What's the yellow stuff on top?"

"They usually place a little butter, made from milk of a cow – a different variety of animal that is raised for food. Do you like it?"

"Yes, but it's not as good as the beef."

Jorge said, "I like this, but it's different from anything I've ever eaten. How long do we wait for a reaction?"

"Not long. People normally aren't allergic to root vegetables. So each try what the other just had."

After they each tried the new vegetable, they asked, "What's next?"

"Now you have a larger portion of what you just ate and a special treat, pineapple juice to drink."

Lucy said, "You can have water if you prefer."

They all started eating the same foods, but Lucy was a little distracted as she was monitoring the alien's wellbeing while she ate. When finished, Hanna asked, "You mentioned earlier about something to do with my ship?"

"Yes, something this size must have huge engines and fuel requirements, can you tell me something about it."

"Actually the engines that power my ship are not that large. They are of simple design by our mentors, The Katz, and the fuel is reaction mass we obtain from large gas giants we encounter in every system we pass through. The designers on our home planet just adapted those used in the Cruisers given to us by the Katz. This Battleship is the second upgrade our planet made to the original design of the Cruisers. The first upgrade was the smaller war ships accompanying us that we call Heavy Battle Cruisers. The original ships were about three quarters that size; however, we don't use the original design in our Battle Fleets now because of their poor laser defense capabilities. We now use them primarily for exploration."

Hinderman asked, "Just how big is this ship and how many crewman are there?"

"This ship is over a mile long and takes about 3,000 crew to operate it. We also have about 1,000 marines for security, in case we are ever boarded by the enemy. The Battle Cruisers require a little less crew. The Battleship can fire twice the number of missiles as the Battle Cruisers and have twice the range of their Laser Cannons. Basically, the Battleship protects the Cruisers. It takes about three times as long to build a Battleship than a Heavy Battle Cruiser and initially when we were building up our fleets we were after numbers of ship hulls. I'm curious, what were your thoughts when we arrived in orbit?"

"We knew something was coming toward our planet that was not natural, but when your ships made orbit beside one of our habitats, we were afraid about your motives."

Hanna gave him a small smile, "That was our reaction when the Katz arrived above our home world. Later, the Fleet Admiral and I were together commanding one of the first Earth ships given to us by the Katz."

"How do you mean together?"

"He was the Captain and I his Executive Officer. None of our ships have lost a battle with the Xones. Earth now has two Battle Star Fleets, and Aqua, the other world like you also has a Battle Fleet."

"You say the other world like us, what do you mean?"

"Aqua and Green are populated by people basically like us down to the same DNA. We have now two examples where Earth and Aqua people have mated, and in the first example have had a child together. My oldest child recently mated with the first example, so yes we are basically alike."

Hinderman looked at her with an open mouth and wide eyes of someone surprised, maybe even in wonder, "What do the Katz and Xones look like?"

Hanna opened a folder and handed it to him, "This is what Admiral Gamma Killa looks like. She is definitely not related to us although she is about the same size and body type. The females rule her society, although the males are stronger physically. Before the Katz arrived our own society was male biased, now it is gender neutral."

She passed him another folder, "This picture is of a dead Xones. When their ships are too damaged to fight they blow them up. They appear to be of reptile origin, but that's just our opinion. They cannot be trusted to abide by a treaty and they attack anyone that appears weaker than themselves. The ships they use have the same capabilities as the ships originally given us by the Katz. The Katz have lost battles with the Xones and we thank they adapted many of Katz designs for their own use; our own newer ship designs are much better than theirs. We made a recording of the one instance the Xones called for a parley, it was very revealing."

Hinderman smiled as he quipped, "I have a feeling you are saving that recording for another time."

"Yes, when your party is ready to parlay tomorrow, Fleet Admiral Bloodworth will show you what transpired. Do you have another question?"

"Yes, I'm very curious about this other race, the Aquas. May I speak to your child and his mate?"

"My son is married to Karrie Becker and they both are Lieutenants in this ships Weapons Section, let's defer that meeting until tomorrow morning after breakfast."

"Why not have a breakfast meeting? I'm curious how she adjusted her meals to what she previously was used to."

Hanna smiled at him, "Very good. You have killed two birds with one stone."

His eyes widened at her word phrasing, "That's a very good analogy. I must remember that."

Hanna thought a moment before continuing; "Let's head toward our Child Care Center. You might find it interesting."

Ten minutes later, they entered the CCC after passing a marine sentry. There were three young children, ages two, three, and four playing inside. Two older children, ages five and six, were studying using hand held tablets. After looking around, they all left and continued their way back to the meeting room.

The General asked, "Are those all the children currently onboard?"

"No, just those whose parents are currently on duty. If I remember correctly, there are twenty-one children on board."

CHAPTER 7

Captain Bloodworth interrupted, "Let's make plans for tomorrows meetings and then we'll settle you each into your own cabin, unless you'd prefer to stay together?"

Jorge quickly said, "The Ambassador and I would like to share a room, Gwen can have her own cabin."

"Very well, tomorrow will start with breakfast with my son and his wife, whose mother is from Aqua, and The Fleet Admiral and I will attend as well. Do you have a purpose for Gwen in our future meetings? If not, we can show her around the ship and she can later tell you her impressions."

Ambassador Pardon seemed relieved with this option. "Thank you; Gwen, when we get back to the Habitat, prepare me a complete report on your impressions."

Hanna continued, "After breakfast my husband will show you a recording of the parley with the Xones Admiral and Earth's determination of future activities regarding the Xones. What do you want to discuss?"

Pardon held up a finger, "We'd like to discuss our future relationship including possible trade."

Hanna smiled at the Ambassador, "Sir, I'm afraid a trade

relationship may be several years down the way – for one thing neither of us has cargo ships to make the trip. No, that's not right, we have resupply ships that can be converted to cargo vessels. Assuming we can come to an agreement of mutual protection and we give you a starter battle fleet, plans for cargo ships might be in the offering."

Both representatives from Green looked at her like she was their fairy godmother. Ambassador Pardon said with a little squeak in his voice, "This is the ultimate purpose of your visit?"

"Yes, of course. You are our cousins and we have a common enemy. It's only natural that we want your help in combating this cancer in our midst. If you won't help us, then we'll leave you to your unprotected fate."

General Hinderman face reflected his understanding, "In other words you won't waste your resources on a planet who doesn't help themselves."

"Yes, Aqua is a planet of people who believed in nonaggression and wanted us to protect them from the bullies of the Galaxy. We took their delegation with us to a battle with the Xones where it was demonstrated that the Xones didn't care if the people they meet were a threat, they just attack everyone they meet. One of those in that delegation became their military leader and is the mother of the woman my son is married to."

Hinderman asked, "How large is their fleet now?"

"Over a year ago their Battle Fleet consisted of one Battleship and eight Heavy Battle Cruisers, and their Home Fleet consisted of ten Heavy Battle Cruisers and six Cruisers. They have their own space yards building ships."

Hanna continued, "Their biggest problem is finding crews for the ships they build. Their world has a strong pacifist core."

Ambassador Pardon looked a little shaken, "Captain Bloodworth, you have given us much to consider for our talks tomorrow and I for one need time to reflect and rest. Could you show us our cabins now?"

"Certainly, however do you have plans for your shuttle personnel while here?"

"Oh, I've been remiss to consider them. Perhaps Gwen can talk with them and be their escort while they stay here until we are ready to leave?"

Hanna turned to Gwen, "I'll assign two marines to escort you to the shuttle and the mess hall for food before assigning them a room. What gender are they?"

"They are both male, so one room for them should suffice."

"I'll place your rooms adjacent to one another in case they need help with the language. Did any of you bring luggage or a kit with you?"

The Ambassador replied, "No, I didn't plan for an overnight stay with you."

"Very well, I'll see to a kit for all of you and I hope you are comfortable in your quarters. By the way, the ships gravity is set at Earth normal, is it different from Green's?"

"No, at least not enough to be noticeable."

"Very well, the marine security will escort you two to breakfast at 07:00 hours ship time. Our time is calibrated to how long it takes for our planet to rotate, which is 24 hours. If you have a personal timepiece, ship time is now 19:10 hours. Would anyone prefer to be awakened at a particular time?"

They all held up their hands, "Would 06:00 hours be sufficient for everyone?"

"The marine security will awaken everyone at that time. Gwen please inform your charges of the wakeup time and when you are ready have the marines escort you to breakfast. Do you think they would enjoy a tour of the ship with you?"

"I believe so. If not, they can return to their cabin."

"After breakfast a guide will pick you up there and deliver you to the shuttle when the others are ready to leave. Any questions or concerns?"

"Okay, until tomorrow then."

The next morning, marine security brought the two emissaries from the Planet Green to the Officers Mess, where a space was cleared for their meeting. Fleet Admiral Bloodworth, Captain Bloodworth, and Lieutenants Adam and Karrie Bloodworth were already in attendance when the new arrivals sat down at the large round table. Introductions were made and then everyone looked at the menu for their selections for breakfast.

General Hinderman asked Karrie, "What choices do you generally make from the selection of Earth foods?"

She smiled at his question, "On Aqua we don't eat animal flesh, so it's generally eggs and potatoes or maybe waffles. Do you eat animal flesh on Green?"

"Yes, but the steak tastes better than from Green, as do the fruit juices."

"Yes, it must be what the animals feed upon and the fruits grow from. We prepare our vegetables differently than Earth chefs, but I make do."

I understand you and Adam are newly married. Is it hard to adjust to Earth's customs?"

"No, we are basically from the same gene pool so it's mainly customs that I have to learn. We both have some differences that we have had to adjust to." She said as she smiled at Adam.

"How long has Aqua been fighting the Xones?"

"Since before I was born, maybe twenty-four Earth years."

"Yes, that measure depends upon where you are from. Green is the third planet from our Sun and takes about 388 days to rotate around our sun."

Karrie replied, "Aqua is also the third planet from the Sun and takes 381 days to rotate around our Sun. That's compared to 365 days for Earth; so, there's really not a lot of difference in our years. I understand that you are considering taking up the fight to defend yourself against the Xones. They are a relentless horde and would eliminate any they encounter."

Admiral Bloodworth interrupted, "The Green people really wanted to verify what Hanna told them about another world whose people were similar to the Earth people and now the Greens. It's a little mind-bending for just how close our people are to each other."

Karrie nodded her head, "Yes, when my mother met her future husband they had an immediate bonding with each other which only got stronger as they were together. Their union brought forth me and my interactions with humans as I grew older didn't match mothers' reaction until I met Adam. I felt an immediate attraction, which he later said matched mine. Our attraction became so strong that we were married within 24 hours of our first meeting. So, for us, our mutual attraction was much stronger than what my parents experienced. I'm telling you this because people from your world may experience what we did."

"So, the second generation female attraction to a human male may be stronger. Were there any other effects of this attraction?"

"We can't tolerate being apart for very long and we know generally were the other is without conscious thought."

"I assume that's the reason you work in the same Section?"

"Yes, and there may be a more severe downside; if one of us dies, will the other survive?"

After breakfast the group returned to the Conference Room where a projection screen was set up. Admiral Bloodworth said, "Gentlemen, the following is a recording of my parley with an Admiral of the Xones in response to the heavy losses they received from our fleets."

The UES Beast, a Heavy Battle Cruiser, stopped broadside to the stationary Xones Cruiser, which was positioned head-on to the Earth Ship 100,000 miles apart. "Comm to Xones ship, what is your purpose?"

Admiral Bloodworth said to Commander Williams, his Chief of Staff, "Now we see if they came prepared to parley."

"But how will they know Universal to answer our request?"

"I'm guessing they've captured Katz ships in the past and used their Learning machine."

"How long do we wait before trying again?"

"Let's give them a chance to figure out what they want to say."

"Sir, I'm getting a reply, "Comm to warship, why do you attack our ships?"

"Comm to Xones ship, you know why. You attacked me personally without provocation and have a history of destroying everything you don't need and other life forms."

"Comm to warship, the Katz lie. They are an old race without the will to wage war against us, so they have found you to fight us."

"Comm to Xones ship, yes, we suspected that was their primary goal; however, we cannot allow you to come any closer to our home worlds."

"Comm to warship, there are more of you? Why is it that we haven't encountered you before?"

"Comm to Xones ship, this arm of the Galaxy has many of our worlds. We did not have the ability to travel in space before the Katz arrived. We are explorers and will now follow your ships to your home World. Do you wish to surrender to us or wait for us to

annihilate   *your*   *species?"*
It was two hours later before the Xones replied to their ultimatum. "Comm to warship, what do you call yourselves?"

"Comm to Xones ship, we call ourselves by many names, my particular race is called Humans."

"Comm to warship, your Human ships are noted on two fronts and are becoming annoying to us. But, we are many more than you can imagine and we will overwhelm you eventually. However, we will offer you a truce to expand no further if you will do the same?"

"Comm to Xones ship, as you noted, we Humans can be very annoying. The Katz were at first reluctant to give us Space because they feared us almost as much as you. You notice we have improved the design of the Katz ships and are even now building better weapons in which to fight you. We are a tenacious race who will destroy you if you continue to fight us."

"Comm to warship, what is your warrior name? Mine is Admiral Sissas."

"Comm to Xones ship, you have the honor of addressing Fleet Admiral Bloodworth. What is your answer to my ultimatum?"

"Comm to Fleet Admiral Bloodworth, I will consult with my superiors and will return here with an answer in sixty units of time."

The Xones ship maneuvered until it was pointed toward the next warp gate, and then accelerated away from them at 3g's. When the ship traveled 50,000 miles it fired two salvos of missiles at them.

Captain Lundberg ordered, "Comm to weapons, fire two salvos of missiles at departing Xones ship and then prepare for missile defense."

"Ma'am, yes ma'am, firing two salvos now."

The Beast shuddered as the salvoes left the ship.

"Science Officer, how long before incoming missiles arrive?"

"Ma'am, fifteen minutes. Short range missiles defense will fire in five minutes."

"Comm to CCC, prepare for missile engagement and take shelter."

"Short range missiles firing."

"Laser Cannons firing."

"Ma'am, incoming missiles were eliminated, no ship damage is

reported."

"*Ma'am, a message torpedo has departed the Xones ship.*"

"*Ma'am, the Xones ship is being engaged by our missiles. One hit...two hits.*"

"*Ma'am, the Xones ship has exploded.*"

"*Any chance the remaining missiles will reach the message torpedo?*"

"*Ma'am, it's a million to one odds.*"

"*Comm to Fleet Admiral; Sir, the Xones ship has exploded and the message torpedo will likely reach its destination.*"

"*Thank you Captain. Please set a return course to the fleet and you may discontinue Battle Stations.*"

Admiral Bloodworth said, "My take on this action was that the Xones Admiral was so frightened by us that he risked his death to try to kill me. It also showed that you couldn't trust the Xones to uphold any treaty they might make."

General Hinderman asked, "The ship you were on was like the smaller ships in your escort?"

"Yes, this action took place about twenty ship years ago. The fleet has been upgraded since then."

"Admiral, how did you find us?"

"We've been looking for others like us ever since we became aware of Aqua. The fourth gate from Earth was the entry to Aqua. From our second Earth warp gate the fourth gate only brought us more battles with the Xones. This last time I played a hunch and sent a probe through the gate at 1g speed rather than our normal 2g's and found you. If the Xones did this as well, you would have been discovered and destroyed. I think it's a fluke that you haven't been discovered before now."

The two Green representatives turned pale as they looked at each other, "Admiral, assuming we sign a treaty with you, what help are you willing to give us?"

"Do you have any warships capable of defending this system?"

"No! We have small ships used mainly to transport cargo from our second planet that we call Raylee. Nothing that can be converted to defend against the Xones."

"We would contact the Katz and have them send a huge portable shipyard capable of producing ships like our Heavy Battle Cruisers and Battleships; however, that will take time. We have a surplus fleet of our original Cruisers equal to what the Xones use and we would be willing to have you use seven of these as your starter fleet until you begin building your own ships like we use now. You would have to train crews to man them and find officers who have the tactics ability to defeat the Xones. Each ship has a Learning machine to teach your crews how to perform their duties. The hard part is finding men and women with the ability to outwit your enemy. Standing toe to toe with them will not work; you need to outthink them. Kill them with tactics that gives you the advantage. Once you have your ships crewed we'll offer your brightest three ship commanders a ride to observe some of our battles with the Xones."

"We are not asking payment for this help, except for an occasional stop to reprovision our food supply. Do you think you can sell this to your people?"

The Ambassador and General looked at each other, and then Ambassador Pardon spoke, "I don't think there will be a problem at all. Give us three days and we'll be back for a signing."

CHAPTER 8

A week later First Fleet was back at the Green Systems warp gate with a treaty in hand with the Green System. Fleet Admiral Bloodworth commed the Fleet with the details of the Treaty before they sent a probe through the gate to make certain that no unfriendly's were in the system. They eventually transited the gate and then sent another probe back through the gate at the normal 2g's speed. The return was negative, so the Fleets second Battleship, the UES Madrid led their half of the fleet through the gate.

When the Flagship reached the fifth system, Captain Samantha Lopez of the Madrid sent a comm to the Hulk informing the Fleet Admiral that no active sensor readings were found and she awaited his orders.

Fleet Admiral Bloodworth anticipating another ambush by enemy missile platforms sent two sensor missiles separated by 100,000 miles toward the next warp gate. These missiles were each programed to emulated the readings of ten ships in the hopes of springing the enemy's trap.

The two ploys were hardly a quarter of the way toward the next gate when they were attacked by two enemy missile platforms of 100 missiles each. The sensor missiles were programed to go silent when they detected missiles headed their way with the hope that they might survive the missile attack.

Admiral Bloodworth led the fleet forward hoping they had sprung the enemy's only trap in this system. An hour later their sensors detected a renewal of one of their sensor missiles continuing to the next gate ahead of them.

* * *

Lieutenant (jg) Hope Bloodworth was well into her second year of medical school at the Johns Hopkins School of Medicine located in Baltimore, Maryland. Fellow student Jeff Fellows joined the study group of Hope and her roommates. Hope and Jeff originally met during last summer's school session and he quickly charmed her roommates at their first meeting. Now their group was a fixture at Norton Hall every Tuesday and Thursday.

The relationship was so productive that everyone was loath to introduce romance into the mix for fear of destroying a good thing. However, Jeff was starting to get a reputation as a lover because of his close relationship with the study group despite the fact that no one had time for romance because of their studies.

One late Thursday, they were ending an especially tiring session when Joey Willoughby asked Jeff, "Are your male friends ribbing you about our study sessions?"

He flushed a little, but gave her a smile. "No, they seem jealous that I've got three of the most beautiful women all to myself."

Olivia flushed at this revelation, "So, they think we're beautiful. Why haven't they made some kind of move?"

He gave a little laugh, "Two things - first I'm always with you studying, and two they've heard that Hope is a black belt in Judo who broke a guy's collarbone when he put the moves on her."

Her roommates looked at Hope sharply. Olivia asked in shock, "Hope, is that true?"

"Well, he didn't stop when I told him to buzz off... It was his own fault!" She said defensibly.

Her roommates looked at her in shock for a moment, and then they started laughing so hard tears came to their eyes. Hope asked, "What's so funny?"

Joey answered, "Us, for thinking we needed to protect you from overeager boys."

"You should have known better. Mother had the marines give me self-defense lessons as soon as I got breasts. However, no one ever tried to take liberties with me until now. It kind of felt good that I could take care of myself."

Joey grinned at her, "Okay, after our mid-term tests are over next week we need to host a party. I'm in the need to have my ego stroked by a male. Jeff how do we get the word out?"

"Make a poster and place it on the bulletin board. You better say BYO booze if desired, otherwise soft drinks and chips will be served - drunks will be ejected."

Joey grinned, "I'll make the poster and go thirds on the refreshments. Hope won't be wearing her uniform for this party, so let's see what happens."

The night of the party Hope's roommates were waiting until she came out of the head, anxious to see how she was dressed. When she finally emerged they both smiled their approval. She was wearing a dress, conservative in that its hem was knee length, but the color was a shocking pink and showed enough of her beasts that it was eye catching.

"Well, do you approve?" She said with a hesitant smile.

Olivia said, "Wow! You're going to need a bodyguard."

Joey laughed, "No, Jeff's reaction is what I'm looking for."

Hope frowned, "What do you mean?"

"Honey, you are clueless, he's smitten with you and you act like he's your brother."

She frowned at them; "You know I'm going back to space when I graduate. We have no future!"

"Oh, but there is if you convince him to intern with you on the Hulk." Joey said with a smile.

"He'd have to join Star Fleet and commit himself for years."

"Honey, if he interns with you he'd already have committed his love to you."

"You really think he feels that strongly?"

"When he comes through that door, look into his eyes and you'll know."

She went over to their full-length mirror and preened, turning from side to side, "Do you really think he loves me? I'm frightened, this is a big commitment!"

They stood on each side of her and smiled at her in the mirror. "Regardless, you need to know." Olivia said while squeezing her hand. If we're wrong, it's better to know now rather than pine over someone who's not interested."

Fifteen minutes later, their first knock sounded from their door. Hope summoned her courage and answered the door, finding Jeff standing there. His eyes widened as he took in her appearance and there was no hiding his passion for her in his expression. She took his hand and pulled him inside and shut the door with her hip as she pulled him into her embrace, kissing him with all the passion she was holding in reserve.

When they finally broke apart he said in awe, "You love me too!"

* * *

Lieutenants Adam and Karrie Bloodworth received new assignments to the Bridge. Adam was assigned to the First Shift and Karrie to the Second Shift and both were assigned to weapons deployment.

The First Fleet was now travelling through the sixth system and had yet to encounter any Xones ships. The fifth system had the ambush waiting for the unwary, but the Admiral took steps to spring that trap without any casualties and Adam was now wondering what yet lay before them.

Adam arrived in their shared quarters first and quickly did some housekeeping chores before his wife arrived. He set aside a bottle of wine to celebrate their transfers as he felt her approaching and quickly dimmed the lighting and turned on the music they enjoyed just as she entered the cabin. Karrie smiled her appreciation before they embraced, savoring each other's scent, before kissing passionately.

They slowly broke apart and Karrie took a seat while Adam poured the wine. Clicking their glasses together, they toasted themselves for finally reaching their goal of a Bridge assignment. Karrie smiled at her husband, "I know dear, we'll eventually get our dream assignment where we're assigned to the Bridge on the same shift. At least we're here at last."

Adam nodded his head, "I know, but I've got the first shift so let's eat and return here for some togetherness and then sleep. It may get exciting tomorrow for both of us."

The next day the Hulk was at the middle point in the eighth system, when its sensor display lit up with three enemy fleets of twenty ships each ahead of their current track. All three enemy fleets were 200,000 miles ahead and about 80,000 miles apart in a staggered formation. Adam hit the Battle Stations button and the ship became awake. XO Bruce Namio asked for the sensor data and after quickly studying it he placed a comm to the Admiral. While he awaited his response, Namio asked Adam for his analysis.

"Sir, all three formations have just fired a salvo. I would recommend that the fleet go to X-RAY 1 immediately and then start firing salvos of our own."

"COMM Flag to fleet, initiate X-RAY 1 immediately."

The fleet immediately split into two separate formations with each Battleship surrounded by seven Battle Cruisers. "COMM Flag to Fleet, Formation 1 Cruisers concentrate four salvoes on left enemy formation, Formation 2 Cruisers concentrate four salvoes on right formation, and the Battleships will concentrate two salvoes on the center formation, Fire when ready."

"Comm to CCC, we are under missile attack, seek shelter now."

"Admiral to Bridge, what's the clock for incoming and outgoing missiles?"

"Sir, fifteen minutes for incoming and eighteen minutes for outgoing."

"Admiral to Bridge, in ten minutes we will move fleet 200,000 miles to our right."

"COMM Flag to fleet, in ten minutes we will move 200,000 miles to our right, on my command."

Captain Bloodworth arrived at the Bridge and assumed command from XO Namio. "What is the status of missile engine cut-off?"

Lieutenant Adam Bloodworth replied, "Ma'am, enemy missile cut-off was normal, so far there have been no early cut-offs for three salvos."

"COMM Flag to Fleet, execute move to our right 200,000 miles – Execute now!"

"Captain to Flag, move has been accomplished, checking now

for trailing missiles – none followed our move. Time to arrival of our missiles is two minutes."

Adam reported to the Captain, "Ma'am, there is some movement by the enemy, but it's too late – our missiles attacking now. All three formations are being hit, one explosion, two, three, many explosions. Ma'am, there are no active readings from any of the enemy formations. It appears to be a clean sweep."

"Captain to Flag, sensors no longer have any active readings except isolated explosions."

"Flag to Fleet, reduce readiness to Battle Ready and resume voyage to far gate in normal formation. Well done everyone."

The eighth system had no further activity and when stopped before the ninth gate, the sensor returns showed no activity. Fleet Admiral Bloodworth decided to return to Earth to begin activities related to the new Green System.

CHAPTER 9

The Hulk was back in Earth orbit after a two and half year voyage. For Hope a little over four years has elapsed. She and her betrothed lover, Jeff Fellows, were ending their first year of internship at the Johns Hopkins Hospital in Baltimore, Maryland.

When she heard that the UES Hulk was in orbit she immediately placed a call to her Mother. Captain Hanna Bloodworth returned her call and was brought current as to her status as a graduate from Medical School and with one-year experience as an intern. Breaking the ice, she then revealed her relationship with fellow intern Jeff Fellows and wanted her to consider taking him on as an intern with her when she rejoined the Hulk.

There was almost thirty seconds of silence before Hanna replied, "Hope, how long have you been together."

"If you mean sharing a bedroom, about a year. However, he's been a boyfriend since the second year. He's willing to join Star Fleet, so that's not a problem."

"Very well, how soon can you two meet me on the Hulk? I want to be sure he knows what he's getting himself into."

"Yes Mother, we'll be there later today if you send a shuttle for us."

* * *

After Hanna arranged for a shuttle, she commed her sister, Doctor Lucy Hendricks. "Yes ma'am, how can I help you?"

"Lucy, I've just heard from Hope and she's bringing her fiancé aboard wanting him to join her as interns aboard the Hulk. Can you use both of them?"

There was silence for several seconds, and then she heard a muffled laugh."

"Dammit Lucy, it's not funny to me!"

"Yes, I can believe that. To answer your question, yes I can use both of them; but I want to interview him first."

"Good, me too. They'll be here in about six hours and I'll let you know when they arrive."

"Does Eric know?"

"No, he's below with the Board explaining about the Green system. I'll tell him when he returns."

"I'd like to be a mouse when you tell him about his little girl."

"It seems our little girl has grown up. I'll get back with you, out."

* * *

Hope watched Jeff's face as the shuttle left Baltimore heading toward the Hulk. He gulped and got a little pale as the (g) forces increased as they gained speed, but when his eyes locked onto the view screen showing the ground rapidly receding she knew he was hooked. His eyes got bigger when he saw the Battleship UES Hulk grow from a speck to something huge that filled the screen. She couldn't help but smile when she said, "Jeff, watch as we approach the ship, we're going to fly right inside and land!"

"What the Hell!" He said, as the shuttle flew right through an open Bay Door and settled into place. The shuttle crewman opened the door, and helped Hope as they both gave support to Jeff as he left the shuttle. He took a deep breath and nodded his head at Hope that he was okay now, before following her toward the OD guarding the entrance to the ship. Hope, who was wearing her

Lieutenant (jg) uniform, saluted the flag and asked permission to board. The OD returned her salute and gave her permission. She then told the OD who she and the visitor were and that the Captain was expecting them.

The OD replied, "Captain Bloodworth left word for you and guest to meet with her in her quarters. Do you know the way?"

"Yes, it's been a few years, but I can find it."

"Come along Jeff, I think we're both going to remember this first meeting."

It took the pair almost twenty minutes before reaching the Captains Stateroom, where a marine was standing guard. She returned the guards salute and told him she was the captains' daughter and was expected. He pushed the entry buzzer, which was answered by Jason Mao, the Captains Steward. He gave Hope a long look and smiled, telling the marine she was expected.

Hope gave the steward a hug when they entered, before turning and taking Jeff's hand as they approached the Captain, who was standing next to her aunt. "Mother, Auntie Lucy, this is the love of my life, Jeff Fellows."

"Jeff, the woman with all the stripes on her sleeve cuffs is Captain Hanna Lundberg Bloodworth, my Mother. The other woman is her sister and is the Doctor of the ship, Commander Lucy Lundberg Hendricks. They both hold our future in their hands."

They stood before the ranking officers and awaited their reaction. Lucy turned to her sister, "She looks older somehow, maybe even smarter than when she left. Do you think she was smart enough to bring us a competent Doctor?"

Hanna gave the two a smile, "Let's sit and talk for a bit and get to know each other. Hope certainly has grown in mind and personality since she left for medical school."

After they took seats facing each other, Hanna said, "Your father is on Earth discussing our

discovery of another race similar to Earth and Aqua. That's going to bring many changes for our future, but for now let's concentrate on you two. You said you've finished a year of internship where you graduated. I'm sure Lucy is going to be interested in what that entailed, but right now I'm interested in you two getting married and staying aboard for years, maybe for your entire working lives. Jeff, has Hope told you about our lives serving Star Fleet?"

"Yes, I think she tried to scare me off with her stories. She told me about how Doctor

Hendricks started and how she followed in her footsteps, getting commissioned and placed on detached duty to attend medical school. Upon graduation, she returned to her ship as an intern for two years and she now appears to be the primary doctor of the ship, on a Battleship no less."

Hanna smiled, "Yes, she has done well, but a Battleship requires more than one doctor and she's been overworked. Did Hope tell you about how time works in warp space?"

"Yes, a voyage of one year for the ship's crew in warp space, is equivalent to about two years on Earth. That's a little hard to believe, but you two don't look as old as you should for people over 100 years of age."

"Yes, you bring up a valid point, if you don't travel with your mate, the person left ashore will soon age beyond what a couple could realistic expect a marriage to survive, that and the long absences between voyages. Have you discussed this with your family?"

He nodded his head, "They don't like it, but this is my life and I can't foresee a future without hope in it."

Hanna looked at her future son-in-law for a moment, and then turned to her daughter.

"You're sure he's the one you want to spend the rest of your life with?"

"Mother, I ache when I'm too long away from him."

"Yes, I remember when I thought I'd never be able to be with your father. You have my approval and don't worry about Erik, I'll convince him if it comes to that. The one you have to convince now is your Aunt. She's the one to convince that Jeff is good enough for an intern for her hospital."

Hope's eyes turned to her Aunt, and then she smiled. "Lucy, I graduated eighth in my class of 212 students. Jeff graduated ninth, and we were both in the top ten percent of our class. He was actively recruited by ten top hospitals to do his internship with them, so I think he's a good pick to intern here."

Lucy looked at the two young graduates with new eyes as she

studied them, "What were your final picks for internships?"

"We've both worked long hours in the Emergency Room this past year."

"Hanna, you better get this young man commissioned before he changes his mind."

"Hope, you know the way to Personnel and by the time you get there I'll have paved the way for Jeff. Afterwards, take him to the Learning machine for Universal language, medical machine operation, and military courtesy."

"Yes mother, what are our rank's going to be so that Jeff can draw the proper uniforms from the Quartermaster."

"Let's stay with your current rank for both of you. Later, after some experience you'll both be promoted to Lieutenant."

After Hanna made her call to Personnel, Lucy smiled at her sister as she said, "Hope has lost all her insecurities she had when she left for medical school. She knows what she wants and isn't shy about the way she goes after it."

Hanna shook her head in sorrow, "She's just like me at that age. Wait until her husband decides she has overstepped herself and learns that marriage is a partnership if it's going to work."

Lucy frowned at her, "You never fought with me over a disagreement. As I recall, you reconsidered and if you were wrong or didn't think the fight was worth the hassle, you capitulated. I never pushed the point if you continued the argument because when you did that you were probably right."

"Yes, but we were sisters and knew each other very well. Jeff and Hope haven't known each other that long and have been under the stress of medical school. We'll see how this learning curve works out with two type A personalities. I wonder how Eric is doing with the Board?"

* * *

Fleet Admiral Bloodworth and Admiral Cochran were arguing with the Board over the no payment for the seven Cruisers promised to the Green System. Bloodworth pointed out that we didn't pay the Katz for the ships we received or charge the Aqua's for the ships we gave them. The Board member who was arguing with him abruptly stopped and reconsidered, before dropping his objection. The Board then formally approved the Green Treaty.

Later, the two admirals were discussing how training the Greens could be speeded up so that they could formally defend their own system. After discussing several methods they finally agreed that when the Cruisers were delivered, that their Earth Crews would train the Green crews until they were proficient enough to operate on their own. At that point they would rejoin the next Earth fleet that arrived.

Bloodworth was concerned that if the Greens were in any kind of battle they currently had no way to replace their missiles. They soon came up with a way to fix that problem and possibly a way to get the Earth crews home sooner. They would send a supply ship with the six Cruisers, have the Greens build a space supply platform where they would store the extra missiles, and use the ship to return the Earth crews home. If the Cruisers were sufficiently trained perhaps they could escort the supply ship to Earth, assuming the threat level is no worse.

Admiral Cochran nodded his head in satisfaction, "Yes, I think this might work if everyone is agreeable. Worse case, they stay until the next fleet arrives. Since the Second Fleet hasn't arrived yet, let's get those six Cruisers prepped and crews selected. You might ask any First Fleet XO's if they want to volunteer for the Captains positions. It would mean they would be selected next for any new ship construction."

Bloodworth smiled, "I'll put all positions needed on as volunteer postings and any positions not filled will have to come from Second Fleet crews. It shouldn't take more than three months to check systems and replenish stores."

Cochran asked, "How long do you need for shore leave after this long voyage?"

"First fleet will need four months this time. Everyone will probably take his or her maximum of thirty days. I personally will need that for Hanna and myself as well. We need it for family reasons."

When Eric returned to the Hulk he had his Chief of Staff send notices to the First Fleet asking for volunteers to serve aboard the six Cruisers being given to the Green's and the positions needed. Those XO's, who wished to volunteer as an acting captain, should first check with the Flag Captain.

Eric commed the Captain, "Yes Sir, this is the Captain."

"Are you free to consult?"

"Yes sir, will our stateroom suffice?"

"I'll meet you there in fifteen minutes."

He reached their stateroom before Hanna and had their steward prepare them hot tea to drink.

Eric was sipping his tea when Hanna arrived, who held up her hand as she hurried into the head.

Later, she sat sipping her own tea, "Hope and her intended met with Lucy and me earlier and they are both going to intern here, and I suppose get married ASAP. His parents live in Kansas City. Is that far from Springfield?"

"Not far, about a three or four hour drive. Do you know anything about them?"

"Not a thing except they tried to discourage him from joining Star Fleet, mainly because he'd be gone so much of the time. They should meet with his parents and discuss where they should get married."

"Let's meet with the love birds and discuss this with them. They could take leave, visit his parents and make their plans."

Hanna pressed a button on her hand unit and said, "Comm to Lt. Hope Bloodworth, contact the Captain ASAP."

"Ma'am, this is Lt. Hope Bloodworth."

"As soon as you and Lt. Fellows can manage, your Father and I have some personal matters to discuss with both of you."

"Aye ma'am, we will be there in two hours. Jeff is presently in the Learning machine."

"Very well, we'll see you after he finishes."

"Crap! I forgot he was going to do that." She said with a frown.

Eric looked at his watch and thought a moment, "Do you think we should contact his parents ourselves? It's 16:10 hours in Kansas City."

"We could introduce ourselves and tell them what they're doing now and ask if they would like to discuss their marriage plans?"

"Without informing Hope? No, that would really make her mad. We could ask her to come here while Jeff is still in the tank and then call them if she's okay with it."

"Let's try, I'd really like to talk to them."

"Comm to Lt. Hope Bloodworth, please return to the Captain's

Stateroom for a short period of time."

"Aye Ma'am, I'm on my way."

When she entered the room and seeing her father, she ran into his arms. "Oh Dad, it's good to see you again."

"It's been too long; Hope, is it true that you've never talked to Jeff's parents?"

"Yes, we never had the time because we both took summer classes."

"How about Christmas?"

"He's Jewish, but not religious. I know, there's something's off between Jeff and his parents."

"Hanna and I want to call them and arrange a meeting, but not without your consent."

"Dad, I don't want to get married until I find out what's going on between Jeff and his parents. Let's call them now."

Hanna said, "I've got their number from his enlistment data. Eric, you call since you're the father."

They could hear the various clicks as the call routed itself to Kansas City, and then the first ring, another ring, before a click as someone picked up the receiver. "Hello."

"This is Fleet Admiral Eric Bloodworth, whom am I talking to?"

There was a short silence, as the person on the line said nothing, then, "This is Shanell Fellows. Is this about Jeff?"

"Yes, Jeff Fellows is planning on marrying my daughter, Hope Bloodworth, and my wife and

I wanted to meet his family before the wedding."

"Oh my dear, Jeff is our adopted son. His family died in a car accident when he was three and my Joseph and I raised him. He told us of his love for your daughter, but we didn't know of any wedding."

"Would you and Joseph like to attend the wedding or would you prefer to also help in the planning of the event?"

"Yes please! I can attend the wedding, but Joseph is in a nursing home after a recent stroke and is not well."

"How is your health? Are you able to walk?"

"Oh, I get around and I'm able to drive to the doctor and grocery."

"Very good! When we have made final plans we will contact

you again. Would you like to speak to Hope, my daughter?"

"Yes please."

"Mrs. Fellows, this is Hope. Jeff and I attended medical school together and are both doctors now. I'm happy that you're able to attend our wedding. How old are you?"

"Oh my dear, I'm a healthy seventy-eight. Don't worry about me."

"Oh but I do. Does Joseph still have his mental abilities?"

"No, bless his heart. I don't think he will be with us much longer."

"Mrs. Fellows it's been a privilege to speak with you. I'll talk to you later."

She disconnected and turned to her father and started crying in his arms "That poor woman's husband is dying and her adopted son is far away. She said the stroke is recent, Jeff may not know of his illness? Jeff and I will have to talk about his adoptive parents before making any marriage plans."

Hanna said, "Hope, look at me! Ask your questions, but before you begin remember how you met him and his treatment of you since. His part in this separation may be innocent and beyond his control, so tread softly with your questions."

Hope looked at her mother with new respect and took a long deep breath. "Yes Mother, Jeff is the most considerate person I've ever met. He doesn't have a mean bone in his body."

Hope looked at the time. "He's still got another hour in the tank and assuming we go ahead with the wedding, do we have it here or on Earth? Mother, both sides of my Grandparents are now gone and only your sister, Clare, is left on Earth. Do you think she'd want to attend?"

"That's a thought; she and Jeff's mother are our last ties to Earth. Everyone else is here aboard this ship." Hanna said softly in reflection, "I'll call Clare and get her response to our problem. Besides, her son Ian is in Star Fleet somewhere, I've lost track."

Erik said, "You talk to your sister and I'll track down Ian. Depending on Jeff's Mothers health, having the wedding here is probably our best choice."

CHAPTER 10

Hope and Jeff Fellows wedding took place aboard the UES Hulk, three weeks after Hope's return to the ship with her intended in tow. Since Jeff had no one to act as Best Man - Adam, her brother, stepped in for that position. Hope was able to arrange for her two roommates from medical school to come aboard as her Bridesmaids, with Joey Willoughby as the Maid of Honor.

Shanell Fellows, Jeff's sixty-eight year old adoptive Mother, was also aboard with wonder in her eyes as she observed things she'd only previously heard about on the news feed. Lt. Ian Lundberg Eiberger was found aboard the UES Beast of First Fleet and was ecstatic about being able to attend the wedding of his aunt and uncle Bloodworths daughter. He was made a groomsman, while Ian's mother - Clare, Hanna's middle sister, was helping her sister Lucy get Hope into a wedding dress borrowed from Clare.

The only people not wearing a uniform were the bride and the civilians present. The wedding itself was being held in the large conference room open to all off-duty crew. After the wedding an open reception was planned.

Later, after the wedding, standing in the reception line, Hope asked, "Jeff, did you have any trouble getting your mother to the shuttle?"

"No, the police escort helped, but she practically jumped into the shuttle she was so excited. I thought she might have some trouble with the acceleration, but she just held my hand and kept her eyes on the view screen all the way to the Hulk."

"I wish your father had been alive and well so that he too could be here."

Jeff nodded his head, "Yes, but his phobia about space wouldn't have allowed him to come.

I'm glad Mom is here as this may be the last time we see each other because of her age."

Hope squeezed his hand, "I know what you mean. I've now lost all my grandparents during our voyages or while attending school."

"When my father heard I was interested in a Star Fleet woman, he just went bonkers. There was no reasoning with him and Mother was the only person I could talk to."

"Jeff, no one is blaming you. It's something you did your best with until the problem resolved itself. How is your mother getting home?"

"Do you mind if we took her back to Kansas City. We can go to Florida from there for our mini-honeymoon, before coming back to the ship."

At her nod of acceptance he looked around at the crowd of people at their reception. "Who are all these people – besides the crew?"

She smiled at him, "Mostly extended family from mothers side of the family. Dad was an only child. See that Lieutenant talking to Aunt Clair, he's her son who got the space bug from both her sisters. That would make him a cousin, I think. Dad said when Ian was little they visited Hamburg, Germany where Mom was from. Anyway, he gave Ian a badge from the Heavy Cruiser UES Beast, which really gave him Space Fever. Dad found him assigned to the Beast, can you believe that?"

"So, he's in Star Fleet now. I guess we get to start our own Star Fleet family branch."

"Yeah, but not just yet. We have to finish our internship and I want to experience being a Doctor before becoming a mother."

* * *

Lieutenant Adam Bloodworth was in his cabin waiting for his wife to come off Bridge duty.

He smiled at his memories of his sister Hope's wedding. It was the first of its kind in the history of Star Fleet, a wedding of a Fleet Admiral's daughter who was also a commissioned Star Fleet officer, marrying another Star Fleet officer onboard the Admiral's Flag Ship, captained by his wife and the mother of the bride. He wet his index finger and made a mark in the air, no one is going to beat that.

He was a little concerned about Karrie. She seemed a bit out of sorts when she replaced him at his Bridge duty station. Maybe it was just his imagination, but it still nagged at him. He finished cleaning their cabin and bagged their laundry for pickup when he felt her approaching.

She entered their quarters and immediately hurried to him with tears in her eyes and as they embraced he felt her emotions racing from joy to dread and back again. "Kay, what's going on?"

"Oh Adam, we're going to have a baby!"

"How did that happen? I thought you were taking birth control."

"Adam, you know we aren't a typical couple! Whatever the reason, it didn't work and I'm pregnant!"

"Did you take the test?"

"No, let's talk to Lucy. I suppose I could be wrong, but I don't think so."

When they arrived at the ships hospital, Doctor Lucy Hendricks took one look at Karrie and smiled. When Karrie started to speak, Lucy said, "I know, I'll get a kit and we'll check to be sure."

After Karrie returned from the head, with the stick in hand she exclaimed, "It's positive!"

Lucy frowned, "You've got the implant, yet here you are pregnant. Come with me, we're going to run some tests. Adam, why don't you go tell your mother she's going to be a grandmother."

Adams face got a little paler as he finally realized he was going to be a father. As he walked out of the hospital, he decided to tell his father first. Maybe, he'd come up with a way to tell his mother that she was going to be a grandmother.

He soon arrived at the ships Flag Office and approached the Chief of Staff's desk.

Commander Dana Williams Sullins looked up at his approach and smiled, asking, "Lieutenant Bloodworth, how can I help you?"

"Ma'am, I have a personal matter to discuss with the Admiral."

She turned and saw that the admiral was not using his comm, "Sure, go right in."

Adam walked up to the clear door and knocked. His father saw who was there and motioned him inside and pointed to a chair asking, "What's going on?"

"I just came from the hospital and Karrie's pregnant."

Eric looked at his son and realized that wasn't the whole story, "What's going on?"

"You mean besides telling mother she's going to be a grandmother?" He said with rueful smile. "Karrie has an anti-pregnancy implant that apparently didn't work. Maybe something else is going on here - is it possible that her body wants this pregnancy?"

Eric looked at his son with sympathy and concern, "Son, what's happening now?"

"Oh, Aunt Lucy's running tests on Karrie now. She told me to tell mom she's going to be a grandmother – did you know she had a wicked sense of humor?"

"Yeah, just like your mother. I'd better comm her to come here, we'll want some privacy when she hears this news."

* * *

Father and son were having coffee when Hanna arrived about twenty minutes later. Seeing her son with Eric she immediately thought someone in the family was hurt. But, from their expressions that wasn't it.

She went over and prepared her own coffee, asking, "What's going on?"

Adam gave her a weak smile, "Lucy told me to tell you that you're going to be a grandmother."

Hanna looked from one to the other and realized it wasn't a joke. *It couldn't be Hope; she's just returned from her honeymoon, so that left Karrie.* "Is Karrie alright? I thought she used an implant?"

"Yes, Lucy's running tests trying to find out what went wrong and if Karrie's all right otherwise."

"Something else is going on! What's the problem?"

Adam gave her a weak smile. "It's our connection with each other! It's getting stronger and that could be the reason the implant failed."

Hanna studied her son's face and could tell he was worried, "Son, you knew when you married Karrie that you were entering uncharted territory. Don't let your concerns worry Karrie; she has enough of that already. Let's return to the hospital and see if my sister has better news for us."

When they arrived they found all three doctors hovering over the test results. When Hope saw them arrive, she immediately came over and asked Adam, "Come with me, we need a sample of your blood to test a theory we now have."

After they left, Hanna asked Lucy, "What's going on?"

"We found something odd in Karrie's blood workup. Hope is getting blood from Adam to confirm a theory we've developed, and Hope has already given blood to act as a comparison."

Twenty minutes later, the doctors returned to Karrie's bedside where Eric and Hanna were waiting. Lucy spoke for the other doctors, "For some reason Adam and Karrie's DNA has changed slightly. They each have acquired some of the others strands, apparently enough that they feel each other's moods and nearby presence. Whether it has anything to do with her getting pregnant despite having an implant is unknown."

Karrie asked, "How about my baby, is she alright and how far along am I?"

"We don't know its gender yet, but you are six weeks into your gestation. You apparently are one of the lucky ones without morning sickness."

"I've felt weird, but so far no sickness."

"Karrie I'm going to clear you for duty, but I want you back here weekly so that I can chart your progress. If you have any problems return here so we can chart it."

Karrie gave a short laugh, "It sounds like you're going to write a book about my pregnancy."

The three doctors gave each other a small smile.

CHAPTER 11

Adam and Karrie Bloodworth were the proud parents of Marie who ruled their household. Captain Mae Fieldspire Becker of the Battleship Trojan Horse, Flagship of the Aqua Navy, was reluctant to leave after seeing her granddaughter for the first time while the Hulk was in Aqua orbit.

Fleet Admiral Bloodworth apprised the Aqua Space Headquarters of his discovery of another race similar to the people of Earth and Aqua, and their plans to ultimately start a third front with ships from Green. This caused jubilation among the people of Aqua and greater interest in manning its new ship constructs.

The combined fleet of Aqua and First Fleet left Aqua orbit with three Battleships and twenty-four Heavy Battle Cruisers. Aqua's Battle Fleet was now one Battleship and ten Heavy Battle Cruisers. During this almost two year cruise they battled six times with the Xones and destroyed 320 enemy ships, with no losses of their own.

Two years and six months later the UES Hulk was back in Earth orbit and Fleet Admiral Bloodworth left his Flagship to consult with Star Fleet Headquarters. Admiral Cochran finished debriefing Bloodworth on his activities out of Aqua and asked, "Eric do you want more coffee before continuing?"

"Yeah Jim, my throat's getting a little dry."

After they refilled their cups, Cochran asked, "I understand you have a new granddaughter; how's she getting along?"

"Marie is almost three now and a climber, causing her parents to watch over her closely.

She's also talking, which has everyone excited."

Eric expression turned serious as he asked, "Jim, what has been accomplished with the Green's?"

"Almost a year after you left for Aqua with First Fleet, Admiral Pavlova left Earth with Second Fleet escorting seven Cruisers and a munitions ship for the Green System. His intention was to leave the Cruisers there for the Green's to crew and learn how to operate them with the help of the skeleton crew that got the ships there."

"So that's the last you've heard from them?"

"Yes, I'd expect that Second Fleet would check on them before returning to Earth."

"That's probably why they haven't arrived yet, how about the Katz? Any word from them?"

"No, It's not like them to stay away too long."

After returning to the Hulk, Admiral Bloodworth sought out his wife to determine how they were going to spend their shore leave. They no longer had relatives living on Earth, except for Hanna's sister, who they last saw at their daughter's wedding aboard the Hulk.

She gave him a thoughtful look as she considered his request, "I'd like to go somewhere with a wide vista of scenery and exotic smells. Do you have an idea that fits?"

"To me that would be in the mountains or seashore. What's your preference?"

"I've never been to Switzerland, how about you?"

"Why not do both, a week there and the next week on a beach somewhere?" He said with a slight smile.

"You just want to see me in a swimsuit. I've heard of a secluded area in the Florida Keys that might fit our needs. Have Dana make arrangements for both places. Your Chief of Staff is very good at making those kinds of arrangements, besides she always takes her leave when you do and maybe she'd want to go there as well."

"How about Clare, we could stop and see her for a few days before coming back to the ship?"

"When we decide when we're going, I'll check to see if it's

convenient for her."

Two days later they received a comm from Home Fleet that a Katz Fleet of ten ships was inbound toward Earth, with an ETA of three days.

When the Katz fleet arrived, Fleet Admiral Bloodworth commed an invitation to Admiral Gamma Killa to a conference to be held aboard the UES Hulk at her convenience. She replied, "I shall be aboard within the hour."

After Admiral Killa's arrival, Fleet Admiral Bloodworth and Captain Hanna Bloodworth escorted her to their quarters. Steward Jason Mao opened the door and bowed to their visiting benefactor, who stopped inside and gazed at the space allowed the senior officers of a Battleship.

Killa turned to the Bloodworths and smiled, "My, you humans know how to build a fabulous warship. I thought your Heavy Battle Cruiser was the ultimate upgrade from our original design, but this appears to be the weapon that's going to win the war against the Xones."

Eric Bloodworth smiled at her enthusiasm, "Yes, with this Battleship leading a fleet we have reached further into the Xones' territory and destroyed many more of their ships. Our voyages are now lasting about two years in warp space, and more importantly we've added another race, much like the Aqua's and ourselves, to the Xones fight. We need another shipyard for them so that they can construct their own warships."

Admiral Killa looked at him in surprise, "What is their technical level?"

"A little higher than we were when you helped us. They have in-system space ships and were not aware of the warp gates within their system. They call their planet "Green," which is the third planet from their Sun. They also use the second planet for mining and agriculture. We saw no evidence of any armed spaceships within the system and they seemed anxious to obtain the seven Cruisers we offered for their defense of their system against the Xones."

"This is great news, but it will take at least six months to get the shipyard to our new allies. You say you gave them seven ships? Do they have any with trained crews?"

"Uncertain, Admiral Pavlova is expected to follow-up with

them when he returns from his voyage, and he's twenty days past due from his ETA."

"Well, I'll wait until his arrival before arranging for the shipyard. In the meantime I want to see more of this wonderful ship."

Hanna said, "Would you like to be guided by my son, Lieutenant Adam Bloodworth? He married the daughter of Captain Mae Fieldspire Becker."

Admiral Killa gazed at Hanna for a moment, "Was their attraction the same as their parents?"

"Yes, maybe even stronger. They were married the same day they met."

"These people from Green, are they mostly the same as Humans and the Aquas?"

"Yes our DNA scan indicates that they appear to be from the same gene pool."

"Interesting, isn't it? Also, they appear to be about the same distance from Earth."

Hanna quirked her eyebrow at Admiral Killa, "Your people have been around for a long time. Have you heard anything about an older race seeding systems as an experiment?"

"There is evidence of an older race with space capabilities, but whether they engaged in such practices is pure conjecture. Still, …"

"It does raise suspicions, doesn't it?"

"Getting back to your son giving me a guided tour; I'd really enjoy that. I would like to meet his wife as well; maybe at a social setting or a dinner?"

Hanna smiled at her interest, "Gamma, I'll arrange a dinner where you can meet all my extended family. Have you met my sister and my youngest child? They are married to members of our crew and have expressed a desire to meet you."

* * *

The next day Lieutenant Adam Bloodworth conducted a tour of the Hulk for the benefit of Admiral Killa starting with the Battleship's enhanced Laser Cannons that had a 50,000-mile range, up from 10,000 miles for the Heavy Battle Cruisers.

Admiral Killa asked, "How have these new lasers performed in combat?"

"Madam, they are the primary missile defense for the fleet. No enemy missile has survived once they enter the ship's range. Those missiles targeting the supporting Heavy Battle Cruisers suffered a similar fate and we have started to retrofit the larger lasers to our Heavies, but due to their larger size it has resulted in fewer laser cannons. Come, let's check out our larger missile salvoes."

The Admiral viewed the larger missiles carried by the Hulk in surprise, "These must have longer range due to their size?"

"Yes, they have a range of 150,000 miles, up from 100,000 miles and they have an easier method to select an early shut down and restart program. In addition, each side has a forty missile salvo, twice that of a Heavy. These can be used on the Heavies as well, but due to their large size limits the inventory that can be carried. We do have two cargo ships that carry additional missiles and food consumables."

Admiral Killa tentatively touched the huge missile, and then followed Adam as he continued the tour.

Later that evening the Bloodworth and Lundberg extended family had their first combined dinner. All those who were members of Star Fleet were in attendance, Lieutenant Ian Eiberger of the UES Beast, the son of Hanna's sister Clare, was given leave to attend this special gathering. In addition, both children of Fleet Admiral Bloodworth and Captain Hanna Lundberg Bloodworth were in attendance with their spouses, Lieutenant Adam Bloodworth and his wife, Lieutenant Karrie Fieldspire Bloodworth; and Lieutenant Hope Bloodworth Fellows and her husband, Lieutenant Jeff Fellows. Last, but not least, Hanna's sister, Commander Lucy Lundberg Hendricks and her husband, Lt. Commander Kory Hendricks.

The dining table in the Admirals Suite was barely large enough to accommodate everyone.

Fleet Admiral Bloodworth made the introductions of their extended family to their guest who stood and gave everyone a short bow.

"I am honored to meet the extended family of Fleet Admiral Bloodworth and his wife, Flag Captain Hanna Lundberg Bloodworth. Their combined efforts have resulted in the withdrawal of our common enemy, the Xones, because of the staggering losses they have suffered. Perhaps with the addition of another ally we can accelerate their withdrawal."

There was clapping of hands from everyone at the table in agreement of this statement. Killa took her seat and gave everyone a short bow of her head before asking Ian Eiberger, "You are the only family member not on the Flagship, but instead serve aboard the Beast. Was this intentional?"

"Madam, no, when I joined Star Fleet the UES Beast was open for posting and I've always wanted to serve aboard her since I was a child. Someday I hope to fill a posting aboard the UES Hulk. "

"What is your specialty?"

"Ma'am, I presently supervise a Laser Cannon section, but eventually hope to have Bridge

Duty."

"Aah, much like your cousin Adam Bloodworth aboard the Hulk."

At Ian's nod, she asked Adam, "I understand you and Karrie Becker have recently had a child?

Karrie answered, "Yes, it is a continuing experience for both of us. We are both happy, but due to our strange meeting and rapid marriage we are uncertain what the future holds for us and our child."

Admiral Killa addressed Hope Bloodworth Fellows, "You are the youngest child of your Parents; what was it like growing up in their shadow?"

Hope looked blankly at her for a moment, "Ma'am, there was no pressure from my parents to become part of Star Fleet, I just assumed I would. My second mother was Aunt Lucy, the ship's Doctor. That's where my interests lay; I want to heal people. I met my husband in medical school and convinced him to follow me back to this ship where I was born."

Killa turned to Lucy Lundberg Hendricks, "Lucy, I've known you for many years, even before you went to medical school in Berlin. How long have you been mated?"

"Madam, it's been three years now, but it seems longer. I haven't told my family yet, but we want to start a family now that we have two new interns aboard."

Hanna quipped, "As you can see our family has its own

surprises and occasional concerns as most human families do. Do Katz families have similar concerns?"

"Yes, but not the same as described here. Our matriarch society concerns are more dictatorial than yours and our birthrate is controlled by our Supreme Ruler based upon factors completely different than yours."

Sensing Killa's reluctance to continue this line of discussion, Hanna said, "Let's eat, everyone may make a selection from the menu beside your plate, except for Admiral Killa and Karrie who have already ordered their meals."

Later, before Lieutenant Ian Eiberger returned to his duty station aboard the UES Beast, Hanna Bloodworth asked him, "Ian, if you desire a posting aboard the Hulk I'm sure I can arrange it?"

He looked at his Aunt with a small smile. "I know, but I'd prefer to make my own way within Star Fleet. I want to eventually become a captain of my own ship and I don't think I can do that aboard the Hulk."

She hugged him tightly before answering, "You are so much like your mother. She wanted to follow her sisters into space, but her family responsibilities kept her on Earth. You are following her dreams; remember when your Uncle Eric gave you the badge from the Beast?"

His eyes became bright with remembrance as he pulled the Beast ship badge from his pocket and showed it to her, "I keep this as my talisman to remind me of my goal. The ship I really want is this one, The Beast."

"Ian, if that's your goal I'm sure you will eventually get it. Let me know if there's anything I can help you with."

He smiled at her before coming to attention and saluting her, which she returned. Hanna was very proud of her nephew as she watched him leave.

CHAPTER 12

A week later Second Fleet arrived in Earth orbit and Admiral Pavlova aboard his Flagship, the Battleship UES Tiger, immediately asked for a meeting with Fleet Admiral Bloodworth. When the two sat down for their meeting they were joined by their Fleet Captains. Admiral Pavlova related, "We left the seven Cruisers and the skeleton crews that were promised to the Green System, and when we returned eight months Green time later we found that they had completely crewed one ship and were almost half-way getting another ship crewed."

Bloodworth interrupted, "That's great news, how was the new crew getting along understanding how the systems worked?"

"Well, while Second Fleet was in the Green System the newly crewed ship was travelling in-system on its shake-down cruise!"

Eric looked at Vlad in surprise, "Really! That's a little faster than we did. Was it because they were already in space?"

"Probably. But they still need to learn tactics before they meet the Xones. I gave that General you talked to a copy of the tactics we've been using. He said they have given their people a test similar to what we used to determine those people with a bent towards tactics."

Admiral Bloodworth replied, "The Greens may be a more

effective ally than the Aquas if they are this pro-active. I'll stop there first on my way to our hunting grounds and see for myself how they are getting along."

Hanna asked Flag Captain Annalisa Hansen about her son, who was now seven. She replied with a wide smile, "Oh, Peter takes after Vlad which sometimes is a hassle. He's always into something trying to take it apart to see how it works and has scored high in his tests."

"Have you thought about having another child?"

"Vlad and I have discussed it and I've finally convinced him that Peter needs a sister to protect."

"Yes, I enjoyed raising a daughter, even when she turned out to be as strong willed as me.

Adam recently married the daughter of Captain Mae Fieldspire Becker. Do you remember her and Commodore Robert Becker's attraction to each other before their marriage?"

At Annalisa's nod, she continued, "Adam and Karrie were married within 24 hours after they met. Their attraction to each other is so strong they can't abide being apart for long, and they now have a child."

Annalisa placed her hand on Hanna's and squeezed gently, "Hang in there. This may be something great rather than a continuing worry. Remember, you have your immediate family with you on the Hulk, the biggest baddest ship the Xones have ever seen."

Eric asked Vlad, "How did you like your ship in battle?"

"Well, I appreciated the larger salvoes, but I couldn't believe the Laser Cannons defensive firepower. It was like opening the fires of Hell where nothing survived."

"Yes, that was our reaction too. How about staying for diner? If I remember correctly we're having steak."

Annalisa laughed, "You said the right word. We've been out of Earth beef steak for over a month."

* * *

Three months later First Fleet left Earth orbit with plans to visit the Green System before continuing on in search of enemy ships. They were also escorting the Katz delegation with news of the arrival of a Shipyard ship.

Upon First Fleets arrival in the Green System, two new first generation cruisers challenged them. Satisfied the ships were friendly, the Green System ships turned over sentry duty to First Fleets B Squadron. Fleet Admiral Bloodworths' A Squadron followed the two Green Cruisers and Admiral Killa's fleet of ten Heavy Cruisers to Green. Upon arrival three days later they found the remaining gifted cruisers in various states of readiness docked around a new space station that appeared to be still under construction.

General Jorge Hinderman soon contacted Admiral Bloodworth asking for a conference aboard his Battleship. Three hours later he arrived aboard a shuttle from one of their gifted cruisers. When Hinderman walked from his shuttle his arrival was celebrated by the playing of pipes and an honor guard. Three other individuals, all wearing similar Star Fleet uniforms, followed close behind him.

Fleet Admiral Bloodworth saluted Hinderman, who was now wearing the uniform of an Admiral. "Admiral Hinderman congratulations on your new position. I see your world has made many changes since I was last here."

"Yes, our military has made several changes since we acquired these fabulous ships. It requires a new way of looking at things. It's well that each of the ships had learning machines that we used constantly to train our crews in all aspects of ship operation and weapons use. I'd like to introduce the three officers I've brought with me. The first is my Chief of Staff, Commander Gwen Spicer, who you've met before. She was head of the Science Department aboard the Space Station you initially parked next to. Next, is Commander Nicholas Pierpoint who is currently the highest point graduate from our Tactics School, and is expected to head our fleet as it develops. Finally, Commander Lauryn Speer is head of Engineering for when we receive our shipyards from the Katz."

Bloodworth shook hands with the three Green Commanders before saying, "Let's move this meeting to our Conference Room, follow me."

Commander Speer asked as they were walking, "Is this Battleship included in the construction plans provided by the Katz?"

"Not yet, but the Heavy Battle Cruiser is. We no longer build the cruisers that you are now using because of their inadequate Laser Cannon protection against missiles."

When they reached the meeting room the newcomers were surprised to meet the Katz Delegation headed by Admiral Gamma Killa. After introductions were made they all took seats at the rooms round conference table.

The newcomers were still a little unsettled by the Katz's appearance, but Admiral Hinderman pushed through any discomfort he felt by asking Admiral Killa a question, "Ma'am, our Earth benefactors have brought us news of your help in fighting our common enemy, the Xones. Do you have news of the arrival of your shipyard so that we can produce our own warships?"

"It is heading this way as we speak, but it may be another three months before its arrival. You realize that the cruisers you are currently using were given for training and defense of your system. They are technically par with what the Xones are using, but the Earth people used such superior tactics that they never lost a battle with them. They have since improved the design to build what they called a Heavy Battle Cruiser that is bigger and contains more efficient Laser Cannons for defense, consequently we no longer construct the original cruisers that you now use."

Hinderman smiled slightly as he replied, "Yes, and today we're aboard an even larger ship."

Commander Speer eagerly asked, "This Battleship is huge! It dwarfs any other ship in the system and it's offensive power must be spectacular?"

Bloodworth smiled at her enthusiasm, "Actually we have another with supporting ships standing guard at the warp gate while we are here. The Battleship Class has a forty missile broadside salvo, double that of our Battle Cruisers and its Laser Cannons have a 50,000 mile range, compared to 5,000 miles for your cruisers. This ship is the primary defense for its supporting ships."

"Why do you build Heavy Cruisers if this ship is so much better?"

"It takes three to four times longer to build a Battleship and we needed numbers to fight the Xones. You are going to need numbers here as well. Before you build a Battleship, you should have at least seven Battle Cruisers. That combination will take you through anything they have thrown at us to date. They have more ships than we do, but they have lost so many that they have to improve their tactics or concede victory to us. Their latest change is ambushes. They lie in wait with engines silent until we pass and then spring their trap placing us between two forces. However, if they maneuver with their formations tightly grouped together we have nuclear weapons that will decimate them."

Admiral Hinderman looked at him in surprise, "You have such weapons too?"

"Yes, we developed them at our last world war over 120 years ago, and we've never used them in a war since until our fight with the Xones. It's an effective weapon in space and they have only recently taken proper reaction methods to guard against its use. At every voyage each of our ships has one nuclear missile aboard. We've never used more than three nuclear devices in a single voyage, and the opportunities have been less each voyage."

Commander Pierpoint frowned as he asked, "Sir, I would be interested in studying the tactics used in those battles. Have you kept count of the number of ships your fleets have destroyed since you've started?"

Admiral Bloodworth looked over at his Flag Captain, "Hanna, it's got to be about 2,000 ships, doesn't it?"

"No, I think it's closer to 3,000 ships."

Admiral Hinderman looked at them in wonder, "Your Battle Fleets total how many ships, forty - fifty ships? The Xones must be worried out of their minds!"

"Yes, that's why you've got to be careful you don't commit yourself without a fallback tactic. Right now their tactics is to throw more ships at us, which has resulted in horrendous losses for them. If they get a smart Admiral that may change."

Admiral Killa said, "Our Intelligence sources think that the Xones have transferred all their warships to this sector of the Galaxy to counter the threat you have provided. They believe you have eliminated at least a third of their warships and they lack the manpower to crew their new constructs."

Admiral Bloodworth chuckled to himself before replying, "When the Green's enter the conflict, they might reconsider their expansion plans and withdraw to a defensive position around their core systems."

Hanna shook her head at him, "Honey, that's wishful thinking. Retreat is not in there nature. I believe they will attack until their last ship is destroyed."

Admiral Hinderman looked at the other senior officers, "Gentlemen, we are ready to take our place in this fight for survival as soon as we have sufficient ships to protect our home system. We are eager to join this fight against our common enemy."

Admiral Killa stood and looked around the table before speaking, "The people of three common systems have now joined with us in our fight against the Xones. We will remain here and help protect this system until the Greens have constructed enough Heavy Battle Cruisers to both protect its home system and have its own Battle Fleet."

Admiral Bloodworth also stood, "Admiral Hinderman, when we leave here we intend to engage the Xones in battle and we would be honored if you would select up to six of your officers to join us and watch how the Xones conduct their battles."

"How long before you return to our system."

"About ten months your time, five months ship time."

"Very well, I'd like to go with you, but I can't be absent for ten months. Commander Pierpoint and five other future ship Captains will join you; when should they report aboard?"

"How much time do you need to get them here?"

Commander Pierpoint replied, "Sir, we'll be ready within four days."

"Gentlemen, we'll depart after they report aboard."

Three days later First Fleet's A Squadron broke orbit of Green and headed toward the warp gate to rejoin the remainder of the fleet. Later, after the fleet was intact the Hulk sent a sensor probe through the gate to determine if any Xones were present. The six Green personnel were present on the Hulk's Bridge watching the procedure as they ascertained the threat level before entering a new system.

When the message torpedo returned with no active readings, the Battleship UES Madrid led her supporting ships through the gate, followed by the UES Hulk and her supporting ships. After the Squadrons of First Fleet arranged themselves in their prearranged defensive positions, the Madrid sent a sensor probe through the fourth gate at the normal 2g's speed and awaited its response.

When the answering torpedo returned it reported many active returns, starting 1,000 miles from the gate was a heavy minefield that extended for another 2,000 miles. There were also three active enemy formations of thirty enemy ships each starting with the first formation 100,000 miles from the gate, the second formation was 100,000 miles further away and to the left of the first formation, and the third formation was the same distance from the gate as the second formation, but was to its right. All were stationary and in loose staggered defensive formations.

Admiral Bloodworth consulted with Commodore Samantha Lopez of the Madrid about her thoughts about this new ploy of the Xones. She replied, "Sir, it's obvious they intend to overwhelm any ships defenses that enters the system to clear out the mine field. We could clear out a narrow field through the minefield with missiles fired through the gate. However, I don't know if we can target any but the closest formation in our first salvoes."

Bloodworth replied, "I agree with your assessment about our first salvoes; however, if we clear the path by destroying the middle formation, then we can send multiple salvoes at the other two formations by turning off our missiles at say 50,000 miles after they have turned toward either the left or right formations and restarted 50,000 miles later giving our missiles time to select individual targets, and if we stagger our salvoes we will eventually overwhelm their defenses."

"Yes sir. How many salvoes for the middle formation do you recommend?"

"The heavies can handle this target as their missiles have the range for full powered flight.

Let's begin with them each firing one salvo of twenty missiles, which will be 280 missiles to clear the minefield and kill the first thirty ships and then wait and see if we need more. We'll use the heavies to clear the remainder of the minefield too; I think your Squadron can handle this action; however if we need more, mine will finish it."

"Yes sir. My Squadron will start firing in five minutes."

Lopez gave her orders and five minutes later they began firing one ship at a time through the Warp gate after checking each ships results, and stopped after the fifth ships missiles cleared the path they desired.

"Comm to Madrid, you may have your heavies fire against near formation as planned."

"Madrid to fleet, Aye sir. B Squadron fire one salvo at near formation at my command. Fire, fire!"

The missiles went through the gate and were upon the near formation in minutes and quickly overwhelmed the enemy leaving nothing but debris and the path open to the far formations.

"Comm to fleet, Sir, May I have the honor of firing first?"

"Fleet to Madrid, concentrate four salvoes at far left formation. The Hulk will follow with three salvoes at the far right formation.

"Madrid to fleet, Aye sir. Firing now."

The first salvoes soon cleared a path through the debris field as the missiles sped toward the enemy ships. Before Madrid's missiles reached their target, the Hulk's missiles were targeting their selected enemy formation and the sheer number of missiles soon overwhelmed the enemy formations defenses leaving two more clutters of debris.

Admiral Bloodworth asked, "Sensors, are there any other activities within the system?"

"Sir, no sir."

"Was there a watcher at the next gate?"

"Aye, sir, but it immediately left when the last two formations were destroyed."

"Fleet to A Squadron, transit the gate and use your lasers to clear the remaining minefield.

When finished rejoin us and we will transit back to Green."

Later, after First Fleet's transit back into the Green System and A Squadrons ships headed toward the planet Green, Admiral Bloodworth held a meeting with the Green observers.

Commander Pierpoint asked, "Sir, how did you know you could fire missiles through the warp gate with any accuracy?"

"Initially we didn't. I saw an opportunity and tested the theory, which worked. In one past instance the Xones sent a salvo through the gate at us, but we were ready for such an attack and were able to destroy all the missiles without damage to our ships."

Pierpoint replied, "Yet, the Xones don't seem to pass along lessons learned by others of their kind."

"Yes, we wondered about that as well. One reason may be because there generally are no Xones survivors in our battles, except for Xones observers left near gates. In addition, the enemy is reluctant to change tactics even when severe losses should have forced such a move. One change they have started to make is to discontinue their ball formations that we decimated with our nuclear weapons. It's been at least three years since we've seen them use it."

"You haven't used nuclear weapons except against their ball formations?"

"Yes, their ships have to be grouped closely together for maximum effect using such a weapon. So far, I haven't found a need to use them except in that instance; however, each of our ships still carries a single nuclear device in case of a need."

CHAPTER 13

Fleet Admiral Bloodworth was pleasantly surprised that the Green Space Fleet now had four of their starships crewed and their shake down cruises completed. The remaining three ships were in the final stages of familiarization by their crews and were scheduled for their shake down cruises in four days.

The six representatives from Green's Space Fleet, who traveled with them at the last battle, left the Hulk upon arrival in parking orbit, and Admiral Jorge Hinderman asked for a meeting to convene at the UES Hulk in three hours. Captain Hanna Bloodworth quickly prepared a conference room in case the Admiral brought others to the meeting.

It was well that she had this foresight as the Green party numbered twenty-six and arrived in two shuttles. Captain Bloodworth personally greeted Admiral Hinderman and his party and escorted them to the conference room where Fleet Admiral Bloodworth and his staff waited to greet the arrivals.

Chief of Staff Dana Williams configured the room to hold a large round table seating fifteen, with additional seating for twenty more behind the Green delegate. After everyone took a seat, Admiral Bloodworth introduced Admiral Gamma Killa to the Green delegation.

"Admiral Killa is our ultimate benefactor and is from an ancient race of people who are known as the Katz. They sought us out because they needed an aggressive race of people to engage the Xones, who are an enemy of everyone they encounter. The people of Green have now joined the people of Earth and Aqua in this fight against our common enemy."

Admiral Hinderman stood and bowed to Admiral Killa, "Admiral, I understand that your portable shipyard is expected to arrive soon, which we are eagerly anticipating. Our fledging star fleet is just now training to defend our system from the Xones threat. Before we join your fight we must build our own battle fleet. Admiral Bloodworth, in the meantime please accept twenty of our ship officers as apprentices so that they might learn how to fight our enemy."

Admiral Bloodworth considered for a moment before replying, "Sir, I would be happy to disperse your apprentices throughout the fleet so that they may receive a diverse education. I would recommend that you train at least an equal number from each gender because of the aging problem for non-warp people. Has anyone addressed this problem?"

Hinderman's face flushed before raising his eyes upwards in self-disgust. "Sir, I remember your cautionary story about your own problems with starship crew aging. I really didn't think I needed to worry about that yet, but obviously if I'm putting together a battle fleet then now is the time to plan for its crews."

He turned to his assistant and asked her a question before looking up at Admiral Bloodworth,

"Sir, the initial group is comprised of 60/40 men over women. I propose that I add four more women to the group for a total of twenty-four, if this is agreeable to you?"

Admiral Bloodworth smiled at the request, "Captain Bloodworth, do you foresee a problem with this number?"

"Sir, no sir. If I spread a mixed pair onto twelve ships they will be easily assimilated. I assume you want them made a part of the Bridge crew for them to learn tactics first hand?"

"Yes, hopefully they will also learn caution when making tactical decisions. Admiral Hinderman does this arrangement meet your approval?"

"Yes, I appreciate the exposure this will give my people. Where will your fleet go next?"

"We return to Earth and then replace Second Fleet at Aqua, and expect to return here in about five or six Green years. Will this be a problem?"

Hinderman thought through the problems this might present before replying, "No, but I should notify my apprentices of the amount of time they will be gone and the reasons why. When do you want them here?"

Admiral Bloodworth queried his Fleet Captain, "Captain?"

"We will be ready to sail in four days. Will that be sufficient time?"

Admiral Hinderman smiled at Captain Bloodworth, "I believe so. Do my people wear their own uniforms or yours?"

"Their own uniforms, so that our crews can readily identify who they are. They will have no command authority unless all other Bridge crew is incapacitated. They should bring at least two changes of clothing; all other kits will be furnished. They will be required to exercise daily as all our ship crews do."

"Very well, may I use this room to address my potential apprentices before we leave?"

"Sir, yes sir. Do you want me to stay to answer any questions they might have?"

"Thank you Captain, that may be helpful."

CHAPTER 14

Commander's Kegan Higgerson and Aundria Eoff of the Green Star Fleet were aboard one of the UES Hulk's shuttles heading toward the UES Joan of Arc. They were told a female, Allison Collins, captained the ship and that she was considered to be a hard ass. Aundria wasn't quite sure what that meant, but she assumed it meant she wasn't an easy touch.

Aundria never had a female commander before, but she assumed it didn't matter. The Captain was God aboard his/her ship and should be treated as such. Their shuttle grounded aboard the Joan of Arc and the two Green officers walked quickly toward a male commander, where they saluted the Earth Flag and asked permission to board. He gave them a steely look before giving them permission.

"Commander's, in the future when entering a new ship you should salute the OD, no matter their rank. I'm this ships executive officer, which means I outrank everyone but the captain. You may address me as Executive Officer Derik Bischof or XO. Follow me and I will introduce you to Captain Allison Collins and then I will hand you off to a junior officer who will guide you through ship orientation."

The two Green Officers followed the XO to the Bridge where

they waited until the Captain finished a discussion with another officer. As they approached her command chair she watched them with a solemn expression. After introductions Captain Collins said, "You will be assigned different watches that will change every three months. I expect you to know your seniors job ASAP so that you will be able to operate it if they are incapacitated. When under Battle Stations you both will report for duty and are expected to observe the tactics used. I will quiz you later on the results and any alternate tactics you might think of. Do you have any questions for me?"

"No...? XO what is there first duty assignments?"

"They are both with the science officer. Eoff is with the first watch and Higgerson is with the second watch."

"Very well, please carry on."

The XO led the two newbie's off the Bridge where a Lieutenant (jg) was waiting. "Lt. Baker take these officers to personnel for processing and then stick with them until they are familiar with ship routine and know where their cabins and officers mess are located."

The three stood and watched the XO walk out of sight. Lt. Baker said, "You can relax now. My name is Max Baker. What are your assigned watches?"

Aundria said, "I'm first and he's second watch."

"Okay, first watch is 24:00 to 08:00 hours, second is 08:00 to 16:00 hours. Check your timepiece, it's now 10:22 hours. Is your time calibrated to twenty-four hours?"

Kegan responded, "Yes, did you say 10:22 hours?"

At Max's nod, he said, "My time is set."

Aundria said, "Me too."

Max asked, "Did you both bring running clothes?"

He replied at their affirmative nod, "Good! The marines run twice a day in storage bay 3f at 06:00 and 18:00 hours. Pick a time convenient for you. It's better to run with the women because their pace is a little slower than the men. Okay, let's get to personnel and have you checked in and receive your room assignments. You both will be assigned a roommate of equal rank; if possible, otherwise you get a single. The singles are really small rooms and your baggage will be delivered to your assigned rooms. After personnel you will go to the hospital for any needed shots. After you finish these tasks, I'll take you to lunch."

Later, both Green officers signed releases to avoid getting assigned to a small single room and if needed, accepted a room assignment with a lower ranked officer.

When they arrived at the hospital the doctor checked their medical records for any needed shots to protect both them and the crew. Aundria asked, "When did you get our records?"

"Yesterday, probably about the time you were selected to come here. You both have all your required shots, so you can go. However, if you feel sick come see me."

Max looked at the two officers questioningly, "Are you ready for lunch? Have you been cleared for Earth food?"

Aundria gave Max a quirky smile, "Mostly, but there are some foods we don't like. I guess we will experiment."

After eating, Lt. Max Baker escorted them to their rooms and wished them luck before leaving. Commander Eoff used her code to enter her assigned room she shared with another officer and finding no one else present she opened her luggage that someone delivered and started putting away her clothes in her assigned closet space. There was also a kit with her name on it that she opened to see what it contained. It was almost like a present someone delivered.

Later, she looked at her assigned bare bed and wondered where the bedding was stored, but before she started looking her roommate arrived. The female Lieutenant Commander stopped just inside the door and gave Aundria a surprised look saying, "Who might you be?"

"I'm Commander Aundria Eoff of the Green Star Fleet on temporary duty and apparently your new roommate."

"Oh! How temporary are you?"

"Until you bring me back to my system, however long that's going to be."

She rolled her eyes at Aundria and closed the door. "Commander, my name is Skyler Still, currently working on port lasers. Where are you assigned?"

"Bridge, first watch. Do you know where the bedding is stored?"

"Under the mattress, here let me help you." She said as she raised one end of the mattress. Working together they soon had the bed made and took a seat facing each other across a desk that doubled as a comm station.

Skyler was a six-foot slim individual with natural blond curly hair cut shoulder length who appeared to be in her mid-thirties. Men would probably consider her pretty, but not beautiful, mainly because of her sharp features and the direct way she looked at others.

While Aundria was considering Skyler, she was receiving the same analysis from Skyler who thought she looked like a normal human. Aundria was her height and slim that came from an exercise requiem, but she had bigger breasts than herself. Her hair had a reddish tint, cut slightly shorter than hers and was about her own age. She considered her face striking, perhaps even beautiful when she smiled.

Skyler said, "I'm on first watch too, so that makes it easier for us. We'll have to eat early in order to get our eight hours sleep. I exercise with several others on first watch at 22:30 hours at SB 3f if you want to join us. That gives us time for breakfast before reporting for duty."

Aundria looked at her timepiece and frowned, "That means we need to hit the sack around 14:00 hours. I just had lunch about two hours ago."

Skyler frowned, "Well, go ahead and get ready for bed and I'll set the time for us to get up later to start our day. I'll see you when you wake up, bye."

Aundria watched her roommate leave and gave the closing door a small smile. *Well, so that's my roommate. I could have done much worse.*

Later, she awoke to a beeping sound that was getting louder and more frequent as she became aware of her surroundings and heard her roommate say, "Last one up has to make the others bed and wait for their turn in the head."

Skyler turned the alarm off and headed toward the shower while Aundria slowly sat up and considered the situation. Then she quickly made her roommate's bed and laid out her exercise clothing, at which time Skyler exited the head and started on Aundria's bed while Aundria took her turn in the head.

When Aundria left the head Skyler was starting to put on her exercise clothing. It wasn't long before the two left their quarters and jogged toward their exercise destination. They already completed their warm up by the time they reached SB 3f. The exercise bay was about a thirty-yard square with a painted oval track where the crew ran. There were easily thirty other people running at a moderate pace in a circle inside the storage bay. Aundria followed Skyler as she edged into a slot between two male groups of runners.

Skyler told her earlier she usually ran thirty minutes at a brisk pace and if she couldn't keep up she should edge herself to the inside where it would be easier for her. Aundria came from a family of three older brothers who challenged her to keep up with them on cross-country runs, so this track was no problem for her.

Skyler's timepiece beeped at her and the two left the circle of runners and returned to their quarters. After showering and dressing for duty they went to the officers mess for breakfast. Skyler led the way and found a table with two male officers she knew and asked if they could join them.

After taking their seats Skyler introduced the two officers to Aundria. Lt. Commander Peter Geoff asked, "You're on temporary duty from Green? What's the story on that?"

"There are twenty-four of us getting command experience before our starships are built, and I'm one of two of us assigned to this ship."

"Oh, that makes sense. Who is the other one?"

"Commander Kegan Higgerson, who follows me on the Bridge's second watch."

Skyler quirked an eyebrow as she said, "I heard that they sent an even number of Greens by gender after Admiral Bloodworth reminded their Admiral of the problem regarding warp time."

Lt. Commander Kyle Maggi said, "That makes sense, their ships should all be gender neutral, otherwise they won't know they have a problem until the person left behind in a relationship suddenly ages twice as fast as the one onboard a starship."

Aundria looked between the officers in confusion, "Is this a joke?"

Skyler replied, "You weren't told about the aging problem on warp ships, whereby they age at about half the rate as those left on the ground?"

"No! Wait a minute, I did hear something like that, but I

thought it was a joke someone started."

Maggi said, "It's no joke, believe me. When I go home on leave my family ages twice the rate as I do. It's really strange."

Aundria mused, "So when I return to Green after a voyage of two years, four years would have passed for my family!"

At Maggi's nod, Aundria replied, "If that's the case, then there are going to be some Heavy Battle Cruisers ready for our group to command."

Skyler shook her head in envy. "Yeah, it's going to take us a lot longer to get our first commands. You are lucky in that regard, but I don't envy you your first command encounter with the Xones. That's going to be a lot of pressure and responsibility."

Aundria grimaced. "Yes, but hopefully I'll be exposed to several battles with you so that I'll know what to expect."

Geoff gave a short laugh, "Yeah, First Fleet generally finds some hairy battle situations, but our battle formations are now so large that we have to sucker them into a fight. The Xones generally only attack when they think they have the advantage."

Skyler added, "We have destroyed thousands of their ships since we've started fighting them. If they were smart they would have begged for a truce, but apparently their honor demands they fight to the last ship."

Geoff said, "It's time to head toward our section. Hope to see you again Aundria."

They all cleared their table off and disposed of their trays and waste before leaving for their duty stations. Aundria was stopped at the Bridge entrance by a marine guard, where she identified herself before entering and headed toward the science station. She was five minutes early and stood aside as she observed its change of shift.

The Science Officer turned to her and asked, "You must be one of the new Green officers we've been expecting?"

"Sir, yes sir. I'm Commander Aundria Eoff and I'm here to learn your duties."

"Very well, I'm Lt. Commander Michael Anderson and it's going to be strange training a higher-ranking officer. Are you familiar with the instruments of this station?"

"Only in what they do according to the learning machine."

"Okay, let's see you use them to determine what ships are in this system."

"Yes sir, may I take a seat?"

"Go ahead, I want to see you operate it as if it were your station."

She sat and scanned the machines settings before pushing the scan button. The screen lit up showing icons of objects surrounding Green and several around the next closest planet. Finally, she noted the home fleet and the other half of Earth's First Fleet near their systems large gas giant planet. She turned to her supervisor and reported her findings, starting with the furthest and ending with those in orbit around Green.

Anderson nodded his head in agreement. "Normally, we leave the machine in passive scan mode while in orbit, which will alert us when there is a change, such as a fleet entering the system. When that happens a red light will flash here." He pointed at a steady amber light.

"The steady amber light is to inform us that it's working. If it changes there will be an audible sound as well; that's in case my eyes are off the machine when the status light changes. Are you still with me?"

"Sir, yes sir."

"That's the only thing you need to know until we break orbit, which is scheduled for 10:30 hours today during second watch. Do you have any questions?"

"Sir, yes sir. Let's assume that there's an incursion at the warp gate and I'm the officer watching the scanner, what's my first duty?"

"You say loudly, Contact at Warp Gate, and then the number of contacts. Command will follow with their instructions, which you address unless I take over. Is that clear?"

"Sir, yes sir. Should I stay here or should I stand and let you continue your duties?"

"The latter, commander."

"Sir, yes sir." She then stood and got out of his way.

Nothing of interest happened during the remainder of her watch and after being relieved by her fellow officer from Green at 08:00 hours, she headed toward the officers mess for lunch. It seemed odd to be having lunch at this hour of the day, but a military unit ran twenty-four hours a day.

When she entered the dining room she looked around for anyone who might look familiar and spotted Lt. Commander Kyle Maggi. She started his way and received encouragement when he looked up and smiled while waving her toward him. He stood and motioned for her to sit facing him, which she did with a smile.

"Commander, how was your first watch aboard the Arc?"

"Initially it was a little exciting, but when nothing happened it got boring."

"Yes, but after a few Battle Stations when missiles are headed your way, boring is under appreciated."

She smiled at his humor, "How do you keep busy when in dock?"

"First we make any needed repairs, and then we do battle sims to keep our edge. When we reach Earth orbit, I'll take shore leave. It will have been almost three years Earth time since my parents have seen me. Every time I go home they seem to noticeably age, while they say I'm ageless. My younger sister now appears older than me."

"I take it you don't have a girlfriend on Earth?"

"Not any more. After my first voyage we returned to Earth after being gone over three years and I found that she moved on and was engaged to another man. I now stick to onboard friendships with the opposite sex."

"Nothing serious?"

"No, not yet, but I'm still looking for that special woman that rings my bell."

They were looking at the menu getting ready to order when Lt. Commander's Still and Geoff sat down at their table. They all ordered before bringing each other up on happenings during their watch, which was nothing of importance.

Aundria asked the new arrivals about any relationships they were currently pursuing, when she caught the quick eye contact between the two. Skyler's face flushed slightly as she kicked Aundria's leg under the table. "Oh, I've been seeing someone but it's too early to determine how serious it may become."

Geoff, seeing how flustered Skyler had become, said, "Same here, but so far its promising."

Aundria smiled to herself thinking, *romance here seems similar to the mating ritual on her own world. I better ask Skyler what birth control methods they use here just in case I find someone for myself.*

CHAPTER 15

The First Fleet was back in Earth orbit ninety-three days after leaving the Green system and found Second Fleet in orbit awaiting their arrival. Admiral Vlad Pavlova sent a comm to the Fleet Admiral requesting an informal meeting at his convenience who commed a reply, "I'll contact you after my debriefing with Star Fleet Headquarters, but I should be available tomorrow on the Hulk at 18:00 hours."

Fleet Admiral Bloodworth held a tablet showing a dispatch from Fleet Headquarters, to his Flag Captain. "They want both of us to meet with the Board at 18:30 hours today. That gives us two hours to get there; perhaps I should bring one of the twenty-four Green apprentices with us so that they may have an idea who we are helping. Who would you recommend?"

"From the feedback from the captains of the ships who are training them, I would recommend Commander Aundria Eoff on the Joan of Arc."

"Very well, comm the Arc and have her ready to be picked up in about an hour."

"Good! You better start getting ready and I'll meet you in our stateroom."

About an hour later a shuttle from the Hulk arrived on the Joan of Arc to pick up Commander Eoff. She hurried to the craft and climbed aboard, taking a seat opposite the two highest-ranking officers of First Fleet.

Flag Captain Hanna Bloodworth told her, "Buckle up, we're going to Star Fleet Headquarters below to meet our governing directors. They speak Universal so they may have questions for you. Fresh air may be a welcome relief for you after being aboard for several months; I just hope you don't have allergies. Here's a allergy mask if you start to have problems."

After landing near the headquarters building, an escorted vehicle took them to its entrance. Exiting their vehicle they stood a moment letting Commander Eoff stare at the headquarters building and take a quick breath of desert air, before they followed their escort inside.

As they walked toward the elevators, Eoff said, "The air here smells funny to me, it's very dry and the flora is strange too."

They continued the conversation on the elevator as it started down, rather than up as Eoff expected. As the elevator passed the tenth floor, she said in awe, "This building is much larger than one would think if there are this many floors underground."

When they left the elevator they stopped before a marine checkpoint and showed their identification. When the Marine Lt. Colonel asked for Commander Eoff's ID, Fleet Admiral Bloodworth vouched for her, "She's an alien from the Green System who's here to meet with the Board."

She pushed a button on her desk comm and asked for help, listened for the response before she disconnected and smiled at the Fleet Admiral, "Sir, you and your guest may proceed."

Admiral Cochran immediately greeted them when they entered the boardroom. Fleet Admiral Bloodworth greeted the Admiral and said, "Sir, this is Commander Aundria Eoff of the Green System, who's an apprentice aboard one of First Fleets ships. She's one of twenty-four who are learning how to command a Heavy Battle Cruiser under battle conditions, and she and her other apprentices will have use of this knowledge when they return to the Green System to man their new constructions."

Cochran's concerned face turned into a smile as he turned to the young officer and asked, "Commander Eoff, did I get your name right?"

At her acknowledgement, he continued, "This is great news! We were worried it would take years for your system to train officers and crew to man your ships as they are produced. Would you do us the honor of addressing our governing board on your plans and ambitions?"

She turned to the Fleet Admiral and asked, "May I speak freely with these individuals and are they aware of our treaty details?"

"Yes, they are aware of the treaty and are worried about your exposure to the Xones. So, speak your mind and if you have any recommendations, tell them."

She nodded her head in understanding and smiled, before saying to Admiral Cochran, "Sir, yes sir, I'll be happy to speak with them."

Admiral Cochran stepped to the table and used a gavel to get their attention. "Board members, we have a surprise guest. Fleet Admiral Bloodworth has brought with him one of the twenty-four officers from the Green System he has aboard his First Fleet ships, who are acting as apprentices to learn how to command Heavy Battle Cruisers. When they return to their system in three or four years they expect to be able to become commanders of their own cruisers. Commander Aundria Eoff has consented to speak with us about her plans. I give you Commander Eoff."

* * *

The board gave the commander a polite welcome of hand clapping as she moved toward the Podium. Commander Eoff, only twenty-six years old, noted that her audiences youngest member appeared to be in her sixties.

"Ladies and gentlemen, when I first started this training cruise I didn't know you. You were as alien to me as I am to you. However, with a common language and an apparent lineage, it was almost like meeting a long lost relative who tells me we have a common enemy who is trying to kill all my people. We, like you are a very aggressive race of people who don't take kindly to the idea of some alien race threatening to eradicate us."

She looked at her audience, gaging their acceptance of her words before she resumed speaking. "Some of our people traveled with Fleet Admiral Bloodworth to a nearby star system where they observed a battle with the Xones. To them it was obvious that the Xones were outclassed in both weapons and leadership ability. Yet, it was also obvious that it was going to take decades at our present strength to eliminate them, because they were not going to surrender to save themselves."

Her audience was hanging on her every word as she continued, "Our people resolved to take the help offered us and as soon as we were properly trained we would open another front in the fight against the Xones. That's why twenty-four of us are training to command as many of the Heavy Battle Cruisers and later, Battleships as we can build. We treasure your friendship in our shared cause."

There was silence for an extended moment, before the Board of Directors stood and cheered their enthusiasm and then crowded forward to shake her hand.

* * *

Admiral's Cochran and Bloodworth shook each other's hands in enthusiasm as they grinned at each other. Cochran asked, "Did you know you had such a firebrand in that group?"

"No, but she was the best in the group they sent us. I think she's a future Green Admiral."

After everything settled down, the board called for Fleet Admiral Bloodworth to give his report of enemy battle actions and anticipated future activities of the Xones. He gave his own viewpoint on how well the Greens were converting into another Star Fleet System and were closely following or surpassing their own rate for crewing its starships. The board gave him their continued support for how well he has conducted their war with the Xones.

Later, on the shuttles return to their ships, Captain Bloodworth asked Commander Eoff, "Would you prefer to spend the remainder of your apprenticeship aboard the Flag Ship, rather than the Joan of Arc? The Hulk would give you a different prospective on where battle orders originate, rather than following orders from the Flag."

Commander Eoff looked from the Flag Captain to the Admiral before replying, "Ma'am, I would prefer working on the Hulk if I'm not too much of a distraction?"

Captain Bloodworth gave her a long silent look, before saying, "Commander, I didn't think I'd ever say this, but your kind of distraction I'm going to look forward to. Pick up your things and shuttle to the Hulk. I'll inform the Captain of the Joan of Arc of your transfer and I'll see you tomorrow during the second watch."

"Yes ma'am, think you ma'am. I'll begin tomorrow during second watch and I really appreciate this transfer to the Flagship."

The following morning, Captain Bloodworth was present when Commander Eoff reported for Bridge duty. Seeing her arrive she motioned for Eoff to approach her command chair.

"Ma'am, where do you wish I should begin?"

"Commander, I've reviewed your previous training stations and you appear to have grasped their duty requirements. Which station would you prefer?"

"Ma'am, I prefer the science officers station. It's boring while in dock, but while traveling there's always the possibility that something exciting will occur."

Captain Bloodworth said with a small smile, "Very well you may cover that station. Lt. Commander Simmons will stay with you and answer any questions you may have, but tomorrow the station is yours. Do you have any questions?"

"Aye, ma'am. How long is First Fleets expected stay in Earth orbit?"

"We generally stay three months to provide for shore leaves and replenishment of consumables. Did you have a reason for this question?"

"Ma'am, yes ma'am. I would like to wander among the nonmilitary populace to gain insight on how they differ from the Green populace."

"Commander Eoff, how long do you anticipate this wandering will take?"

"Ma'am, I'm not sure, but I'll need to learn the language of the country I visit and I should probably have an escort to keep me out of trouble and offer advice on travel procedures."

"Very well, let me consider the ramifications of this request and I'll get back with you. In the meantime schedule time on the learning machine to be taught English. The United States is a country that has the largest area with a common language. You may carry on."

"Yes ma'am, thank you ma'am."

* * *

Three weeks later Commander Aundria Eoff and Gunnery Sergeant Tricia Fender were wearing civilian clothing after stepping off a shuttle from the UES Hulk that landed at the Springfield/Branson Air Terminal in Springfield, Missouri. Fleet Admiral Bloodworth had arranged for the shuttles landing here because this was his hometown and had made many trips home while his parents were alive.

Gunny Fender stood an inch shorter than Aundria, but there was no question which of them was in charge. They gathered their traveling bags and hurried to the waiting ground shuttle that took them to the air terminal, where their flight to Denver was waiting for them.

They climbed the outside steps to the terminal connection to the aircraft, where they walked a few steps and entered the aircraft. Leading the way, Fender showed the steward their first class tickets, who then took their bags and stored them while they found their nearby seats. Aundria breathed a sigh of relief as she took a window seat, while Tricia slid in next to her in an aisle seat.

Aundria asked Tricia, "How long is this flight to Denver?"

"Not long, about an hour. When we get there where do you want to go?"

"I want to meet people; no, I want to observe them, listen to what they say."

"Okay, after we land we'll check into a hotel, then we'll go to a nearby mall to observe civilians."

Three hours later they were in a food court of a mall where they were drinking a fruit drink while Aundria eavesdropped on the conversations around them. When the people at a table near them left, four older teenagers of mixed gender immediately filled it. One of the girls was excited about receiving notice of her application to enter Star Fleet. Two of the others were concerned about them never seeing her again after she left for the stars.

The girl they called Ginger, replied, "Silly, I'll be back and look you up when I return to visit my parents. Joe, you sent in an application too, haven't you gotten a reply?"

"Not yet, I sent mine in almost a week after you did and my scores were almost as good as yours, so I'm hoping I'll get in too."

Ginger gushed, "Oh, wouldn't it be something if we are in the same class."

Joe smiled at her and held her hand, "Yeah, but lets be realistic, I've heard that they have opened another school because of the high enlistments. Are you still trying for officers training?"

"Yes, I want to drive one of those starships!"

"I heard that if they accept you, they'd pay your way through expedited college courses toward a special college degree."

One of the other girls said in obvious awe, "Did you hear about them finding another star system like Aqua that has people like us on them?"

Joe said, "Yeah, I wonder how many other systems have humans on them?"

Ginger said, "Well, I know what it means now. When they get their act together we'll have another front opening against the Xones."

There was a chorus of approval sounds before they started eating the food they brought to the table.

Tricia looked at Aundria and asked with a wide smile, "That the type of information you were looking for?"

She nodded her head and grinned at Tricia. "Yeah, it seems the Xones war is receiving wide support here. How about the rest of Earth? Is it the same?"

"When you get back to the Hulk check the nationalities represented by the crew. Starting at the top, the Admiral is from the U.S., his wife, the Flag Captain, is from Germany. Her sister, the ships doctor, is from Germany and the marine detachment is mainly from the U.S. The remainder of the crew has members from every major country. Ship captains are from Russia, Italy, France, U.S., Great Britain, Spain, and Germany. It's well we converse in Universal."

Tricia continued, "Do you want to call it a day or do you want to talk to someone?"

"Where do we pick up our shuttle when we want to return to the Hulk?"

"Someplace like where we landed so we won't cause a big stir."

"Okay, let's stick around here for a while so that I can observe more people. I'd like to have a nice dinner tonight and leave tomorrow for Springfield. I can talk to people at the air terminal if the opportunity arises."

Tricia checked her handheld for information about flights back to Springfield and found one leaving early tomorrow morning. Tricia went to the head so that she could have privacy while arranging a shuttle pickup in Springfield tomorrow. On their taxi ride back to their hotel she asked Aundria, "Have you ever eaten bar-be-que," and then described what it was.

"No, but I'm game if its not too spicy."

Before leaving the taxi Tricia got the name and location of the best in Denver. Because of their early morning flight, they decided to eat early. Later, while getting into the taxi Tricia asked the driver his opinion of the best bar-be-que restaurant and received the same answer as the first driver.

It was well that they arrived early, as the restaurant was almost full and there was a short wait before they were seated. They both ordered the special that almost everyone around them was eating. Tricia had Aundria look at the others plates and then described what each item was.

Aundria looked at her in surprise, "I can't eat all that, that's twice what I normally eat!"

Tricia smiled as she said, "Don't worry about it, I'll eat what you don't. This is my favorite food."

Tricia was disappointed as Aundria not only ate her own portion, but was also starting to eye her own plate. On their ride back to the hotel Aundria asked, "Why don't they serve this type of food on the ship?"

"I'm not sure, maybe it takes a special cooking method for the pork, beef and chicken they prepare?"

CHAPTER 16

It was gratifying that when First Fleet arrived into the Aqua System they were met by its home fleet that included a Battleship and ten Heavy Battle Cruisers; a defense force that would have given an attacking Xones Fleet five times its size phase for concern. If the Aqua Battle Fleet happened to be present, all bets were off.

Fleet Admiral Bloodworth counted two Battleships and twenty Heavy Battle Cruisers of Aqua's Battle Fleet in orbit and with First Fleets equal number of ships, they would bring a impressive amount of firepower in their next foray into Xones territory.

Bloodworth invited the leaders of the Aqua and Earth's Second Fleet Battle Fleets to a conference aboard the UES Hulk.

Almost immediately, Admiral Vlad Pavlova answered with, "Expect us for a dinner conference at 18:00 hours." Captain Mae Fieldspire Becker response was "Please have our children in attendance."

* * *

At the appointed time Lt. Commander Karrie Becker Bloodworth met her parents when they arrived in the shuttle bay. After the arrival ceremony she hugged both her parents, Aqua's Admiral Robert Becker and Fleet Captain Mae Fieldspire Becker. There were some tears from both mother and daughter as it had been about two years ship time since they had seen each other.

Mae asked, "Where's Marie? At her age I won't even recognize her it's been so long since I've seen her."

"Adam has her. He thought you'd rather see me than him at this reunion. Besides, she's really a daddy's little girl; when she doesn't want to do something she'll stick her tongue out at me, but when he gives her the look, she'll do it without complaint."

Mae snorted back a laugh, "You were the same with me and Robert. I guess we just like men more than women. Do you and Adam still have the same attraction to each other?"

Karrie smiled slightly, "Yes, maybe even a stronger connection. Right now he's brushing Marie's hair."

Mae touched her daughter's arm, stopping her. "That's more than my connection with Robert, and you say it's getting stronger?"

"Yes, and he feels what I'm doing as well. We better get going, I understand there will be others joining us at the dinner table."

Karrie led them to a small conference room rather than the Admiral's stateroom because of the large number of expected guests. Adam and Marie met them at the door where the grandparents stared at the youngster smiling up at them. Mae went to her knees before the child, saying, "Marie, I'm your grandmother – your mother's mother, and this tall man is your grandfather. I can't get it through my head that you're almost five."

Marie looked at her mother with a puzzled expression, "Mommy, I think I remember my Grammy, but Grandfather's uniform looks different."

"Yes, he has been promoted from a commodore to an admiral."

"Oh, but it's not the same as Admiral Bloodworth."

Admiral Becker said, "Admiral Bloodworth is the top admiral in Space and outranks all the other admirals out here."

"Oh, will mommy and daddy become admirals too?"

"Probably; time will tell."

Mae pulled Karrie aside and whispered, "Have you tested her IQ level?"

"No, it's too early to get an accurate reading, but it's obvious she will test high."

* * *

Flag Captain Hanna Bloodworth spoke up, "Friends and relatives I want to introduce an officer from the Green Star Fleet, Commander Aundria Eoff. Commander, come stand with me while I introduce you to my family."

"You already know Fleet Admiral Eric Bloodworth; this couple is Rear Admiral Robert Becker and Fleet Captain Mae Fieldspire Becker of the Aqua Star Fleet. Next, are Lt. Commander Adam Bloodworth and his wife, Lt. Commander Karrie Fieldspire/Becker Bloodworth, who you probably already know from your Bridge duties? The young girl is their daughter, Marie. Adam is our son and Karrie is the daughter of the Becker's. Next are Lt. Commander Kory Hendricks and Commander Lucy Lundberg Hendricks. Lucy is my youngest sister and is the ships primary medical doctor. Now, this handsome commander is my nephew, Ian Eiberger, who is the new XO of the UES Beast."

"Ian, snap out of it! Aundria, what's wrong? Lucy! Crap, it looks like we have another coupling here!"

Adam took charge of Ian, while Karrie took Aundria's hand and they led the two dazed officers to chairs. The two besotted individuals sat and stared into each other's eyes for a few minutes and then they took each other's hands and pulled themselves to their feet and into each other's arms and kissed passionately. When they broke apart they each had flushed faces, realizing their actions.

They said together, "What just happened?"

Hanna said, "Let me guess. You both felt an extreme attraction for each other that was like nothing you've felt before with anyone."

They both nodded their heads, while still holding hands. "Karrie, you explain how you and Adam met and what happened between the two of you."

Before Karrie could begin her explanation, Aundria took Ian's hand and led him to a chair and then sat in his lap with her head on his shoulder. "Now, that reaction is even stronger than mine with Adam. Ian, how are your reactions to Aundria?"

"Strong, stronger than any I've experienced before. I don't feel that extreme longing with her in my lap and my desire to touch her now seems satisfied."

"Ian, I want you to try something that satisfied Adam and my reactions. I want you and Aundria to kiss each other again. Don't worry, we won't let it get out of hand."

Ian and Aundria looked at each other passionately until they started kissing each other with such passion that both would later complain of bruised lips. Eventually, they slowly broke apart enough that they could stare into each other's eyes before they slowly smiled at each other. Aundria stood and then helped Ian to his feet.

She was still holding one of his hands when she said, "How is this going to work. I don't think I can stand being too far away from Ian. Ian let's experiment, let go of my hand. See, we can now function apart. Karrie, you two can work apart aboard the same ship, can't you?"

"Yes, but your attachment to each other seems even stronger than ours. However, we've developed the ability of knowing what the other is doing, which eases our anxiety over not being near them. We married each other the same day we met. Is your feelings toward each other lust or romance?"

Aundria face flushed as she stared at Ian. "For me it's both."

Ian nodded his head and replied, "Yes, I can't foresee life without her. How is this going to work, we aren't in the same navy?"

Hanna looked at her husband thinking hard for a fair solution for everyone. "For now, we need to keep you both aboard the same ship. Ian, you're the XO of the Beast and we can transfer Aundria to continue her training aboard your ship's Bridge. Aundria, does your world have any problems for the two of you getting married or mated?"

"It's a moot point. We would be the first for such a bond. My uncle is Admiral Hinderman and he would quash any attempt to break us up. Worse case situation, maybe I can join your navy?"

"Let's not borrow problems. You can be married aboard this

ship tonight and return to the Beast with Ian. We'll be sorry to lose you, but I don't see a better solution for now."

"Ian, do you agree to all these changes to your life with me?"

He pulled her into his arms and kissed her deeply. When their lips parted, he asked, "Aundria, will you be my wife?"

"Yes, Ian I will marry you and will follow you to whichever navy we are in."

Fleet Captain Bloodworth commed the Chaplin and the couple were married. Suddenly, everyone was famished and the family gathering, now wedding party, sat down to a feast that no one remembered eating as they watched the newlyweds at their table.

Karrie turned to Adam and smiled, "Honey, do you remember those first hours after we were married?"

"No, it's all a blur. The only thing I remember from that time was how much I loved you and wanted you in my bed."

"I was pretty much the same, but my overriding emotion was my love for you. Look at her! You can't see it but she has her leg touching his, rubbing it slowly. Now he's picking up her hand and bringing it to his mouth and kissing it. Oh, they won't last long doing this little passionate dance."

Adam got up from his seat and approached his mother and spoke softly in her ear. "Those two are about to copulate here on the table if we don't get them to a room."

She looked at him in surprise, then down the table at the newlyweds. "Sh.., Ian! Grab your bride and follow me. I'm taking you two to a room and I'll comm your ship to prepare you a larger cabin as you are bringing your bride aboard tomorrow. I'll also clear it with your captain for Aundria to stand her watches on the Beast's Bridge. Comm me tomorrow when you're ready to return to the Beast."

"Aye Aunt Hanna. Thank you for understanding our situation."

The next morning Fleet Captain Bloodworth accompanied the married couple to the Beast where Hanna had scheduled a meeting with its captain, Kelly MacLachian. Upon arrival, Captain MacLachian met the group and led the way to his stateroom.

The four took seats in its dining area and after they were settled Hanna filled Kelly in on the past history of the relationship of Admiral Becker and Captain Mae Fieldspire of the Aqua Star Fleet, followed by Hanna's son Adam, and the Becker's daughter

Karrie, and now the recent similar episode involving Hanna's nephew Ian and Green's Aundria Eoff.

"Captain MacLachian each of these relationships started with some kind of compelling reaction between the parties involved, some stronger than others. Ian and Aundria's seem stronger than the other two, but not by much. When we return to Green our two systems will have to agree upon a solution similar to what my son and Aqua's leaders arranged. Hopefully, both will remain together with us, but that's not certain. Whatever's decided they have to remain together or they may both perish. With your permission, Commander Eoff will continue her apprentice on your Bridge where she will be in close proximity to Ian."

"Captain Bloodworth, that's the craziest story I've ever experienced. I've heard what I've thought were wild rumors, but this beats even those. Of course I'll accept your proposal and I hope when we return to Green everything will work out for everyone. Ian, you weren't even dating anyone here; how did you attract someone like this beauty?"

Hanna said with a grimace, "They didn't have a choice in the matter. Something in the woman's blood picked her mate! This much we do know, the female carries the gene that causes the attraction in the male that has the opposite gene factor it is looking for. So far, women from two alien races have met human males and caused this reaction. Women from these alien planets never had this reaction with males from their own planet."

"Have any of these women had multiple reactions with human males?"

"No, from their reactions they are extremely attracted in the male first selected. Captain MacLachian looked at the two officers with sympathy before saying, "Commander's Ian Eiberger and Aundria Eoff Eiberger you both have a day off to make changes in personnel matters and obtaining larger married quarters. XO, report back for Bridge duty at 08:00 hours tomorrow. Commander Eiberger you start tomorrow at 2nd watch as well. The XO will determine your duty assignment. Any questions? No, then you are dismissed."

Kelly asked Hanna, "What's going to happen when we return to Green? What we did here was simple, but her home planet's reaction may be something else."

CHAPTER 17

First Fleet's presence in the Aqua system resulted in three successful battles with the Xones in which the combined battle fleets of Aqua and Earth participated. After each battle Aundria was quizzed by the Captain and XO about the tactics used and if she could think of any faults or another tactic that might have achieved the same results.

Aundria replied, "Sir, in this instance it's hard to argue against a successful outcome, but I wonder if the Admiral considered the possibility of another group of enemy ships lying in ambush to our rear."

The captain said, "XO would you answer her question?"

"Sir, yes sir. Commander, our fleets have already encountered such a ruse and in that instance the fleet immediately fired nuclear missiles after the Xones lit their engines revealing their presence. We then moved the fleet's position out of range of the incoming missiles. We had to delay our movement because of the staggered missile firings of the enemy."

Later, after their last battle, Commander Aundria Eiberger asked, "Sir, the last battle was obviously an attempt to ambush the fleet from another warp gate. I've read the report where this was tried before and the Admiral countered by setting his own trap for the Xones. Why the change in tactics this time?"

XO Eiberger said, "This time we had two battleships with their awesome laser protection that we didn't have before, plus the large number of Heavy Battle Cruisers in reserve. The Admiral actually wanted them to attack him because he knew they would lose most of their attacking ships, ships they can't afford to lose."

"Sir, I can hardly wait until our Green Fleet is ready for battle."

* * *

Now that they were back in Earth orbit, Commanders Ian Eiberger and his wife, Aundria Eoff Eiberger were aboard their shuttle from the UES Beast, heading toward Hamburg, Germany. Ian's mother, Clare Lundberg Eiberger, did not know of his recent marriage and he was nervous about her accepting an alien as his wife.

The shuttle landed at a small aircraft airfield outside Hamburg, where Ian told the crew to pick them up in three days. They each carried their luggage to the terminal and took a cab to Ian's family home, after first calling and making sure his mother was at home.

They arrived without incident an hour later and the two approached the duplex with some anxiety. Ian rang the door buzzer and pasted a smile on his face as they awaited his mother. Instead, his father answered the door and upon seeing his son, he grabbed him into his arms in a tight embrace. Breaking apart they both had tears in their eyes and it was then that Jasper noticed Aundria standing on the stoop and looked to Ian for an explanation.

"Dad, this is my wife, Aundria Eoff Eiberger."

"Your wife! My God, you've gotten married. Clare! Come meet Ian's new bride!"

* * *

Clare came bursting from inside to see what the ruckus was about and stopped open-mouthed upon seeing the beautiful woman dressed in an unfamiliar uniform.

"Mom, this is my wife, Aundria Eoff Eiberger."

Clare immediately pulled Aundria into an embrace, and then led her into the house telling the men to handle the luggage. She stopped in the kitchen, and told Ian's bride to take a seat while she checked on the meal she was preparing. Satisfied, she sat before Aundria and took her hands in her own and said, "Tell me your story, and knowing Ian, there's got to be a great story."

Aundria smiled at her new mother-in-law, glad now that she'd learned German before coming here. She started by telling her how they met and her own background. When she finished, Clare looked at her with an open mouth of astonishment. She turned to her husband and asked, "Jasper, did you hear all that?"

He nodded his head. "Ian, we were beginning to worry about you finding a wife, but why go to another world?"

Ian warily smiled at his parents, "Initially, we really had no say in the matter. Apparently something in our blood DNA clicked. At first it was desire, and then lust, as we had this overwhelming desire to touch one another. Now, we need to work near each other and even when apart we know where the other is located."

Clare asked, "Aundria, is it still lust or do you love my son now?"

"Oh, we love each other. If we didn't we would both be very unhappy. Ian goes out of his way to show his love for me and I do the same for him. Have you noticed how we are always trying to touch each other?"

Clare looked at her son and his wife and nodded her head in agreement as a tear trickled down her cheek. She then laid her hand over theirs, and immediately felt a warm glow emitting from their connection. She somehow knew that this marriage was important and their connection had meaning other than their love for each other.

* * *

They spent three days with Ian's family before returning to the Beast and resuming their duties. That evening alone together in their cabin, the couple lay in bed contemplating their time on Earth with Ian's parents. Aundria said, "Clare is really an unusual woman. I don't know if I could have accepted an alien woman as my son's wife."

"Mom was stuck with me while both her sisters and later me

went into space. My aunts are both together now on the Hulk, something she would give up almost anything to join them in space. Now, she lives her dreams through us."

"Ian, have you considered transferring to Green's Star Fleet as a advisor, much as Admiral Becker did at Aqua so that he and Mae could stay together?"

"Yes, I have no objection to such an arrangement, but Admiral Grantsman may not agree. He's your uncle, what do you think?"

"I'm his favorite niece and I got him to include me in this training venture. I'd like to be a Captain to your Commodore in a Green Fleet ship, rather than a lower ranked officer in an Earth Fleet. However, I'll go wherever you go whether it's in your navy or mine."

* * *

Seven months later First Fleet crossed through the third warp gate into the Green System after sending through a message torpedo announcing their arrival. The Home Fleet welcoming them consisted of two Heavy Battle Cruisers and all seven of the original cruisers given to the people of Green.

After consultation with the commander of the Home Fleet, they led the A Squadron of First Fleet back to Green while B Squadron guarded the gate. Three days later they were in Green orbit awaiting a visit from Admiral Grantsman and his staff to be held aboard the Earth Flagship, the UES Hulk.

Commanders Ian and Aundria Eiberger were already aboard the Hulk awaiting Green's delegation that was due to arrive within the hour. Later, standing at attention in Shuttle Bay 1, as the Green Shuttle settled inside, they both nervously mentally touched minds for mutual support.

Admiral Grantsman and three others followed him down a Marine Honor Guard corridor to Earth's Flag, which he saluted and asked permission to board from Flag Captain Hanna Bloodworth. Admiral Grantsman noted his niece's presence with a raised eyebrow before following Captain Bloodworth into the ship toward their meeting room.

When they arrived at their meeting room Captain Bloodworth asked, "Does anyone like refreshments before we start, we have sticky buns?"

Jorge Grantsman smiled, "You remembered my fondness for them! Yes, I can't pass up something that we can't quite duplicate."

Hanna replied, "I think it's the sugar you use, its flavor is different from ours."

Jorge lifted one of the buns to his nose and inhaled deeply, before shaking his head in disappointment. "It also has a different smell."

Hanna approached Jorge and spoke softly so others could not hear. "Admiral, your niece and my nephew are married or mated, whatever term you use. It didn't involve a normal courting behavior and represents the third time this has happened between a human and an alien, twice with an Aqua and now with a Green. I think it's wise to discuss this with them before we start our meeting."

He looked at her closely and seeing her earnest expression, he nodded his head in agreement. Hanna nodded her head at the newly-weds when she had their attention and they followed their elders to another nearby room.

After everyone was inside she motioned for a marine to stand guard outside the door. Once seated, Hanna told Jorge what happened during the couple's first meeting, their marriage, and how they had been assigned duties near each other.

Jorge asked Aundria, "Is this true?"

"Yes uncle, I've never felt this way with another man. We love each other beyond anything I'd ever heard or experienced before, and Ian feels the same toward me."

He asked, "Captain, you say there have been two other instances?"

"Yes, the first was between Admiral Becker, who was on loan to the Aqua Navy, and their Captain Mae Fieldspire. They had a daughter, Karrie, who met my son, Adam, in a similar situation as these two. They have a daughter despite using birth control and in all three instances they cannot bear being separated from each other; in Adam and Karrie's case they know where their mate is and what they are doing when they are separated."

Jorge looked at the two for a few minutes while considering their dilemma. "Captain Bloodworth, you have been supervising their performance since their marriage, how would you rate their abilities?"

"Ian, has been the Executive Officer of the UES Beast for almost three years and has performed well. If there were an opening I wouldn't hesitate promoting him to a captain of a starship. Aundria has no command experience, but she has command presence. She addressed our Star Fleet Board when she was on Earth the first time. They wanted to see what an officer of the Green Navy looked and acted like. After they heard her speak, they gave her a standing ovation. She was with us for three battles with the Xones and scored high in tactics."

Admiral Grantsman hesitated a moment before replying, "Captain, we have four Heavy Battle Cruisers ready or almost ready for the beginnings of our Battle Fleet; however, we don't have experienced commanders to lead them. Would you consider lending to our Star Fleet your Commander Ian Eiberger to act as Commodore for our Battle Fleet?"

"Admiral, what position do you contemplate for Aundria? She needs to be nearby for this to work."

"I was thinking XO to her husband until she gains command experience."

"Didn't you initially plan on another officer to command your fleet?"

"Yes, he's married to someone on the planet, so that didn't work out."

Hanna asked, "Ian, can you live with this transfer? You probably won't be able to visit Earth for many years and your mother will be devastated not being able to see you."

"Perhaps we can send video's back and forth until I can return for a visit. Aundria and I gamed this as one of the possible options we were going to be offered and agreed to take it if offered. Besides, I believe with me as the buffer between the two fleets we will get better results."

Admiral Hinderman frowned, "I hate to be so transparent, yet Aundria knows me well and has done this before; however, I still think I'm getting the best deal."

* * *

The following day, Ian and Aundria transferred by shuttle to a new unnamed Heavy Battle Cruiser of the Green Navy. Pipes music welcomed them aboard, a tune unfamiliar to Ian, but bringing a smile to Aundria's face. They both saluted Green's Flag and asked permission to board from a young Lieutenant (jg), who returned their salute and granted them permission. She called a nearby marine to guide the officers to the Bridge.

When they stepped across the threshold of the Bridge, the marine announced, "Captain on the Bridge!"

Captain Ian Eiberger was wearing a white beret, a custom he intended to carry across to Green's Star Fleet. His XO was Aundria and they stood and observed the crew at their stations for a slow count of three. "At ease, carry on."

Everyone relaxed as the two walked toward the command chair. Ian said, "Lt. Commander, what is your name and normal duty station?"

"Sir, my name is Quinn Norval and I normally have duty as the Science Officer."

"Very well, Lt. Commander Norval, I am going to assume command to make an announcement and then return the Con back to you."

"Sir, yes sir. You have the Con." Norval said, and then stepped down from the Command Chair.

Captain Eiberger took his place and touched the all-ship intercom. "Attention for all crew aboard this ship, this is your Captain Ian Eiberger speaking. My XO, Commander Aundria Eoff, and I have just arrived aboard this unnamed Heavy Battle Cruiser. Every crewmember will submit a possible name for this ship to their Department Heads, who will submit to me a recap of these names by this time tomorrow. In addition to being your captain, I am the Commodore for Green's Battle Fleet, which will make this ship the Flagship of the Fleet. I am on permanent loan from the Earth Battle Fleet and have participated in over fifty battles with the Xones. Your new XO is my wife and a native of your planet. She has also participated in three battles herself. That is all."

CHAPTER 18

The UES Hulk was awaiting the response from the probe sent through the third warp gate, when suddenly enemy missiles burst through the gate headed toward First Fleet. The laser cannons from the fleet's two battleships quickly destroyed that problem. Ten minutes later they received a message torpedo from their probe, which revealed a single enemy cruiser departing the gate area and three loose groups totaling ninety ships that were stationary 300,000 miles from the gate.

"COMM, Admiral Bloodworth to UGS Tiagerfish. When in position, fire one salvo at the departing cruiser. Inform me when in position."

"Tiagerfish to Flag, we are in position."

"Flag to Tiagerfish, you may fire one salvo. After firing clear area for the Hulk and Madrid to transit the gate. Unless Flag informs fleet otherwise, the remaining ships will follow us through the gate one hour after we transit the gate."

"Tiagerfish to Flag, one salvo fired and clearing the area."

"COMM, Flag to Madrid. After gate is cleared, follow the Hulk and when in position fire three salvoes at the left formation and two salvoes at the middle formation. The Hulk will do the same for the right and middle formation. Expect to be fired upon soon after leaving the gate area and take standard defensive measures."

"Madrid to Flag, aye sir. Madrid will fire three salvoes at the left formation and two salvoes at the middle formation when in position."

The two battleships transited the gate and immediately assumed firing positions, whereupon they fired upon the three enemy positions. The two battleships then assumed defensive positions and awaited six salvoes fired at them by the enemy ships in response to their attack.

Admiral Bloodworth asked, "How long on the clock for incoming missiles?"

"Sir, twenty-eight minutes for incoming missiles and our missiles will reach them beginning in twenty-one minutes."

"COMM Flag to Madrid, maneuver 150,000 miles up on my command... Execute maneuver now."

The Xones three fleets failed to react to the incoming First Fleets missiles other than launching their short-range defensive missiles at them, which had little effect. The first salvo took out at least a third of the Xones ships, then less than two minutes later the second salvo struck them with even greater devastation, leaving less than ten ships in each of the three enemy fleets. The remainder of the enemy fleet disappeared when the third salvo hit them.

Now it was the battleships turn to defend themselves as 900 enemy missiles approached them in the first of six salvoes, or 5,400 total missiles. The two ships were 20,000 miles apart, but their laser cannons had a range of 50,000 miles, which allowed them to mutually defend themselves. The first three enemy salvoes completely missed both ships; however, the remaining salvoes must have had an early shutdown instruction because both battleships received almost 200 attacking missiles from each of these salvoes. None survived the defending laser fire to come within 10,000 miles of either ship.

The UES Hulk sent a message torpedo to the remainder of the fleet to join them and upon their arrival gave them a recap of the battle. Admiral Bloodworth also reported the departure of one enemy observer from the system after the battle.

* * *

The combined First Fleet and Green Battle Fleet returned to the Green System to report their success in this great battle. The Commodore of the Green Fleet, Ian Eiberger and his XO and wife, Aundria Eoff Eiberger, joined Admiral Bloodworth aboard the Hulk, where they had a conference with the head of Green Fleet, Admiral Jorge Hinderman.

Admiral Hinderman, after a review of the battle recordings, was ecstatic at its results and how Green's own small part was performed without any problems. He congratulated the UGS Tiagerfish and its crew on their performance.

Later, after the conference broke up, Admiral Hinderman took his niece and her new husband aside for a family discussion. "Aundria, your family is anxious to meet your mate and although you have performed a mating ceremony according to Earth's customs, they demand that you also perform another according to our customs."

Aundria's face expressed her concern as she held her husband's arm in a fierce embrace. "Ian, since you weren't vetted by my family before our marriage, according to our customs you must perform a series of trials before they can accept you into the family."

"What do you mean, a series of trials?"

"That's up to my mother. Maybe I can smooth things over when we meet her."

"You're not kidding me are you? Admiral, you realize we can't be separated for very long before we're both adversely effected."

"Yes, but her mother is not convinced. She believes you've done something to Aundria to somehow control her mind."

Aundria grimaced, "If only it was that simple. Ian, let's ride down to Green with Jorge and get this taken care of. Besides, I miss mother and my family and I want to show you off to them."

Ian nodded his head in agreement and they made arrangements with Admiral Hinderman to meet him at his shuttle in thirty minutes after they packed for the trip. Later, on the shuttle heading toward a confrontation with Aundria's family, Ian held her hand gaining solace from this contact.

The shuttle landed at a new space shuttle port near the large city of Port Locke. They took a ground car limo to the family home located over thirty miles away in a small rural community. While travelling Aundria gave Ian some background on how their planets mating procedure normally occurred. After the prospective groom was introduced to the mother of the bride, a background check was made if not already known to the family.

However, Ian's background as an alien from another planet made this procedure unworkable for the family. They had to break new ground in how they were going to give permission for this union.

When they arrived at the family home it was late, well past their normal bedtime, but only mid-evening for the locals. Aundria's mother, Maile Eoff, gathered her daughter into a long fierce embrace before releasing her and confronting her new alien husband. "Daughter, introduce me to this interloper!"

"Mother! This is my husband, Ian Eiberger, from the planet Earth, which gave us a means to fight our enemy, the Xones."

Ian stepped forward and surprised Maile with a kiss on her cheek. "Aundria has told me of her fiercely protective mother. I'm happy to meet you and have learned your language for my first meeting with her family."

Maile touched her cheek with a stunned expression on her face. "Daughter, is your husband normally so generous with his kisses?"

"He honored you by this show of affection toward the mother of his wife. It is a normal tribute to family members."

"I see; however, I seem to have a lingering reaction to his kiss. Is this normal?"

"Mother, you and I share much of our DNA. When Ian and I first met we both felt a shockingly strong attraction to each other without touching. So your lingering reaction to his kiss would not be beyond reason."

"Does this happen for all meetings between Earth men and Green women?"

"No, I've met many Earth men before Ian and I never felt anything unusual before. Ian has no special power over other women, only alien women with a matching DNA. Actually, it's the woman who apparently carries the spark that ignites the flame between us. Our attraction initially was so strong neither of us could do anything but try to touch the other. When that occurred something clicked between us and the mating desire was so strong that if others had not been present we would have joined right there."

"This has happened before?"

"Yes, twice before with another alien race women and human males. They immediately knew what was happening to us and arranged a mating ceremony before we lost complete control."

"Daughter, what is his background?"

"Mother, he is the nephew of the Captain of the Flagship UES Hulk who is married to Fleet Admiral Erik Bloodworth. They have a son married to an Aqua woman under the same situation as Ian and me."

"So, it's in his family DNA and apparently ours for this to occur."

"Yes, we believe so. To the best of our knowledge this has only happened three times and Ian and my attraction is the strongest so far. We don't know why, only that it is something in our blood that causes it. We have a need to remain close to each other, so we work near each other on the same shift. In addition, we always know where the other is when apart and what they are doing."

"My dear, I think I am finally beginning to understand your situation. I feel an attraction toward Ian as well, not sexual, but still, a definite attraction. Jorge, how long will it take for us to get enough of the family together for a mating ceremony?"

"If I start in the morning, three days minimum. This is going to be a big event for the planet because of the family ties to the Bloodworth clan and ours. We may have to move it to a larger venue to hold everyone who want to attend."

"Very well, it's gotten late and we need our rest. Daughter, can you sleep apart from you future mate?"

"Yes mother, but it will be hard for both of us. If it will help we will agree not to have sex until after the mating ceremony."

Maile pulled her daughter into a tight embrace and spoke softly, "Very well, take him to bed in your old room and we will start fresh in the morning."

Later, when they were both in bed, Aundria said, "Did you kiss mother as a test to see if she had a reaction, or as a courtesy?"

"The latter, I was as surprised as you when she had a reaction. We should write down the various things we've discovered about our new condition and ask the others if they have had similar reactions."

Aundria spooned against her husband's back and playfully kissed his neck. "Hey, no fair you promised your mother no hanky-panky."

"Darn, and she would probably know if we did because of her connection to you. I guess we better get our rest because tomorrow promises to be busy for us."

The following morning the couple made their way downstairs when they heard noises from the kitchen. Maile looked up from her food preparation when they entered the room, "Did you two sleep well?"

"Yes mother, can I help you with anything?"

Maile looked at her youngest daughter with affection and concern. "You're not pregnant are you?"

"Not that I'm aware. Why do you ask?"

"You have a glow about you, much like Lillian did when she was carrying her last child."

"We've both been taking precautions, but even so that wasn't enough for the Bloodworth couple who have a child. Are my siblings coming today?"

"Yes, Lillian and Kasson should arrive by mid-day and they will be bringing their families as well. Everyone wants to see your new mate and hear your fascinating tale. Aundria, I've been worrying whether you'd ever find a mate and you bring home a potential world shattering problem."

Ian smiled at Maile, "Yes, I've found that she can rock the foundations of whatever stands in her way. When Uncle Bloodworth took her to the Board of Directors of our Space Fleet she certainly impressed them and recommended that she be groomed for a high position in the Green Space Fleet."

Maile turned her attention to Aundria whose face had turned a bright red in embarrassment. "This is the first I've heard about such a meeting."

"Mother, a lot has happened since I've been gone. Our current problem is but the most recent unusual happening for me. Most has been wonderful, like meeting Ian, but others are just career development. Some I haven't even informed Uncle Jorge."

Ian said, "She currently is the Executive Officer of my Flagship, the UGS Tiagerfish, one of our first Heavy Battle Cruisers, gaining experience before becoming its captain."

Maile looked sharply at Ian. "Your Flagship! That's right; Jorge said you were the Commodore of our Green Space Fleet. That would make Aundria your second in command when she becomes captain."

"Technically, she already is. You have a really bright daughter."

"Yes, however; I guess I haven't given her the credit she deserves. Aundria, what does your mate eat for breakfast?"

"Let me fix him something that's similar to what he is used to eating. Mother, please sit down and talk to Ian while I fix us both something to eat. He really is interesting and his family background is similar to ours."

Later, after the meal and cleanup they moved to the living room area and continued their conversations until the first guests arrived. Everyone jumped a little when the front door slammed open and two children ran into the room and looked around before running toward Maile, screaming "Grandmima!" Then they jumped into her lap and hugged her.

Aundria said over the noise, "That's Lillian's twins, Kellyn and Maylyn."

A woman looking slightly older than Aundria quickly followed her children into the room and stopped, smiling at the spectacle enfolding before everyone. She then caught sight of her younger sister as she stood, and quickly hurried towards her where they embraced each other for a long moment. When they broke apart they had tears in their eyes.

Lillian quickly caught sight of Ian and asked, "Is this the cad who bewitched you?"

Ian came over and quickly kissed Lillian's cheek, saying, "Hardly that, it was more a mutual bewitching."

Lillian touched her cheek where she had been kissed and looked at Ian with wide eyes. "Aye, I can see how that can happen."

Aundria shook her head at her sister. "No, what you felt in that kiss was but a thousand times less than what we both experienced by just being close to each other. When we touched, it was like an explosion inside our bodies. A longing like I've never experienced before and when we embraced it was like I was now complete, a whole person. When we are apart my mind reaches out to him and I can feel where he is and what he is doing."

Lillian asked Ian, "Do you feel the same as Aundria, the same longing for her, the feeling of completeness when touching?"

"Yes, even more so when we make love. It's as if we merge together."

Lillian touched her sister's cheek tenderly. "I envy you your love for each other. It's like nothing I've heard of before."

Ian said, "We're the third couple who've had this experience and apparently ours is the strongest attraction toward each other. My cousin, Adam Bloodworth and his mate, Karrie Becker from Aqua, are the couple before us. Her mother and a Earth human were the first occurrence."

* * *

While they were talking, Lillian's twins left their Grandmima to check out this new man talking to their mother. As they got closer their eyes widened as a strange feeling came over them. Watching this fascinating man they grabbed their mother's skirt and Kellyn asked, "Mama, why does your friend glow and why do Maylyn and me want to touch him. I know I shouldn't, but both of us have a need to touch him."

Aundria's face suddenly turned pale as she said, "Oh, oh. We may have a problem with the children. Lillian, ask them how strong is this feeling to touch him and explain about the glow they see."

Lillian dropped to her knees bringing herself to their level. "Twins, pay close attention to what I say. How strong is this urge to touch the glowing man?"

The twins whispered to each other, then Maylyn replied, "Remember the strong wind we walked in yesterday, it was mostly like that. We feel a pull, but know we shouldn't, so we resist. Is that what you were asking?"

"Yes, thank you twins. What does this glow look like since us adults can't see it?"

The twins conferred again and this time Kellyn replied, "His skin has a bluish glow and he has red hair."

"How strong is the glow from the man, is it faint or stronger?"

The twins conferred again and after agreeing on an answer, Maylyn replied, "It is strong enough to be noticeable, but we don't consider it strong."

Lillian asked her sister, "Should we let them touch Ian and see what happens?"

"Their reaction is stronger than yours, but doesn't reach our reaction to each other. I think our whole female family is keyed to him in some respect. The glow factor is new though."

Aundria motioned for Ian to come closer and they watched the children's reaction as he came closer, but when the twins started to move toward him she told everyone to "Stop!"

"Ian, do you feel a draw towards the girls?"

"A little, but more than a desire to talk to family."

"Girls, has your desire to touch him increased since he's closer?"

Maylyn replied, "Yes, it's much stronger now. It's even stronger than wanting to touch Grandmima. My fingers are starting to tingle a little now too."

"Kellyn, do you feel the same?"

"Yes, Mother. Now my feet are tingling too."

Aundria asked, "Ian, what do you think is happening?"

"Remember when we were drawn together until we actually touched each other. Well, this is the same thing only at a much lower attraction. I think if we touch, they will get a connection established. What happens then is anybody's guess."

Lillian asked, "Twins, do you feel flustered that you can't touch him?"

Maylyn replied, "Yes, is this man Aundria's mate?"

"Yes, why do you ask?"

"She doesn't try to touch him like us. Why is that?"

Aundria replied, "Because I've already made a connection with him. I'm almost sure the twins will be alright if they connect with Ian."

Lillian's face showed her inner conflict, but after a minute she said, "Twins step up to your Uncle Ian and touch him and let us know what you are feeling."

The girls swiftly covered the remaining distance between Ian and themselves and each grabbed a leg and held him tightly. Kellyn said with a relieved smile, "Mother, the longing has passed after I felt something connect, now Uncle Ian is my favorite relative. He even smells good."

"How about you Maylyn?"

"The same I guess. He is better looking than our other man relatives. Oh, his glow is no longer there, but he still has red hair."

Aundria replied, "Twins, Earth people with red hair are more common than on Green, just not as many here."

Lillian asked, "Twins, come to me and let's see if your longing for Ian returns."

"Well, any tingling or other reaction towards Ian?"

They shook their heads in the negative.

Lillian sighed in relief, "Well, I'm glad that's over and since Kasson has twin boys, she probably won't have this reaction from her children."

CHAPTER 19

Aundria's oldest sister, Kasson, entered the living room with her twin boys and found everyone watching them expectedly. She looked around and asked, "What's going on?"

Aundria stepped forward dragging Ian with her. "Kasson, meet my mate, Ian Bloodworth."

Kasson felt an immediate icy shock, followed by a strong urge to touch Ian as she stepped forward with her hand out to him. "Ian, it's nice to meet yoou, ooh, what's wrong with me. Aundria! What's happening to me?"

Aundria put her arms around her sister and asked, "Do you feel better now?"

"I think so. Your mate certainly gave me a turn, and he's really very attractive. I bet you have to beat other women off with a stick."

"But not you, do I?"

"Certainly not! Aundria I'm married with kids, I wouldn't poach my own sisters mate!"

Aundria smiled at her sister and kissed her cheek. "No, I'm not worried about you, but you gave me a scare there for a moment. Ian has the ability to emotionally draw women to him from our family, especially me."

"What do you mean?"

"When I first met Ian we were twenty feet apart ready to be introduced to each other when we each had an extreme urge to copulate with each other. By extreme, I mean it was all we could think about as we pushed people aside so that we could touch each other. We were formally married less than two hours later because we were about ready to tear the clothes off each other."

Kasson looked at her sister in wonder. "He bewitched you!"

"Actually, we bewitched each other and now we can't be far removed from each other. We even work the same Bridge shift aboard our Flagship, the UGS Tiagerfish."

Kasson pulled her sister close and they stared at each other with tears running down their cheeks. "Kasson, we do love each other very much and would kill anyone who would harm our mate."

"Aundria, he is a very attractive man. I shiver a little when I look at him."

"That's because we share similar DNA, which apparently is the cause of our attraction to him. Other women don't share our attraction to him, at least not to the extent we do."

Kasson looked at the twin girls and then with apprehension asked, "Even the twins?"

Kellyn, who had been following her Aunt's conversation, said, "We love mother lots more than Ian, he's just our favorite uncle."

"Lillian has about the same attraction to Ian as the twins do. Ian's attraction to females is limited to me. I'm his whole world."

"Wow, aren't you lucky to have such a lover."

"Yes, but I'm in the same situation, he's my whole world."

"Well, what's the status of the mating ceremony?"

Their mother, Maile, replied, "Jorge called earlier and he's almost got everything arranged for the mating ceremony to be held in the town hall at six p.m. local time. He wants Ian and Aundria to wear their space fleet uniforms and for all Aundria's family to be in attendance, including himself. Ian's family will be represented by Earth's Fleet Admiral Eric Bloodworth and his aunt, Captain Hanna Bloodworth."

Kasson replied, "Wow, that's a lot of VIPs who will be here. No wonder they wanted the ceremony to be held in the town's biggest venue."

She turned to Ian, "It's good that you've got us behind this union, otherwise according to our customs you might have had to fight our families' champion."

When Aundria saw the distressed expression on her mate's face, she squeezed his hand, saying softly, "Don't worry, that hasn't happened in over 200 years and he survived with only the loss of his left hand."

Ian, now sure they were putting him on, said, "I hope everyone realizes that I'm the fastest runner in the fleet."

Everyone laughed at his comment, including the children. Ian spoke to his mate, "We better make sure our uniforms are prepared for this ceremony, pressed and all our medals properly displayed."

Aundria quickly turned to the children, "Girl's you can help me, while the boys help Ian. Now let's get busy."

The girls, including their mothers, followed Aundria while the boy's followed Ian. When they reached their bedroom, Ian picked up his luggage and started looking for another room to work on his uniform. One of the twins, Jomar, said, "Let's try the laundry room. It has room to hang clothes and you can press your uniform there if it's needed."

Ian followed the boy's downstairs to their suggested room and found it suited his purpose. He quickly pulled his uniform out of his luggage and checked for wrinkles. He needn't have worried since all its material was of a new generation wrinkle-free substance. He looked at the boys' faces as they collectively gasped when they saw the uniform jacket.

The fourteen-year olds were almost Ian's height, but their bodies had not yet filled out. He took the jacket off its hanger and held it for Jomar to put on, who turned to his brother holding it closed over his thin body to display it better. "Mark, look at me, I'm a Commodore. Now, you try it on."

After Mark had his turn with the jacket, Ian placed it back on its hanger and looked at the battle ribbons and medals displayed on its left breast. There were three ribbons representing medals for valor. He opened his bag and drew out the cases containing the medals, and after replacing the ribbons with the actual medals, the "fruit salad" looked quite full.

Jomar asked, "Uncle Ian, what do all the ribbons and medals mean?"

The ribbons represent battles I've been present at and the stars on the ribbons mean I've been at the same location more than once. The medals represent that I've been cited for valor during a battle."

Mark said, "Uncle Ian, two of those medals have gold stars on them. Does that mean you've gotten this medal more than once?"

"Yes, a silver star means a repeat of this award. A gold star means multiple repeats of this award."

Both boys' mouthed the word, "Wow!"

After making sure everything looked proper, he put the jacket on and turned to the boys and asked, "Does it look right to you?"

They nodded their heads, faces glowing with obvious hero worship. Mark said, "You better have Aunt Aundria look at it too, because we're no expert."

"Okay, I'll put my pants on too and we'll go upstairs and check on her."

When he knocked on the door, Kasson answered and upon seeing her boys, said, "Boys go get his luggage and bring it back up here and leave it outside the door, then go help your Grandmima."

After they left, she let Ian into the room, where her sister and nieces were fussing over Aundria. She looked up and upon seeing her husband, winked at him. Ian said, "Do you have all the battle ribbons you earned?"

"All but the last battle. You've been in that system before, do you have an extra?"

"I think so, I'll check when they bring my bags back up here. Girls step aside and let me look at my wife for a moment."

Aundria earned several battle ribbons with her service attached to Earth Fleet and later while aboard her own Green Battle Cruiser. "I think you have everything except for the last battle. Put your beret on and let's see how the whole package looks?"

She placed the beret on her head and turned to him. Ian started with her beret and slowly examined her uniform down to her shoes. He then walked around her and stopped to remove a piece of white lint off her uniform before returning to stop before her. He frowned and adjusted the beret slightly before smiling at her.

"Perfect, now you do me."

She smiled at him, and then examining his medals said, "Ian, I didn't realize you had so many valor medals." She then continued her examination until finishing after walking around him.

"You look fine, but that ship emblem representing a Tiagerfish is not fierce enough for what it is."

"We'll work on it. You do realize that we'll probably get medals from your planet for that last battle?"

Her eyes widened, "You really think so?"

"With all the VIPs here, how can they not waste the opportunity?"

Maile said, "I want a recording of you both in uniform for my own memories of this mating ceremony."

They went through various poses of just themselves, and then with Aundria's mother, followed by her sisters, and finally with the whole family. It was difficult getting everyone in the last grouping.

After everyone left the room except the mating pair, Ian found another battle ribbon, among his case of awards, which represented the missing system where Aundria fought a battle. He added the ribbon to her other awards, and then kissed her lips softly. When he started to move away, she laid her head on his chest. "Honey, the family has accepted you as one of their own and I can't be any happier than I am at this moment."

Ian replied, "I wish my mother was here for this moment as well; maybe we can get pictures of this event sent to her."

* * *

Three months later the First Fleet was returning to Earth for resupply and crew leaves before departure to the Aqua system. Captain Hanna Bloodworth, accompanied by her Fleet Admiral husband, was planning on visiting her sister, Clare, in Hamburg, Germany. She was bringing recordings of her son's mating ceremony and visuals of his wife's family.

Two weeks after First Fleets arrival in Earth orbit, the Bloodworths took a weeks shore leave to recharge their own batteries and visit their remaining relatives left on Earth. Their shuttle settled at their usual landing site at a small aircraft airport outside of Hamburg. Clare met them and after a tearful reunion between the sisters, her husband drove them to their new downsized retirement home.

Erik sat in the front with Jasper, while the sisters rode in the back seat catching up on the news they missed while Hanna was in space. Erik asked about their new retirement home located in an area designed for people their age without any children left in the home. Jasper said, "It's caused us to make some adjustments in our lifestyle, but overall we both like the change. Clare and I have made new friends, and some carryovers from before retirement who also live nearby."

Their new home had a spare bedroom for visiting relatives and after settling in Hanna decided that she should now broach the subject of Ian's meeting with his wife's family and the mating ceremony. Carrying the small case containing the material, they rejoined their hosts.

Hanna said, "Clare I've brought some material recorded on the planet Green regarding Ian and his new wife, Aundria. You and Jasper take a seat while Erik sets the recordings up."

While Erik did his thing, Hanna explained what Ian's wife's family required of Ian to be accepted as his wife's mate. At Hanna's nod, Erik started the recording of the actual mating ceremony.

The two paid rapt attention as the recording continued until fifteen minutes later it ended with the pair kissing, sealing their relationship. As the recording ended Clare fell into Jaspers arms, finally letting loose her heartbreak at how far away Ian and his family where from them. Hanna waited until Clare's emotions settled somewhat before saying, "We've also brought visuals of the mated pair and her family."

The first picture was that of the pair together in Green Space Fleet Uniforms. When she handed it to Clare she looked at the pair in rapt attention. "Oh Jasper, look how beautiful they look together. I didn't realize she was such a beauty; he's really done well for himself."

"Now might be a good time to tell you that she is pregnant and may have already delivered her child."

"What! Did they know what gender the child was going to be?"

"When we left Green that information was not known. They have very good medical facilities that are at least equal to Earth's. She plans on staying aboard their ship to raise her child, much like I did."

"Oh my! This is wonderful news; I may already be a grandmother. Let's look at the other pictures."

Clare was particularly interested in the picture showing all Aundria's sisters and her mother. "So this is my opposite family and the child's other grandmother."

Hanna said, "Aundria's sisters had twins. It makes me wonder if she will have twins as well?"

"I wonder if I'll ever see my grandchild?"

Hanna and Eric spent three days with Clare before taking a side trip to a Hawaii beach, and then returning to the UES Hulk. First Fleet added another Battleship and four Heavy Battle Cruisers to its numbers, which caused Eric to delay his departure for Aqua because he wanted to consult with Admiral Pavlova of the Second Fleet regarding adding a Third Fleet.

Ten days later Second Fleet arrived and Admiral Pavlova reported to Fleet Admiral Bloodworth aboard the Hulk. Accompanying him was his wife, Flag Captain Annalisa Pavlova. The meeting was a combined dinner and business gathering as Vlad, an avid beefeater, was in severe withdrawal for fresh beefsteak.

While the men were talking about fleet business the woman were bringing each other up to date on what was happening in their families. Annalisa's son, Peter, was still unmarried and was a senior Bridge crewmember aboard their Battleship, the UES Tiger. Hanna brought her the current news on her own two children and the continuing unsettled marriage relationship of their son, Adam. She then told her about her nephew Ian's encounter with the Green woman, Aundria Eoff, and their quick subsequent marriage, ending with an urgent statement, "If I were you I'd keep Peter away from any female from Aqua or Green."

Admiral Bloodworth interrupted the women's conversation. "Captains, we want your opinion about adding another Earth Fleet. Combined First and Second Fleets have two Battleships and fourteen Heavy Battle Cruisers. We have an additional unassigned Battleship and three Heavy Battle Cruisers; Home Fleet has one Battleship, eight Heavy Battle Cruisers, and twenty Cruisers not active - but kept in standby readiness reserve. What's your recommendation?"

Hanna thought for a moment, and then replied, "If you wanted an independent unit, you would need to draw one Heavy each from First and Second Fleet, leaving them six Heavies to support each Battleship. The new unit would have five Heavies to support its Battleship. I personally would recommend giving the Battleship and Heavies to Home Fleet and defer adding another fleet until there are enough Heavies to support all the Battleships." Annalisa smiled at the men, "I concur with Hanna. Home Fleet needs another Battleship to cover both of Earth's Warp Gates. Any future construction will go to the eventual establishment of another Battle Fleet."

Erik smiled at Vlad, "Well, that's final then. I need to contact Home Fleets Admiral Jason Schmidt on the Battleship UES Mars, and get his recommendations for the Captain of his new Battleship. He can do his own picks for the Heavies."

* * *

Commodore Eiberger's Green Fleet now consisted of three Heavy Battle Cruisers and seven Cruisers. All of the Green's ship construction has been Heavies and they were now laying the foundation for their first Battleship. His command, while small, could defend the Green System from all but an all out Xones attack. Their system had two Warp Gates, much like the Earth system and most other systems they entered.

The Katz, while an old race, didn't know whom the advanced race was that established the warp gate system they were currently using, as it was present when they started their own space exploration some eighteen thousand years ago. They had not yet found any other evidence of the Ancients' existence in their explorations.

Ian came up beside the Command Chair where his wife was sitting. "Aundria, how are you feeling?"

"I'm feeling better; it's been three days since my last morning sickness and I'm hoping I'm now past that part of my pregnancy."

"Have you thought of a name for her yet?"

"I think we should give her a historic name, because I've got a strong feeling she will bring change to our worlds."

CHAPTER 20

"Mother, I know you're frightened for Celena, but she's sixteen now and legally mature enough to make her own life decisions."

"Aundria, how can you let her travel to Earth alone to meet her paternal grandmother??"

She hugged her mother closely to her chest. "Mother, Captain Hanna Bloodworth is her great aunt and the sister of Celena's Grandmother. She will be travelling aboard their great Battleship, the UES Hulk, so she's hardly in any danger from the Xones."

"I know, but I'm going to miss her so much while she's gone. How can you let her out of your control?"

"Mother! How can you even ask that question? You know she's the third child of something so big that we can only guess at its ramifications. The second child is also aboard the Hulk, so they need to interact and exchange information during their voyage to Earth. I'm also curious about her meeting with Ian's mother; no one knows why Celena is driven to visit Clare, not even Celena! I'd like to be a spider on the wall at their first meeting."

* * *

Two weeks later Celena Eiberger stepped off the shuttle aboard the UES Hulk, and was greeted by a female Commander. Celena was a little intimidated by the dark beautiful woman who greeted her as she was used to being the most beautiful woman in the room, and it wasn't her striking red hair alone that brought everyone's eyes toward her. Even if blind people surrounded her, something she naturally projected would attract them to her.

"Celena? I'm your escort, Commander Karrie Bloodworth. Besides being your cousin, I'm also related to you in another way. I'm the second to your third child in this mystery we are both living. Follow me and I'll take you to Captain Hanna Bloodworth who will explain the itinerary we have planned for you."

It wasn't long before she found herself on the bridge of the Battleship. It was much bigger than the Battle Cruiser her parents commanded, yet she immediately knew what each station serviced. Her father nicknamed the Command Chair, the Kirk Chair, after an old video series he called Star Trek that she hadn't seen. As they approached the Command Chair she smiled at the things her mind drudged up.

Commander Karrie Bloodworth said, "Ma'am, passenger Celena Eiberger has arrived."

Captain Hanna Bloodworth looked at her with a critical gaze, "Celena, do you have any long term goals for your life, such as college?"

"I'd like to join my world's Space Fleet eventually after finishing my higher education studies."

"How much, if any, have you already accomplished?"

"I've already finished two of my four years computer college study courses and I've brought the remainder with me to finish if I have the time."

"Very good. Commander Bloodworth will show you your quarters and explain the routine while you are with us. You will dine with the Admiral and me tonight at 19:00 hours in our cabin and you may dress civilian casual for the meal. Please wear a ship suit that will be provided when you travel throughout the ship for meals and other tasks. Any questions?"

"Auntie, how long will the trip take to reach Earth?"

"After we break Green orbit it will take about 96 days to reach the Earth system. It will go faster if you keep busy and you should address any pressing questions to Commander Karrie Bloodworth. She will take care of you until you are comfortable with the ship's routine."

Celena followed her guide off the bridge until they reached an official looking office called "Personnel". Karrie explained to the Lt. Commander in-charge who Celena was and what they needed from his office. Karrie asked Celena, "Do you want a single room or one with a roommate?"

"I assume you mean a female roommate?"

"Yes, she can help you get around the ship easier than being in a single room."

"Yes please. If we don't get along I can always get a single, can't I?"

Karrie looked at her with a raised eyebrow. "Why did you ask that question? You know that you'll never have that problem because other people are naturally attracted to you!"

"I haven't had any experiences with Earth humans except Dad and he doesn't count. I guess I'm a little afraid no one will like me for who I am, not because of the mojo that I project."

Karrie placed her hands on Celena's shoulders, "Look at me! You're a strong person. You would never consciously hurt anyone. Other people know this subconsciously and are drawn to you because of it even if you didn't have your so-called mojo. So, you want a roommate. What languages do you know?"

"Universal, Green, and German."

"I think you need English as well. I'll schedule you for a session in the tank for that and you'll also need to be cleared by Medical. Have you met your Aunt Lucy before?"

"No, and Dad told me I have a cousin in the ship's hospital as well."

"Yes, Dr. Hope Fellows. She'll probably take direct charge of you when you arrive in the hospital. Now let's see, room, medical - oh yes, you need a portable locater. Here take this, if you want to find a person or location just ask the device and it will tell or show you where it is. Also, you need to be measured for ship suits and shoes, and that should do it. I'll leave you here in their capable hands and if you need me use the locator, otherwise I'll see you tonight for dinner."

Later, Celena made her way to the hospital where she

encountered a corpsman manning an entrance counter. She gave her name and said, "I need to speak with Dr. Hope Fellows regarding a medical clearance. She's also a relative."

She gave Celena a surprised look, but quickly paged the Doctor. A middle-aged woman wearing a white lab coat soon arrived and stood gazing in speculation at her for a moment, "Celena?"

At her nod, Hope quickly crossed to her and gave her a hug of welcome. "Come with me, your Aunt Lucy is expecting you with great anticipation."

When they entered Dr. Lucy Hendricks' office, she looked up at Hope and then realizing who the young woman had to be, she quickly stood and rounded her desk to hug her niece tightly to her chest.

Stepping back she studied Celena's face for a moment before saying, "Thank you God, you must have inherited the face of your mother. How are your parents? They in good health?"

Celena smiled at Lucy's welcome. "Yes, they are both well. I think my hair is the major thing I received from Dad. My Mother's contribution was major however. Can you feel anything from me?"

Lucy and Hope looked at each other and nodded their heads in agreement before Lucy replied, "Yes, we both feel your influence, much more than we could from Adam and Karrie. It's obvious that you are stronger in this regard. We need to draw your blood and compare your DNA with those of the other infected people to see if we can detect something, anything that makes sense of what is occurring."

Hope spoke up, "She needs inoculation against Earth deceases as well before she travels to visit Clare."

Celena asked, "How is Grandmother Clare's health?"

Lucy replied, "She's the oldest of our sisters and is quite well for a woman of ninety-plus.

She didn't have the benefit of traveling in warp space that Hanna and I did. I'm sixty-one and the youngest, Hanna is the middle sister, but I'm not going to reveal her age under penalty of death."

Both doctors smiled at that statement before Hope asked, "Is there anything we can help you with while we are traveling back to Earth?"

"I'll let you know, Aunt Bloodworth seemed a little brisk when

I met her earlier. Is it something I should be concerned about?"

"She's concerned about what you represent, the uncertainty that your presence represents to all three human worlds. It has nothing to do with you personally. All the family aboard ship will be present tonight for dinner and you'll get a better read of her when she isn't the Captain of the Flagship of the First Fleet of Earth's Star Fleet."

After Celena finished with the medical part of her acceptance aboard ship she used the finder device to locate her cabin. After punching in the door code, it sounded its acceptance and she slowly entered the room, not knowing if her roommate would be present.

A Lt. Commander looked up from her computer monitor at her entrance into the room and said, "You must be my new roommate?"

"Hello. Yes, I've just arrived from the planet Green and my name is Celena Eiberger. My father is Commodore Ian Eiberger of the Green Star Fleet."

"Oh, so you're what we call a VIP. My name is Tricia Fender and you must be aboard for our return to Earth?"

"Yes, I'm travelling to visit my grandmother, who I'm going to see for the first time. She's the sister of Captain Bloodworth."

Tricia stood and said with an arched eyebrow, "Definitely a high VIP!"

She held out her hand for Celena to shake, but Celena hesitated looking uncertainly at the outstretched hand, "Before I touch you I should warn you that you may receive unwanted feelings from me."

Tricia immediately withdrew her hand, "I don't understand?"

"Do you know my cousins, Commanders Adam and Karrie Bloodworth and the story behind their marriage?"

"I know the rumor! Are you saying that it's true?"

"I'm a much more powerful carrier than Karrie. Do you feel anything emanating from me?"

"Only a feeling of good will that I usually don't feel toward anyone until I've known someone for a long time."

"If I touch you that might change to an even more stronger attachment that you might think is love, or not. These feelings vary according to the person, that's the reason I warn people before touching them."

Tricia brought her hand back until it touched her heart. "Wow, you must live an interesting life. What are you sixteen - seventeen years old?"

"Sixteen. Yes, interesting is a good word. I've had to adjust how I interact with others – mostly I stay close to home and my relatives."

"Your luggage already arrived and they've delivered your ship suits and shoes. They're piled on your bunk over there. Are you traveling only as a passenger or will you have duties?"

"Mostly as a passenger. I plan on studying for my college degree before reaching Earth, and then applying to the Green Star Fleet for a position."

"Celena, if you wore a glove would that blunt the effect you are guarding against?"

"No, a glove is no protection. I try to stay away from a male from Earth or Aqua until I'm sure they're not a match for me."

"How close do they have to be before you have a reaction?"

"I don't know. I may not even be old enough for such a reaction, so I stay wary of all non-Green men."

"Whoa, I don't think I want to be in your shoes. You're going to be in constant danger until you return to Green."

Tricia soon left to begin her shift at 16:00 hours to end at 24:00 hours. Celena emptied her luggage and stowed her clothing, made her bunk, and examined the shared head. She decided to shower and don fresh clothing for her dinner date with her family at 19:00 hours. After her shower, she took a short nap before leaving the cabin and followed the locator to the Captain's suite.

She buzzed the door for admittance and was surprised when an Asian steward answered the door. She gave her name and he smiled, bowed, and gestured her into the room. Celena suddenly realized she was the first to arrive when she found herself face-to-face with Fleet Admiral Eric Bloodworth.

He knew enough not to offer her a handshake and said, "Hanna's still in the head. Do you want a fruit drink while we wait on the others?"

She nodded her head and replied, "I really liked the taste of your orange juice."

Eric said, "My steward, Jason Mao will get it for you. Take a seat over here and I'll have the same Jason."

After they were settled he asked, "How do you like your roommate? Lt. Commander Tricia Fender isn't it?"

"Yes, she's very nice. She was very understanding of my reluctance to touch others after I explained my problem. Sir, I was wondering if I could arrange a female marine to escort me when I take my meals. I don't want a repeat of what happened to my father if I can avoid it."

Hanna spoke up startling Celena. "I think you have made a good suggestion, but let's reduce the risk further by you taking your meals at least two hours off of their peak times, say 09:00, 14:00, and 20:00 hours. Will that work for you?"

"Yes Auntie. Thank you for supporting me in my effort to know my grandmother before her advanced age robs me of the opportunity."

"Clare has often lamented to me that she'd never have the opportunity to know her granddaughter, and now here you are seeking her out. She only knows of you from the recordings sent to her by her son, your father."

The door buzzer sounded again heralding the arrival of more of her family. After everyone arrived there were nine members, Aunt Hanna and Lucy, Cousins Adam Bloodworth, Hope Fellows, Marie Bloodworth, and their spouses. Marie, who at twenty-three, is the unmarried daughter of Adam and Karrie Bloodworth, who technically was at risk as much as Celena.

However, as the evening progressed it was evident that Celena was stronger than either Marie or her mother, Karrie. When Celena brought up the risk to Karrie, she replied, "We think because we are on an Earth ship, the only risk would be males from the other two human planets. If we keep Marie away from them we think she'll be safe."

Celena told everyone about her father's reported experience with her mother's female relatives when he arrived on Green for the required mating ceremony. Apparently her mothers mother, two sisters, and young twin daughters all were drawn to touch him. Once that occurred their urge to touch him disappeared, but he so impressed the women that there was no further problem from them opposing his marriage to Aundria. Hanna smiled, "Yes, I remember a little of that ceremony and your mother was initially anxious about it. By the time of the ceremony it seemed everyone loved Ian."

Marie asked her cousin, "Celena, you're very brave to travel on an Earth ship. Why take the risk?"

"I've got this almost overwhelming desire to meet my paternal grandmother and it's only increased as I've gotten older. I need to fulfill this desire before she passes from this life."

Hanna smiled at her niece as she spoke, "Celena is very brave for someone her age who is starting this voyage knowing the risks she faces. After finishing college she told me she wishes to join her own Star Fleet to battle our common foe, the Xones."

All her family raised their glasses to her as they answered, "Here – Here!"

Celena returned to her cabin some three hours later still buzzed from the welcome of her family. She quickly made preparations for bed and was asleep within minutes and only vaguely noticed when Tricia entered the cabin after her shift.

The next morning when Celena left the head she found her roommate awake. She told her about her expected marine companion for breakfast to arrive at 09:00 hours, and asked if she wanted to join them.

"This, I want to observe."

They were both dressed and ready when their door buzzer sounded and Celena quickly answered the door and found a female Marine Lance Corporal standing outside. Celena quickly told her escort what was expected of her and they closely followed her to the Officers Mess and were lucky that they didn't encounter any male crew during their journey.

Celena stood aside and looked for an unoccupied table far from any others. Her Aunt Hanna correctly selected a time for breakfast when the room would be occupied by few males. Those occupants curiously watched the three women as they selected a table as far away from the males as possible. What really peaked their interest was the noncom marine accompanying a young civilian and an officer. Any deviation from normal activity would interest anyone aboard a closed society like a military spaceship.

All three tables now appeared to be discussing the new arrivals until one Lt. Commander left his table heading toward them. Lance Corporal Marie Johnson quickly left her table and intercepted the officer. After a quick discussion the officer returned to his table where he obviously told the others what he learned.

When the marine returned to the table with a small smile on her face, Tricia asked, "What did you tell him?"

She looked at Celena and winked, "I told him the young girl was from Green and was under conditional quarantine for another thirty days."

"Wow! Lance Corporal you're quick. I foresee a promotion in your future."

Celena picked up her menu and said, "Now that those guys are satisfied what's good that I can eat?"

After they ordered their meal, Marie asked Celena, "Why are you so concerned about being close to a man?"

Celena looked at Tricia and rolled her eyes. "Did you hear any rumors about Adam Bloodworth and his wife, or more recently when my father, Ian Eiberger met his wife Aundria Eoff, who was on temporary duty here from the Planet Green?"

The marine's eyes opened wide in surprise. "Really, you are related to what happened to them?"

"Yes, but I'm apparently a much more powerful a carrier than either of those women. I think my match is a male from either Earth or Aqua, and since I'm on a Earth ship full of potential mates, I have to be careful who I meet or come close to."

"My, you do have a problem. What should I watch for when a male approaches us?"

"First, try to keep that from happening. As a last resort watch his facial expression as he approaches. If he begins to have a dazed look, grab my arm and pull me away from him as fast as possible. I may resist because I will be attracted to him as well, but do your best to get me away from him. If we touch, we are both lost to the reaction and nothing can be done for us except delaying our mating."

"Why are you on this ship if there is so much risk for you?"

"Something is drawing me to Earth to visit my parental grandmother before she dies, and the risk to me is secondary."

"Your grandmother must be very important?"

"She's the older sister of Captain Bloodworth."

The women looked at Celena in surprise and then at each other in confusion. Celena nodded her head, "I don't know why the

Lundberg family is so involved in this either?"

CHAPTER 21

The remainder of the passage to Earth passed without any compromising encounters for Celena. She was growing impatient to leave the ship to visit her grandmother since the Hulk had made Earth orbit over a week ago. Captain Hanna Bloodworth finally notified her that they would leave tomorrow at 07:00 hours. Earth time (Germany) would be 21:40 hours when the shuttle was scheduled to touch down near Hamburg.

Celena was now worried that Grandmother Clare would be too tired to visit with her when they arrived at her home. Auntie Hanna told her that the timing couldn't be avoided and they would make adjustments, if needed, to see her.

The next day the two were on the shuttle descending toward Earth and Celena was watching the monitor showing a water world similar to her own birth world Green. It had less land mass than Earth which gave it a more colorful view with its brown desert, blue oceans, and green land areas. There was even a large white circular storm area in its largest ocean.

After the shuttle landed, they traveled to where Celena's grandmother lived; it was 22:50 hours when they arrived at her home. Hanna had a key to the house and they silently let themselves inside and shared the guest bedroom, trying not to wake Clare.

Although not tired they catnapped until 06:00 hours local time when they heard someone moving around in the kitchen. They quickly dressed and joined Clare, who ran into her sister's arms. When they broke apart, Hanna said, "Clare, this youngster is your granddaughter, Celena Eiberger."

Clare looked at Celena with a surprised look of pure joy. "Celena! I'd given up hope of ever seeing you. Come here and give your old grandmother a hug and a kiss."

Celena hurried into her arms, but when they touched they both felt a jolt of pure energy enter their bodies. Clare started to fall as she lost consciousness, but Celena, while shaken herself, held her up in her arms while calling for help from Hanna.

Hanna was a strong woman and easily carried her into the living room where she placed Clare on a sofa. Hanna asked, "What happened?"

"We both felt a jolt of energy and she collapsed. Wait, she's waking up."

Clare blinked her eyes and stared up at the two women hovering over her. "Wow! That was a rush. I haven't felt this good in twenty years. Let me sit up and we'll see if I still feel this good."

They quickly got out of her way, but were still near enough to help her if she needed it. Sitting upright on the couch she wiggled her fingers and moved her arms and shoulders a little to see if she experienced any pain. "Youngsters, I don't know what happened, but it sure put the jive back into this old body. Stay close while I stand up and lets move back into the kitchen. I've started something for breakfast that I need to look after."

They followed her into the kitchen and watched while she moved around preparing a meal for them. After shoving a tray of biscuits into the oven, she sat down with them at the table. "Celena, you zapped me when we first touched each other. What was that about?"

"Grandmother, for some reason I've had a pressing desire to see you. Maybe to do what I just did?"

"So you didn't consciously zap me. This is really weird. Hanna, do you know what's going on?"

"No more than you two. Everything about these unions defies

understanding, and now we have Celena who appears to be the strongest woman yet. I say woman although she's only sixteen."

Clare looked at her granddaughter with new eyes. "Sixteen or not, she's still a beautiful woman and that red hair she got from Ian is spectacular."

Hanna replied, "Let's think about Celena's compulsion to visit you and when you first touched each other, this happens! Why, what reason other than to revitalize Clare did her arrival here bring? Celena, do you have any other desires since you touched your grandmother?"

Celena held out her hand to Clare, who quickly grabbed it with both hands. She smiled at her grandmother while they were still in contact. "No, I feel only deep love for her... No, that's not quite right. There's something nagging at me while I'm touching her, but it's not clear. The smell of those biscuits is distracting me. Maybe we should eat and come back to this later?"

After breakfast they returned to the living room to continue their conversation. "Grandmother, how are you feeling now?"

"I haven't eaten that much food in years! My body and mind feel much better since you arrived and the only change to explain it is that jolt we both felt when we touched. Celena have you brought any more pictures with you of your family?"

She held up a finger and quickly left them to retrieve a video device in her luggage and soon returned with it in hand. She set it on the floor pointing at a blank wall and pushed the play button, and for the next ten minutes Clare was enthralled with images and sounds of her extended family.

When the device turned itself off, Clare's face was damp with her tears of happiness. She asked, "Those twin girl's belong to your mother's sister? Everyone seems to adore my son Ian, and he appears quite at home with your family. I'm so glad that he has a family so far away from his native Earth."

"I know, but some of that closeness is because of my parents abilities. Father really does love his adopted family and he wanted you to know he misses you very much. Mother was reluctant to allow me take this trip because of the apparent risk of meeting my matching DNA mate. However, so far that hasn't happened."

"Auntie Hanna, you are probably the most intelligent person in our family. Can you guess what all this is leading toward?"

"No, but right now you are the most powerful of our family's women. We will watch over you and learn as events unfold. For now, until we learn more, that's all we can do."

Three days later Hanna and Celena returned to the UES Hulk. When Earth's Second Fleet arrived in orbit, Celena transferred to the UES Tiger, Admiral Pavlova's Flagship. She would accompany them back to the Green System.

* * *

Thirty days later First Fleet broke Earth orbit and headed toward the Aqua system. Captain Hanna Bloodworth was still mystified by what happened when Celena and she visited her sister Clare on Earth. By the time they left, Clare seemed to be much stronger and apparently shed years from her body's age. It was a mystery she intended to pursue when she returned to Earth in about three years.

* * *

Celena was placed with another female fleet officer when her quarters were assigned aboard the Tiger. A female marine non-com escorted her to her cabin and buzzed for admittance. A short auburn haired Lt. Commander answered the door, and upon seeing a marine escorting an apparent young female civilian, stared at them while speculating on what was happening.

Lance Corporal Kelly McCall said, "Lt. Commander Alexandra Robbins, the Captain has assigned this civilian to bunk with you until we reach Green orbit. You are to offer any assistance and/or aid she may require during her stay with you; however, you will continue your assigned duties as before. A marine escort will be provided for her meals at times yet to be decided. Any questions?"

Robbins looked at her new roommate with great interest. "Does she need to be processed by personnel or medical?"

"No, that has already been taken care of and her luggage will be delivered here later."

"Very well, the remainder of my questions will be addressed to my new roommate. Please step inside and let's get to know each other."

Celena smiled at the officer who appeared to be in her late twenties, "I assume my bunk is the one that is unmade? Help me make it and I'll answer your questions as we work."

"Fair enough, what's your name and age?"

"I'm sixteen and my name is Celena Eiberger, the daughter of Commodore Ian Eiberger of the Green Star Fleet, and the niece of Captain Hanna Bloodworth of the First Star Fleet."

"So, a very important person. You must have come to Earth from Green with First Star Fleet and now are returning to Green. May I ask what you were doing on Earth?"

"Yes, I was visiting my grandmother, who's in her nineties."

"So this was a family visit to your grandmother, who is also related to Admiral or Captain Bloodworth?"

"Very good. You have great deductive reasoning. My Grandmother is the older sister of Captain Hanna Bloodworth."

After they finished making Celena's bed they both sat on it and looked at each other, until Alexandra asked, "What was the purpose of your visit? It seems strange you made the effort just to see your grandmother?"

Celena then gave a short history lesson of her families' past and her own apparent risk being on an Earth starship.

"Wow! You really are a brave young woman. I don't think I would have taken the risk coming to Earth with that hanging over my head?"

"Don't forget I was under a strong compulsion to travel here to visit my grandmother."

"So, now that's been accomplished you're heading back home to Green. What are your plans now?"

"Same as before, I'll finish college and join the Green Star Fleet."

Their door buzzer sounded and Alexandra answered it to find that Celena's luggage was delivered. After storing her belongings Celena asked, "When does your shift start?"

"Not until 16:00 hours. When did you last eat?"

"Early this morning at 06:00 hours."

"It's 13:20 hours now and I need to eat soon myself. I wonder when the marine is coming to pick you up?"

Celena shrugged her shoulders, "I have no idea."

Just then their door buzzer sounded and they smiled at each

other.

Celena's marine escort didn't know what she was guarding against, so she had to explain about any possible males who might go bonkers when they drew near her, what their tale-tale signs were and what the marine response should be in getting her away from him. Lance Corporal McCall looked at her strangely, but she had her orders no matter whether they made since to her or not.

Their cabin wasn't far from the Officers Mess and they didn't meet anyone who showed any interest other than she was a young civilian. Ten minutes later they stopped just inside the doors of their destination, scoping out who was inside and the best place to sit. Alexandra pointed out a table that fit their needs and they followed their marine escort to their remote pick.

Four other tables were occupied with male and female officers, so the marine chose a route that didn't come close to any of them. All the officers watched them enter because of their marine escort and the young female civilian. After they took their seats, apparently one female's curiosity became too much for common sense to prevail, and after speaking to her tablemates she walked directly to their table.

The Commander was the ranking officer in the room, which may have colored her judgment somewhat. Arriving at their table she said, "I'm Commander Joyce Still and I wasn't aware that we were carrying a civilian to Green. What's going on?"

Celena stood and addressed the officer. "Commander, obviously you weren't informed about my presence because it wasn't any of your business. Flag Captain Annalisa Hansen cleared my presence aboard the Tiger at the request of Flag Captain Hanna Bloodworth, who happens to be my Aunt. If you want to pursue the matter I recommend that you consult with Captain Hansen."

Celena returned to her seat after she finished speaking, but continued eye contact with the commander, whose face blushed scarlet with anger. Finally, realizing the futility of continuing the conversation, she turned and stalked back to her table where she had a short conversation with her tablemates before leaving the room in obvious anger.

The two female officers looked wide-eyed at the departing Commander, and then switched their attention to Celena, who winked at them. Both women suddenly smiled at Celena, who was now their best friend.

Alexandra placed her hand over her mouth smothering a laugh. McCall held her clinched fist up to Celena, which she bumped with her own.

Alexandra finally got control of her emotions and said, "It's well that you're a civilian or Commander Still would find a way to get even with you. She's a vindictive bitch."

The other officers in the room observed what transpired and were laughing among themselves and smiling toward their table.

Celena suddenly had a thought and said, "You two better tell your supervisors what just happened in case she comes after you, and I'll do the same with Captain Hansen."

They ordered their lunch, ate and returned to their cabin without further problems. Celena, true to her word left a message with Captain Hansen detailing her conversation with Commander Still. Later, the captain sent her a message acknowledging receipt of her message.

While Alexandra was away working her duty shift as Assistant Weapons Officer, Port Missile Section, Celena worked on her computer college courses. Two weeks later they broke Earth Orbit toward the Green System.

Second Fleet was two weeks into its voyage when the cabins door buzzer interrupted Celena's computer college course study. She was alone because Alexandra was on duty, and not knowing what to expect she took a deep breath and opened the door. Facing her was Commander Joyce Still, who said, "May I come in, I have something to discuss with you?"

Celena studied her face searching for a clue as to her intensions and noted that the commander was becoming increasingly agitated at her delay in inviting her inside. She gave the commander a slight smile and waved her inside.

Celena pointed to a vacant chair and said, "Please make yourself comfortable, I'm sorry that's the best I have to offer."

After they were seated, Celena waited for Joyce to speak, a smile still on face as her guest looked around the cabin and frowned. "I would of thought Captain Hansen would have arranged better accommodations, given your status as niece of the Fleet Captain."

"Auntie Bloodworth made it clear to Captain Hansen that I was to be given the treatment I'm currently being shown."

"I was curious about why you have a marine escort?"

"Commander, why are you here interrogating me?"

"So, it's your decision to play this close to your vest. I have my own ways of finding out what I want to know. I don't believe we should give you any special favors, allies or not."

"I'm curious commander, just what do you think is going on?"

"I don't know, but you appear to be more than a young teenager from an alien world and I'm going to get to the bottom of it if it's the last thing I do!"

Celena pointed to the door. "Commander, if that's all, you may leave. Maybe I'll see you in the Officers Mess again."

After the commander left her cabin, Celena took out the small recording device and replayed their conversation. Satisfied, she included it with another message to Captain Hansen. Afterwards, she smiled to herself with the thought; *maybe the entire day wasn't wasted.*

CHAPTER 22

Three days later, Lt. Commander Robbins came off-shift with news she was bursting to tell Celena. Finding her at the computer studying, she gushed, "Take a break, I've got something to tell you. Commander Joyce Still has been demoted to Lt. Commander and transferred off the ship!"

"Oh, how did that happen?"

"I don't know! Everyone I've asked hasn't got a clue. Even Lt. Commander Still hasn't spilled why. It's really odd that no one's talking."

"Oh well, maybe it'll come out eventually. Besides, it couldn't have happened to a more deserving person."

"Yeah, you got that right. It's just strange the way this happened. Usually, everyone knows why it happened. Hey, when is your marine escort arriving, I'm getting hungry?"

Celena looked at the time before replying, "She should be arriving about now, are you going to eat with us?"

"Yes, maybe I can get some gossip from someone there."

Celena was ready when her escort arrived and the three women headed toward the Officers Mess with Lance Corporal McCall about twenty feet ahead of them. When they were getting close to their destination, a group of five male officers came out of its doorway headed toward them and when McCall was almost upon the group, one of the officers suddenly stumbled and almost fell, causing the others to stop and help him. McCall quickly ran back toward the two women motioning for them to turn and run in the opposite direction, but Celena was now having problems too. McCall and Robbins grabbed Celena's arms and dragged her away from the male officers.

By the time they returned to her cabin, Celena was almost back to normal. She sat in a chair and took a deep breath before asking, "Did either of you notice who he was?"

They both shook their heads no and then looked distressed about missing the obvious. Celena sent a message to Captain Hansen explaining what happened and asked for the identity of the male officer.

Robbins asked Celena, "What did it feel like when you felt his presence?"

"Have you ever been hit in the head, yet wanted to get close to the one who did it?"

McCall said, "Yeah, but only because I wanted to return the favor."

Celena got up and went into the head to look at herself in the mirror. Her face was pale, with red rings around her eyes. She rotated her head and then stuck out her tongue, which looked the same as before.

McCall said, "I'd recommend going to the hospital, but he might already be there."

"Yeah, I don't want a repeat of that."

Just then their communication device sounded with a message. Celena read it aloud, "From Captain Hansen – Do not go to the hospital. Stay in your cabin and await further instructions and meals for the three of you will be brought to you."

McCall said, "I should message my sergeant about my status."

Celena replied, "Yes, go ahead. Just say Captain's Orders. Ladies, I'm going to lie down, I'm still a little woozy."

The next thing Celena knew was that someone delivering them food awakened her. Robbins and McCall were spreading it out on the cabin's small table when she joined them. "I must be feeling better because this sure does smell good."

McCall said, "Good to know because I was starting to get worried about you."

"How long was I out?"

The others looked at each other and then Robbins said, "About forty minutes, but you were out like a light as soon as your head hit the pillow."

They soon finished their meal and cleaned up their mess. McCall soon had the room shipshape while they awaited further developments and orders. Two hours later their door buzzer sounded, with Lt. Commander Robbins answering it. Upon seeing who their caller was, she stepped aside to let Captain Hansen enter, who told McCall to guard the door.

Hansen looked around the room at the three women. "Lance Corporal McCall and Lt. Commander Robbins, you both did an excellent job of getting Celena back to her cabin. I've brought with me the personnel file on the Lt. Commander you all almost met. His name is Seth R. Steele and he just arrived aboard from a transfer from the UES Shark. As far as we can determine he has no other blood relation aboard this ship and he's assigned to Engineering, so you all shouldn't ever meet him except when dining."

Celena said, "That's how we met him this time. Is he alright, any lingering effects?"

"None that we can tell. When I talked to him he appeared normal, much like you. What were your symptoms?"

"For me it was almost like walking into a wall, only with a compulsion to get closer to someone ahead of me. My escorts pulled me far enough away that the compulsion disappeared, but it still took me some time to get back to normal."

"Yes, it was well that you thought an escort might be needed if you met your match. I'm sorry about the other problem you had, but happy that you gave me the excuse I needed to eliminate the problem."

"I was happy to help you in any case. Let me look at his picture so I'll know him if I see him again, and how are we going to keep Steele away from me?"

"Here's his picture, he's not bad looking, see? You sure you want to pass on him for your mate?"

The other two women looked over her shoulder at the man who

was apparently her DNA match. Both gave appreciative quick intakes of breath when gazing at his face and Celena smiled at the others approval and did see their point. He was a good-looking man, heavily muscled, blond hair, and according to his file was a little over six feet tall – equal to her height. She wondered if her children with him would have red hair.

"People, remember I'm only sixteen. I want to be part of Star Fleet before I mate with him. Captain, can you put him on ice until I'm ready for him?"

* * *

Hansen smothered a laugh at the thought. *This young woman is destined for great things. Maybe she would give Steele a little background on their likely future relationship. He probably wouldn't believe a word of it. I better get a copy of his file to Captain Bloodworth as well, she has a better use for it than I do.*

For the remainder of the voyage to Green, Lt. Commander Steele's modified meal times were at least one hour different than Celena's. Her Marine escort was continued in the off chance that there might be another male aboard that would be a close DNA match to Celena.

They arrived in Green orbit without any more incidents aboard the Tiger. The UGS Tiagerfish sent a shuttle to pickup Celena to return her to her parents' control. On the ride to Green's Flag Ship, Celena was already missing the friendship she developed with Alexandra and Kelly. They demonstrated a genuine concern for her well being.

Her parents met her when she stepped off the shuttle and after receiving their hugs her father held her at arm's length. "Celena, you look different somehow; come, let's get you settled and you can tell us about your trip."

They were in the Admiral/Captain's suite, settled into their chairs with their drink of choice in hand, when Celena dropped her bombshell. "I've found my potential future mate aboard the Tiger."

Aundria looked at her daughter in surprise for a moment before replying, "You used some kind of protective buffer around you?"

"Very good mother. While aboard Earth ship's I requested a female Marine escort when going to and from the Officers Mess. I did this to give me an early warning in case we met in the hallway. My Marine escort and my roommate dragged me back to my cabin while his friends were helping my match. He, like me was having the classic compulsion attack of trying to get closer to the other. That stopped when the girls got me further away from him."

Ian said, "Thank God for minor miracles!"

Aundria said, "I think it was good planning on Celena's part. What do you know about him?"

She smiled at her Mother, "He's very good looking. Here take a look at his personnel file."

Ian quickly came around and looked at the file over his wife's shoulder. Aundria's eyes widened when she looked at his picture. "Yes dear, he *is* a handsome man. Let's see, Lt. Commander Seth Robert Steele, born 2043 in Prescott, Arizona, USA. So he's about nine years your senior. He's assigned to Engineering, and he's shown as single here. Did you check to see if he was in a serious relationship?"

"Yes, I had my Marine friend check for me. She said he was dating several women, but none seriously. Apparently, he's pretty popular with the female officers."

"Well, that won't be a problem once you're mated, you'd be committed to each other at that point."

"Yes Mother, you both know I want to be an officer in the Green Space Fleet before I mate. Everything changes when that happens. However, perhaps we can start to make some moves that will bring him into my universe."

Aundria looked at her daughter with new respect. "Does he have any idea what's in his future?"

"I'm not sure, but I think Captain Annalisa Hansen of the Tiger may have told him something, but even so I don't think he would believe such a wild story."

Ian said, "But he did have that attack and at some level he's going to be worried."

"Well, I'm going to make sure that when it's time to mate, that I'm the most beautiful women he's ever seen."

* * *

Six months later First Fleet was back in Earth orbit and Captain

Bloodworth received a message from Second Fleet's Captain Hansen of the UES Tiger for a face-to-face meeting regarding Celena Eiberger. They agreed to meet the following day aboard the UES Hulk for lunch, while their husbands talked about the Xones War.

When they met the following day Annalisa told Hanna about Celena's close call with her DNA match and then gave her a copy of Lt. Commander Steele's personnel file. Annalisa watched Hanna's face tighten as she read the file. When finished, Hanna thought, *I should have him under my direct control to ensure these two don't meet again until we want it to happen.*

"Annalisa, I purpose an exchange of personnel between our ships. I'll take Lt. Commander Steele off your hands and give you his opposite aboard the Hulk?"

She looked at Hanna with a smile and asked, "What are you planning?"

"My sister, Commander Lucy Hendricks took a blood sample from Celena when she was last aboard the Hulk, and I'd like to compare hers to Seth Steele. Maybe comparing all the DNA samples from the women affected by this strange occurrence we can get some answers?"

"Yes, it's strange that the match's involve women from Aqua and Green and men from Earth. That has to be a key factor."

"Maybe, and my family appears to have something to do with it as well."

* * *

A week later, Lt. Commander Seth Steele's supervisor called him into her office for a meeting. "Lt. Commander Steele, apparently somebody above my pay grade has taken an interest in you. You're being transferred to the UES Hulk, First Fleet's Flagship. Do you know what this is about?"

"I'm not really sure. Maybe it has something to do with a Green woman we were transporting."

"I don't understand!"

"Captain Hansen told me a story about the Green woman that was too crazy to have been true, but now this. I really don't know what to believe."

"Well, good luck on your reassignment and I'll miss your smiling face."

The next day Lt. Commander Steele arrived aboard the UES Hulk and after requesting permission to board, the OD gave him written orders to report to the Captain upon arrival. As a Marine escorted him, he wondered what was going on.

The Marine knocked on the Captains Day Cabin, and upon acknowledgement he opened the door saying, "Lt. Commander Steele delivered as requested."

"Thank you Gunny; Lt. Commander Steele please enter and close the door."

He did as requested and stood before her desk at attention. "You have an excellent performance report, but that's not why you stand before me. You are here because you are an apparent DNA match to a female from Green."

Hanna then proceeded to tell him the history of the strange matches between couples beginning with the now Admiral and Captain of the Flagship UAS Trojan Horse on the Aqua Star Fleet, their daughter with her son, the connection of a woman from Green and her nephew, both now the heads of the Green Star Fleet, and finally their daughter who appears to be a DNA match with you."

"This woman is only sixteen and doesn't want to mate with you at this time. She desires to join her own Star Fleet before meeting you formally as a potential mate. Before you ask the question, why me and I've never even met her, the questions are moot. When you meet there is something in your blood that will demand that you touch each other. When that happens you will both be lost to a fierce compulsion to copulate. This compulsion has gotten more severe at each meeting of the couples until now. Celena is the strongest of the women so far and we fear you may harm each other and we want to take some precautions before you meet."

"What happens to the couple afterwards? What if they don't even like each other?"

"So far they all have a strong compulsion to be near each other. The two recent marriages even know where their mates are and what they are doing when apart. They need to be close at all times, so they are paired together in duty assignments."

"So, this Celena wants to delay this meeting to age herself and become part of her Star Fleet before meeting me so we can work together as the others have?"

"Yes, mostly. But Celena is so strong there might be other factors in play. When she was on Earth, she visited her grandmother, my older sister. She's in her mid-nineties now, but when they first touched, something passed between them that caused some positive improvements in her health. It's been about three years now and I'm going to visit her soon to see if she's still physically improving. I want you with me to judge for yourself, since you may eventually be part of my family."

"When I had that physical episode where I had that extreme longing to be with someone ahead of me, was that her I was looking for?"

"Yes, and she had the same feeling for you; but, she had taken precautions and her escorts dragged her away from you until she was far enough away that the connection was broken."

"This Celena, you say is sixteen, must be an intelligent person to protect herself this way. But why risk this voyage?"

"She was suffering a compulsion to visit her grandmother, which eventually brought you two together."

"Oh, I'm beginning to understand the thing about your sister now. Yes, I'll be happy to accompany you when you visit your sister."

CHAPTER 23

Ten days later a shuttle from the UES Hulk carrying Captain Bloodworth, her husband, Fleet Admiral Bloodworth, and Lt. Commander Steele were heading toward Hamburg, Germany. Seth Steele's family was originally from Germany, but he and his father were born in the United States. He was curious about what he would discover while there and was taught German and the Green languages by the learning machine before making this trip.

The shuttle landed at its usual location outside Hamburg at a small aircraft airport where the three officers took a cab to Clare's home. They left the shuttle in place because they didn't anticipate staying overnight.

Upon arrival, Clare didn't seem surprised when she opened her door to find her sister Hanna standing on her front step. She grabbed Hanna in a tight embrace and held her for several moments before stepping aside and motioning the others inside while giving Seth a sharp look before closing the door and telling everyone to find a seat.

After her company took seats, Clare took her favorite seat in front of the TV and asked, "What brings everyone here today?"

Hanna smiled at her sister, "Clare, somehow you knew I was

coming, didn't you?"

"Yes, but not this good looking young officer. Let me guess, he is somehow involved with my granddaughter, Celena?"

"Clare, you look like you've shed at least ten years since we were last here. How do you feel?"

"Wonderful, and I picked up your and Lucy's thoughts as soon as your ship arrived in Earth orbit. That's something new for me. So, this young man is her future mate. Does he know what his future will bring?"

Hanna replied, "You can't read his mind?"

"No, nor Eric's. Just my sisters and a little of Hope's. Seth, don't be afraid because this is new to me too. Maybe after you're part of the family I'll be able to read your thoughts, but not now."

Eric said, "Hanna, I think we should bring Clare back to the ship with us and observe how she is changing. I'm sure Lucy and Hope would be ecstatic to look after her and study her physical and mental changes."

Hanna smiled at Clare, "How about it, do you want to go into space with us. This is finally your chance to achieve your dreams."

Clare looked around the room for a moment. "Can I place a hold on this place while I'm gone?"

Hanna smiled, "I'm sure we can, but if we can't and you want to return here, I'll get you an even better place. Do you want to pack anything?"

"I've already done it. My luggage and a box of keepsakes are in the bedroom and I've cooked a meal for us to eat while we wait for a cab."

A little over three hours later they were in the shuttle heading back toward the Hulk. Clare's eyes were huge as she watched the monitor showing the ground disappear under a layer of clouds and later the large ships of First Fleet appeared. She licked her lips in anticipation, as the huge Battleship grew larger on the monitor.

Lt. Commander Steele was sitting next to her holding her hand telling her what the features on the ship were as they headed toward an open shuttle bay, where they soon settled into position. He held her back explaining about the ceremony given a Fleet Admiral and her Captain when returning aboard. She was surprised when she heard the shrill welcoming pipes as the two senior officers walked between double rows of Marines leading to the welcoming OD.

When the ceremony concluded, Lt. Commander Seth Steele helped Clare from the shuttle and they made their way to the OD and asked permission to board before joining the other two senior officers. It was 21:30 hours, so Hanna thought it advisable to show Clare her new quarters and have her start her new life aboard the Hulk tomorrow.

Seth left them for his own quarters, while the others settled Clare into her cabin. Hanna said, "Clare, I'll have a Marine escort guide you to my quarters at 07:00 hours for breakfast and then a very busy day will follow starting with you learning the Universal language."

She showed her sister how to set her wake-up call, the door code for when she returned to her cabin, and wished her a good night before leaving. As Hanna was leaving, Clare's luggage and other items arrived.

The next morning, Clare's door buzzer sounded which she opened to find a tough looking female Marine. "Ma'am, I'm Gunnery Sergeant Amy Cox here to escort you to breakfast at the Captain's cabin. Are you ready?"

"Yes, thank you Amy."

"Very well Ma'am. Please address me as Gunny, Sergeant, anything but my given name. That tends to reduce my effectiveness as your escort."

"Okay, lead off Gunny Macbeth and I'll follow your lead."

A slight smile crossed the Gunny's face as she led the way, making several backward glances to make sure she wasn't walking too fast for the older woman. The crew they met gave the pair curious glances, but no one dared to speak to Clare with the Gunny present.

After breakfast they headed towards what the Gunny termed "the tank," where she learned Universal and Green languages. Later Clare was shown around the ship hitting most of the high points before returning to her quarters where the gunnery sergeant told her, "Rest up until I return at 18:00 hours to escort you to the Captain's quarters."

"Gunny, what are 18:00 hours?"

She looked at Clare in surprise for a moment before replying, "I'm sorry ma'am, I'm used to dealing with military personnel.

01:00 is one A.M., 12:00 is noon and 24:00 hours is midnight."

"Oh! So 18:00 hours is six p.m.?"

"Yes ma'am, you've got it right. Any other questions?"

"No Gunny, I'll see you at 18:00 hours."

Later, after picking up Clare and arriving at the Captain's stateroom, Gunnery Sergeant Cox pushed the button for admittance. The captain's steward answered the door and admitted the two into the room and Hanna smiled at her older sister with some concern.

"Clare, how do you feel? I keep forgetting your advanced age, especially since you now look so much younger."

"Oh Hanna there was no need to worry, Gunny Macbeth here kept up a good pace, but I did okay. When am I going to see the rest of the family?"

Hanna raised her eyebrow at the Gunnery Sergeant, who shrugged her shoulders with a smile. "Gunny, stand watch outside until my sister is ready to return to her quarters, and you may ask for a relief from your OIC if needed."

"Ma'am, yes ma'am." The sergeant said before leaving the stateroom.

Clare made her way into the stateroom and found a comfortable chair. "My, I can't get over how well you live aboard this ship. My quarters are not nearly as opulent."

"Your quarters are similar to what we assign to a single senior officer. Captain's and visiting dignitary's quarters are the best aboard this ship."

Hanna, seeing immediately the reaction that statement generated said, "Clare, don't say it!"

Clare gave her sister a small smile before looking around the room. "Where's Eric? Is he doing admiral things?"

Hanna decided not to rise to the bait and replied, "Lucy, Adam, Hope, and their mates will be joining us soon for dinner. Is there anything you want to know about them before they arrive?"

"Do their mates know about me yet?"

"No, and I'm not sure we know everything about you either."

"Well, maybe my family can determine what's happened to me and if it has any far reaching effect for others."

It wasn't long before the family started to arrive beginning with their sister Lucy and her husband, Commander Kory Hendricks. Commander Lucy Lundberg Hendricks was the head doctor aboard the UES Hulk.

When Lucy entered the room her eyes immediately went to the oldest looking women, and then with eyes full of tears she immediately went and tightly embraced her oldest sister. When they finally broke apart, both had tears in their eyes. Lucy said, "This handsome man is my husband, Kory Hendricks. Kory, this is my sister, Clare."

"I'm happy to finally meet you, the only member of your family who's not in Star Fleet."

"Lucy! My, you did marry a handsome man. Why haven't you got any children?"

He replied, "I'm afraid that's my fault. Although, Lucy and I wanted kids, a childhood accident prevents me from doing my part."

"Oh Lucy, I'm so sorry."

"That's alright, I've adjusted by following the exploits of Hanna's and your kids. They have given me more than enough adventures to follow and now you've arrived to stir it all up again with something new in the mix."

Hope interrupted, "Aunt Lucy, I'm fascinated by Clare's apparent youthful appearance and can hardly wait to find out how it happened and if it can be duplicated."

Lucy rolled her eyes in consternation, "You know what caused her change in appearance! It was Celena, her granddaughter who touched Clare and caused a physical reaction in both of them."

"I know that! What I want to find out is what actually passed between them and if the long-term effects are permanent."

Hanna finally had enough of this family bickering and shook her head in disgust. "We know all this. What my question is when do you want Clare to report to the hospital for tests?"

Lucy replied, "07:00 hours sharp and nothing by mouth except water before you get there. After we draw blood you can have breakfast. Clare, you've been to the tank to learn Universal, haven't you?"

"Yes, I picked up Green too. I'd like to visit my in-laws when we get to Green if at all possible."

They were interrupted by the arrival of Adam Lundberg

Bloodworth and his wife, Karrie Fieldspire Bloodworth. He quickly kissed his Aunt Clare on the cheek and introduced his wife, "Auntie, this is my wife Karrie. She's the daughter of the Flag Captain of the Aqua Star Fleet. Both she and her mother had episodes similar to Aundria whose married to your son, Ian, producing Celena, your Granddaughter."

"My, this is interesting. It seems the Lundberg family figures predominantly in what's happening. Hanna, I'm sure you and Lucy have already noticed this and it's probably the reason you're suddenly interested in what's happening to me."

"Yes, when Celena expressed this overpowering desire to meet you, both Lucy and I suspected something was going to happen with you and Celena. You may be the breakthrough for us in understanding what this is all about."

Fleet Admiral Bloodworth joined them, breaking up their conversation. "Well, it looks like I'm the last to arrive. Anyone besides me hungry?"

Hanna hugged her husband while saying, "Trust you to bring the conversation to food. Everyone let's adjourn to the dinning table. Steward Mao has ordered a proper feast for us now that we are back in Earth orbit."

* * *

Two days later the doctors were reviewing Clare's lab results and Lucy, Hope, and Hope's husband Jeff Fellows all came to the same conclusion that Clare had the physical body of a fifty year-old woman. This was despite being almost fifty years older. Her brain readings were unusual, perhaps due to her ability to read the surface thoughts of others.

The three doctors of the Battleship UES Hulk sat looking at each other after reviewing Clare's medical files. Hope shook her head in obvious anger, "Aunt Clare's only obvious medical abnormities are her youthful appearance and her brain functions. We still don't know how Celena caused these changes in Clare."

Lucy sat back in her chair and looked at her staff while contemplating their next moves. "Perhaps we can map her brain activity when she's reading peoples' thoughts."

Jeff shook his head in bafflement and with some concern said,

"Yes, but that doesn't explain her getting younger or even if she's currently at a stable age."

Hope smiled at her husband and while touching his shoulder said, "Jeff, I know it's frustrating, but we have to start somewhere. Maybe we'll stumble across something while researching her ability to read our thoughts and if this ability extends to others to the same degree."

CHAPTER 24

First Fleet arrived in Green orbit after being welcomed by the Green Home Fleet. The UGS Tiagerfish, Flag Ship of the Green Star Fleet, escorted them toward their home planet.

Admiral Bloodworth noted that the Green welcoming fleet consisted of five heavy battle cruisers and he assumed the systems other warp gate was guarded by a similar number. He wondered if their Star Fleet had started constructing a battleship. Their recommendation to the Green Star Fleet was to wait until they had at least seven heavies before building their first battleship because of the time needed for construction.

Admiral Ian Eiberger, the son of Clare Eiberger, requested an early conference with Admiral Bloodworth and he was informed that his mother was aboard the UES Hulk.

When the Tiagerfish's shuttle arrived, Admiral Bloodworth gave Admiral Eiberger the full welcoming ceremony given to the head of a visiting foreign Star Fleet official. The welcoming pipes started as he left the shuttle with his wife, Captain Aundria Eoff Eiberger, and continued as they walked between the two columns of marine honor guards until they stopped before Fleet Admiral Bloodworth and his Flag Captain, Hanna Bloodworth. They saluted each other and Eric welcomed them aboard the UES Hulk.

When they started inside the interior of the ship Clare welcomed her son with a tearful greeting as he picked her up in his arms and gave her a hug, before introducing her to his wife.

Clare was reminded of her daughter-in-law's beauty from when she first met her shortly after her marriage to Ian. "Aundria, I'm reminded again where your beautiful daughter got her looks. The pictures she brought of her family didn't do either of you justice. No wonder Ian lost his heart when he met you."

"Yes, we both love each other very much; however, our first meeting was mind boggling as you can imagine from reports of others who share our fate. Celena told us of your meeting with her, but she didn't know what the results would be."

Hanna interrupted, "I'm glad you didn't bring Celena with you because we have her opposite on board, presently confined to quarters until you leave"

Aundria grimaced, "She didn't want to take any chances of connecting with Lt. Commander Steele until she was ready for it to happen."

Hanna quietly said, "Well, let's go to my quarters and catch up on what's happened since we saw each other last."

After reaching her opulent quarters they broke into two groups, the two Admirals and the women. One was concerned with the war effort and the other with the apparent escalating factors involving the three human-type races.

While the women were ordering refreshments Admiral Bloodworth asked Ian, "I noticed that you have a battleship under construction?"

Ian smiled with pride. "Yes it may even be ready for space trials before you leave/ We've made some changes in her design that you may find interesting."

"Oh, what changes did you make?"

"We tinkered with the range of its Lasers, instead of 50,000 miles we have expanded it to 70,000 miles plus. With that range our BS can approach any Xones battle group and burn their missiles almost as they're launched."

"Great!! How confident are you of the Lasers new range?"

"We tested the Lasers on a stand-alone platform and were amazed at their performance. I used 70,000 miles as a conservative range. If we upped the wattage, I think we can approach a 100,000 miles range, but I didn't want to risk a burnout."

"Before trying that on a BS, I recommend that a single Laser be tested on a platform until you know its limitations."

"Yes, I agree and we are almost ready for that test. Do you want to observe?"

Eric's face suddenly became almost ferocious as he realized what this could do against the Xones. "Yes, I would like that very much!"

* * *

The women, along with the doctor's husbands sat together with their choices of refreshments getting to know each other again after the long years away from each other. Clare dropped her personal bombshell when she informed Aundria, "In addition to shedding almost 50 plus years and counting, Celena gave me the ability to read other humans minds. My range with family members is the greatest. I could read Ian, Aundria, and Celena while they escorted us to Green. With other humans I'm limited to no more than a mile."

Aundria's eyes were wide with shock. "When did you first pick up our thoughts?"

"As soon as we came through the warp gate into the Green System I could read Ian's mind. It was the same with Hanna and Lucy when their ship entered the Earth System."

"When you say that you can read our minds, do you mean surface thoughts or memories as well?"

"I haven't tried to read memories. Your surface thoughts are as if you were talking to me, only not as clear."

Hanna said, "What do you mean by that?"

"Sometimes you don't think in a straight line, it's disjointed which makes it hard to follow.

"How about others, not close family. Is it easier or harder to follow their thoughts?"

"It depends on the individual, if they are mentally strong generally they are easier to read."

Aundria stared at Clare with an open mouth for a moment, and then stuck out her tongue at Clare. "You'd be fascinated too if you were in my place and you are really going to blow the mind of

Maile, my mother. I can hardly wait until I introduce you to her."

"I think Celena already knows about me. When I read her surface thoughts, I thought she knew I was with her."

"What do you mean?"

"She didn't react like you did. When I first entered her mind her thoughts froze for a few moments, but then she opened herself to my scan. I'm sure she knew I was in her mind. She didn't mention it to you?"

"No, but she did say I was in for a surprise when I met you."

"Does Celena have this ability too?"

Aundria thought back through their recent conversations until suddenly she said, "That little tigger. I'm certain she does as well, maybe not as powerful as you, but I now recall conversations where she remembers things I've never spoken to her about."

Clair looked startled for a moment and then she held up her hand for quiet. She nodded her head several times and smiled before she visibly composed herself. "Celena just now mentally contacted me and asked me to convey her misgivings for not being with you, but the risk to her was too great aboard a Earth ship. Besides, she'd hoped to be able to participate this way."

The others in their group stared at Clare as if she'd just given birth before them. Aundria then shook her head in understanding before speaking. "Yes, that's Celena. Only she would think to surprise us with this kind of announcement."

Clare said with a smile, "Don't be too hard on her. Perhaps she wasn't sure we could communicate this way and didn't want to disappoint anyone."

"Maybe I know her a little better than you Clare. This fits her personality perfectly. Very well, since we now have Celena present, what should we do?"

Clare nodded her head in agreement, "Celena suggests we travel to Green and consult with the head of the family. Perhaps your mother will have something to contribute."

After Hanna consulted with everyone, it was decided that Hanna, both her sisters Clare and Lucy, Hanna's son Adam and his wife Karrie, and Clare's son Ian and his wife Aundria would travel to Green to meet with Maile. Celena would join them in the Eoff's family home on Green at a time dictated by its family head.

Aundria contacted her family through her uncle, Admiral Jorge

Hinderman, who relayed the message that they would be expected to arrive the next day at 10 A.M. local time, or 07:00 hours ship time. A shuttle from the Hulk would pick up those from the Tiagerfish at 06:00 hours to ferry everyone to the meeting. Since this meeting was expected to be historic everyone was expected to wear formal uniforms.

On the shuttle the next day, Aundria noticed that Clare was uncomfortable with the clothing she was wearing. "Clare, don't worry about your dress. I'm sure my mother has something you can wear if it comes to a historic picture being taken."

Clare nodded her head and smiled her thanks for her consideration. When she left Earth, none of her clothing she brought with her would be appropriate for what this might turn into. These flights in a shuttle were the most exciting things she'd done in fifty years, and now she was getting ready to set foot on Green, another Earth-like planet.

The shuttle landed near the large city of Port Locke, in a small rural community near their destination. Admiral Hinderman arranged for transportation for their group of eight people. He also thought to include a police escort.

Clare looked at the countryside and marveled that it didn't look that different from what one would see on Earth. The trees and some foliage looked a little strange, but she didn't see anything that different. They arrived at their destination in about twenty minutes and after leaving their vehicle she gazed at the large two-story dwelling before her. The style was a little alien, but not that different than her own home where she raised her child.

Ian and Aundria escorted her to the front door where a tall woman stepped outside with her arms wide to accept her daughter home. Tears were flowing from both mother and daughter, but then the youthful Celena joined her welcome embrace as she welcomed her granddaughter home. The three embraced for several minutes, but then reluctantly broke apart holding hands.

Aundria held her hand out to Clare, "Mother, this is Ian's mother, Clare Eiberger. The woman Celena went to visit on Earth."

Maile Eoff disengaged from her family and smiled at Clare before saying, "Come closer so that I can see for myself what made my granddaughter so anxious to meet you."

Clare smiled at Maile as she approached and hugged her mother-in-law and said softly in her ear, "No, he didn't get the red hair from me, it's from his father."

Mailes' eyes widened, but when Clare winked at her, she slowly smiled. "Everyone come inside, I've got to hear the story of Celena's visit to see Clare."

After everyone entered the house and took a bathroom break they gathered in the large living room and found seats. Maile stood until everyone was seated and then pointed at her granddaughter, Celena. "Alright, you can begin with your tale."

* * *

Celena looked at her family and all the extended members present in the room. Their minds were all open to her, which made her smile as she thought, *They have no real idea what Clare and I are capable of. Clare suspects, but she would probably quake in her shoes if she knew what the future holds for us.*

"I felt an extreme need to travel to Earth to meet Clare regardless of the apparent risk to me. I didn't know what the purpose of the meeting would be; all I knew was that I had to meet her as soon as possible. During the return voyage from Earth my fears of personal risk were realized when I met my opposite, but I was rescued by my escorts who took me away from his influence and later made sure we didn't meet again during the voyage."

Maile jumped to her feet and loudly interrupted, "What! You met your future mate!"

"Yes Grandmother, but unlike mother and dad, I wasn't close enough to him for it to take control of us. My escorts pulled me away until the effect dissipated."

"Okay, I'm sorry. Go ahead and finish your story."

"When I arrived at Clare's house and we were being introduced by her sister, Hanna, I stepped toward her with my arms raised to embrace her; however, when we touched each other a sudden jolt of energy went from me to her and then back to me causing both of us to collapse. I recovered quickly and helped Aunt Hanna with Clare. When I initially touched Clare I passed out for a short period of time and I don't think Hanna even knew it happened."

"No, I didn't. I was concerned about Clare because of her

advanced age and you didn't seem to be affected that much."

Maile said, "Advanced age? She looks to be about fifty. What do you mean?"

Hanna replied, "Clare, at the time of this meeting was ninety-three. She may still be getting younger."

Celena continued, "Please hold your questions until I've finished. I heard of Clare's reverse aging, but didn't know about her other ability until she arrived in our system and attempted to read my mind."

Maile drew a quick breath and started to stand when Celena pointed her finger at her, at which time she stuck out her tongue at her granddaughter and resettled in her chair.

"I was startled at the attempt, since I didn't know she had this ability as I thought I was the only person with this talent. Later, when mother and father visited the Hulk I mentally followed their conversations and discovered that Clare suspected I also had this ability, so I mentally confirmed her suspicions. Now, any questions?"

Maile stood and hugged her granddaughter. "Smartass, you should have told me about your ability. Now, Clare what can you tell us from your prospective?"

* * *

Clare stood before the others and she realized, *most were looking at her from a fresh prospective, one that here before them stood a ninety plus old woman who was getting younger and now appeared to be in her low fifties. Never mind that she could also read others minds, she was getting younger!*

"When Celena arrived at my home, I saw a beautiful red-haired young woman who was the daughter of my son, this was my granddaughter! When she touched me something exploded in my head and I awoke sometime later with my sister and granddaughter hovering over me wanting to know if I was all right. I felt okay, and later as I got my wits back I realized that I hadn't felt this good in years."

"As they were fussing over me it seemed they both were talking over each other and it was confusing for me. It took a while to realize that I was hearing their thoughts and I asked Hanna to get me a glass of water, which left me alone with Celena. She didn't speak, but I could hear her thoughts. She was afraid she had harmed me by coming here, but I appeared to be okay now and she was grateful to the gods that she hadn't harmed me."

"I placed my hand on hers and told her that I was feeling better now and whatever she did seemed to have made some improvements and not to worry about me. After they left, I noticed that my body was getting younger and my ability to read the minds of others improved as well. As far as I know, that's my story."

Maile stood and placed her arm around Clare's shoulder saying, "No, that's not all, there's something missing here. Celena, your trip to see Clare doesn't end there does it? What are we missing?"

Celena stood and approached the two elders, "I think I know what's coming, but to prove it we need to meet the enemy. The two of us together using our psi powers."

Clare looked at Celena as if she had lost her mind. "Us! Just the two of us against the Xones! What do you know about our powers that I'm missing?"

"I've been thinking about the placement of the three human populated planets and how these strange encounters between women, on systems located on either side of Earth, have had with Earth men. These encounters have eventually resulted in two women with psi powers. If the purpose of these encounters was to produce people with psi powers, the most obvious reason was to counter an alien threat. A threat like the Xones, who destroy all they encounter."

Hanna held up her hand for attention. "I'm not saying you're wrong, but if this is the purpose of what's been happening, who arranged all this? The rumored Ancients?"

Celena said, "You got it in one. Who else can it be? It's obvious our three planets were seeded with humans and we were wondering to what purpose? Somehow they engineered our DNA to respond to those from the other planets, which occurred when we started fighting the Xones."

Hanna nodded her head, "You may be right with your theory and it won't cost us anything to see if you're right. I'm sure I can convince Eric to test your theory."

Aundria said, "Great! Let's have that family picture now before we leave! Mother, do you have something nice for Clare to wear?"

While they were upstairs Aundria called her sisters to come over and witness a historic event. It didn't take long before the pictures were taken and they were returning to their ships. Celena thought she should stay with Clare aboard the Battleship UES Hulk.

It didn't take long to convince Fleet Admiral Bloodworth that their theory was worth checking out and a small battle fleet from Green would join Earth's First Fleet when they next encountered the Xones.

CHAPTER 25

After the combined fleets arrived before the Fourth Warp Gate the returning probe reported three concentrations of Xones ships totaling sixty warships. They were about 400,000 miles from the gate and were in loose formations about 100,000 miles apart.

Admiral Bloodworth commed the Fleet and announced that the UES Hulk and the UGS Tiagerfish would transit the gate and confront the enemy. The remainder of the fleet would wait one hour before joining them unless otherwise instructed.

After the two human ships had passed through the gate, Eric commed Clare and Celena and asked, "Can you understand their thoughts?"

The two looked at each other and then Celena commed, "Yes Sir, we will now begin as planned." Previously, the two agreed upon a strategy of projecting an image of a large expanding Laser blast from the battleship heading toward the Xones at nearly the speed of light. If that didn't work, they would try another agreed upon ploy.

The two joined their minds for added strength, and then projected their image. The two fleet ships held its breath while they awaited the enemy's reaction, if any. After five minutes the three enemy fleets started to break apart as if they were taking evasive maneuvers away from something after them.

The telepaths went to the second phase of their attack plan, making the enemy crews think the Laser blast was specifically targeting their ship. This caused even more dramatic maneuvers that caused some collisions with other ships as the enemy ships made desperate changes of courses without any coordination. Suddenly, a ship exploded, then two more, and then almost all the remaining ships blew themselves up. Only two enemy ships remained of the initial sixty.

The telepaths mental laser projection appeared to show the laser beam turning toward the remaining Xones, as if it had a life of its own, causing both ships to self-terminate at almost the same time. Clare and Celena hugged each other after they realized their ploy worked beyond their expectations, and then softly placed their foreheads together as homage to each other.

The Bridge crew responded with a loud "YES!" They then looked at the Command Chair for a rebuke from their Captain, but instead saw her pumping her fist in glee. Hanna stood at her chair for a moment before retaking her seat and informing the crew that the enemy was destroyed. Even the Bridge felt the vibration as the crew reacted to the news.

Fleet Admiral Bloodworth sent a message torpedo to the remaining fleet that their secret weapon had worked and the enemy was destroyed and ordered the Fleet to come through the gate and observe the results of their recent action.

Captain Hanna Bloodworth quickly made her way to the two psi-talents and gathered them into a group hug. "You did it! You both did it! Was it hard for you?"

They looked at each other and smiled before Clare answered, "No, not after we learned to combine our minds. What's next?"

"I'll have to ask Eric, but we'll likely go to the next gate to see if anything's there."

Admiral Bloodworth soon arrived on the Bridge to offer his own congratulations and after they all settled down he pointed at the Captains office, "Let's meet in there and plan our next moves."

Eric looked at Clare with respect. "Hanna told me you've always wanted to join her in Space. After what you two have accomplished I want to offer you both a commission in the Earth

Space Force stationed here on the Hulk."

Clare looked at her sister and winked, "Hanna, what rank should I ask for? Celena is a Lieutenant."

Eric interrupted, "I think you both should be Commanders, since you're the only psi officers in our Space Force."

Celena grinned as she quipped, "Hey, I like where this is going; however, we should stay together until we defeat the Xones."

Eric frowned as he thought ahead. "I'm going to check out the next gate and if there are more enemy, let's take them out before we return to Green. It's going to take us three or four days reach the other gate, are you two going to be rested enough to do this again if needed?"

Celena said, "I'm ready now, but I'm much younger than you grandmother. How do you feel?"

"I think I'm okay, but right now I've got a buzz from what we've done. I'll know better tomorrow."

Celena looked questioningly at Hanna, who nodded her head. "Clare, why don't you and Celena take a break. Since Celena is restricted to quarters because she's at risk aboard Earth ships, I'll send meals to your shared cabin."

The telepaths left the Bridge under Marine escort, while Fleet Admiral Bloodworth and his Flag Captain settled into comfortable seats with coffee in hand, Eric asked, "How should we make their uniforms different from other Star Fleet Officers?"

Hanna thought a few moments before replying, "They are going to be different from our other officers because they won't normally have a path to command authority, and they may even become feared because they are telepaths. I think a simple change in the color of their berets would be more than sufficient."

Erik looked at Hanna in surprise as he replied, "Hanna, I don't know about that. Those that fear telepaths will go out of their way to avoid them."

Seeing the small smile on his wife's face, he gave her a smile as well. "Oh! You want to generate a mystique attitude toward them. But there are only the two of them, how is that going to work?"

"Celena will eventually mate with her DNA opposite and will produce a child. What do you think the odds are that the child will also be a telepath? I know my sister is a little long in tooth, but she is still getting younger. It's possible she may marry again and maybe even produce another child. These children will eventually increase the telepath numbers. They will start small and hopefully events will produce the mystique over time."

* * *

When Celena and Clare reached their cabin they smiled at each other as the door closed behind them. Celena asked, "Did you hear the mind of my future mate screaming his anger at being confined to quarters again now that I'm back aboard?"

"Can you mentally contact him and try to soothe his distress. After all, since he's your future mate don't you think you should get on his good side. Right now he's thinking that you must be some kind of ogre to put him through this."

Celena's face sobered as she reconsidered her previous position of avoiding him entirely. "Okay, let's see if I can ease into his thoughts without him going bonkers. *Lt. Commander Seth Steele this is Lt. Celena Eoff, your future mate speaking to you. In case you haven't heard I am one of the two known telepath's in Star Fleet. Please settle down and try to calm yourself.*"

Seth stood with his mouth open in surprise as he listened to the voice in his head. *Crap, you really exist! What's this future mate stuff you and the Captain are talking about?*

Well, it's true and what's happened to us has already happened three other times between women of Aqua and Green when they encountered their DNA match in an Earth male. Apparently, you and I have a similar match and since I'm only seventeen, I need to prepare myself before we go through the emotionally charged mating procedure. You've been briefed on what happens when we have a close encounter?

Yes, but I didn't really believe it. You're not pulling my leg are you?

Think about it! It's happened before, so get over it. You are stuck, just like me. Apparently, after we touch we become permanently mentally attached to each other and cannot abide being separated from each other. So far, the couples also become hopelessly in love with each other.

So, how long do I have before you want to mate?

I'd like to wait until I'm at least twenty, but circumstances may not let us wait that long. Clare and I are the lead force in defeating the Xones through our newly gained telepathic skills. It may depend on what we encounter in our pursuit of this goal.

I shouldn't need to be kept locked up if you can now monitor my location. If we stay apart what's your risk?

I don't know that you're my only DNA match aboard the Hulk. You can freely move about, but I'll still need to be careful of others. I'll talk to Aunt Bloodworth about getting you released, so take it easy and enjoy your leisure time as it may soon end.

Celena turned to Clare and asked, "How did I do? Do you think I put him at ease?"

Clare shook her head at her granddaughter, "Honey, I was monitoring your telepathic conversation with Seth and his attitude toward you went from anger at the beginning to frustration when it ended. The two of you already have ties to each other from that first abortive meeting. I think his attitude toward you won't change until your first touch. This attraction toward him may get stronger until you are forced to begin the mating bond."

Celena looked down at the deck and shook her head in frustration. "Gran, we've got so much to do and this mating bond is going to complicate matters to no end. But seventeen is just too young for me to start a family. I'm going to try to delay it as long as I can."

"You better contact Hanna to release Seth from his confinement to quarters, as its no longer needed. However, I'd keep the Marine outside in case there's another DNA match to you aboard the Hulk."

* * *

Three days later they were stationed before the next warp gate at Battle Stations while they were waiting for the response from their probe, which seemed like eternity until the torpedo returned reporting that there was no activity beyond the gate.

Fleet Admiral Bloodworth commed his fleet that they would return to Green where future plans will be discussed.

Six days later First Fleet was back in Green orbit awaiting the delegation from Green Star Fleet. Soon, Admiral Jorge Hinderman, Vice Admiral Ian Eiberger, and Fleet Captain Andria Eiberger exited their shuttle aboard the UES Hulk. The delegation was given the highest honor guard display for these allied Star Fleet representatives.

Among the delegation greeting them was Captain Andria's mother-in-law, Clare Eiberger and her daughter Celena who were both wearing the uniform of a Commander. However, she and her daughter were wearing a red beret rather than the standard black color.

Before she could ask any questions, Flag Captain Bloodworth said, "Let's head to my quarters and we'll bring you up to date on what's happened."

When they were settled in the Captain's Stateroom, the Bloodworths explained their success against the Xones and how the telepath's plan had succeeded beyond expectations. Fleet Admiral Bloodworth then explained, "Hanna and I thought that the two should be the start of a new psi department, separate from the normal chain of command, hence their rank as Commander and the red color of their berets."

Flag Captain Eiberger asked, "Celena remains a Green officer while assigned to the psi department aboard the Hulk?"

Fleet Admiral Bloodworth replied, "Yes, hopefully we will find others from Aqua and the other two planets that will join the department. The two joined their minds in projecting the images against the Xones. Until we find a better way they should stay together."

Aundria Eiberger smiled, "Those red berets are really going to make them stand out as different, much like the white berets did for ship captains, except now there are only the two of them. Celena, Clare, how does it feel to be in the spotlight?"

Celena placed her arm around Clare, "Grandma, how does it feel to be so essential to the war effort after watching most of your family go into Star Fleet?"

Clare placed her hand over her mouth to stifle a laugh. "When I arrived aboard the Hulk the first time, I thought to myself, I've finally made it into space!"

Celena looked at her mother and frowned, "Mother, when I mentally talked with my future mate I realized as I get older we are both going to experience an increasing pressure to mate. My desire to wait until I'm at least twenty may become unrealistic. What do you recommend?"

Aundria looked at her husband for help in answering their daughters' difficult question. Ian's face registered his conflicted feelings as he spoke. "Celena, I can only speak from the male's prospective, but based on your mother's recollections her experiences appear to be similar to my own. I would recommend that you wait as long as you can so that your emotions can mature to match your body. At seventeen, neither your body nor your emotional health is ready for what you're going to experience. I think your initial goal of twenty is logical and hopefully you will be able to achieve it."

"Mother, do you agree with Dad?"

Aundria placed her arm around her mate and nodded in head. "Yes dear. We both went through a blizzard of emotional feelings toward each other. I'm not sure you're ready for that yet."

"Well, in that case I need to stay busy to keep my mind away from that subject as long as I can."

CHAPTER 26

The First Fleet was on their way to the Aqua System to attempt a modification of the telepath's first attack against the Xones. Initially the two psi talents combined their minds when they attacked the Xones near the Green System. They did this for a maximum effort, not knowing how much psi power was needed to create the illusion used.

This time Clare would attempt the same illusion alone with Celena as backup in case more power was needed. They wanted to split the team between First and Second Fleets if it was possible.

According to the ship's doctors, Commander Clare Eiberger's apparent age continued to decline and she now appeared to be in her late forties, rather than her actual age of ninety-seven. There was no known way of measuring the two telepaths' powers other than observation of how one performs a task alone compared to the other. After six months of testing, Celena seemed to have a slight edge over her grandmother.

When they arrived in Aqua orbit and had Admiral Robert Becker and his Flag Captain Mae Fieldspire Becker aboard the Hulk for their usual briefing, there was also a family reunion between the Becker's daughter and granddaughter, Commander

Karrie Bloodworth and Lt. Commander Marie Bloodworth.

After the family reunion greetings were finished, Commander's Celena and Clare Eiberger were introduced as Star Fleet's new PSI Department members, and how that came about including the great victory against the Xones using their telepathy powers.

Mae Becker's eye's opened wide in surprise as she exclaimed, "What! Are these the most recent result of what's been happening when there's a mating between women from the two outer star systems and men from Earth?"

Hanna nodded her head before replying, "Yes, but in this case Celena is the granddaughter of Clare. She was mentally compelled to leave Green and meet Clare, where the transformation occurred."

Mae asked, "They are the first with these powers? I wonder if the whole point of these matings were to achieve these results?"

Lt. Commander Marie Bloodworth interrupted the conversation, "I have a confession to make to everyone, especially to you Mom and Dad. I'm a telepath too. I got my powers about the time I turned twelve, when I got my first period."

Karrie's face turned white in consternation as she said, "Why didn't you tell us?"

"Fear, I guess. Then it was fun listening to other people's thoughts, especially the boys. I thought I was the only telepath and I didn't want to call attention to myself that way, everyone thinking I was a freak. Now that I'm not alone, maybe my abilities can be of use?"

Celena said, "You must have a natural block on your thoughts because I can't get a read on your thoughts at all. Can you read me?"

"Yes, you are wondering how powerful my powers are since I've had them for over fourteen years."

"Can you do anything besides reading the thoughts of others?"

"I've had to be very careful so I've only experimented when I've been alone. I can move small objects, but my strongest ability is as a telepath. I can read the minds of others and I followed what you and Clare did against the Xones, but didn't participate."

"How far away can you read the minds of others?"

"I could read Grandmothers mind as soon as we entered the Aqua System. When we were fighting the Xones I could feel their terror as they tried to avoid what they thought was our Laser fire."

Clare came over and hugged Marie, "Obviously, you're one of us and we now have one telepath from each of our worlds. After we have experimented with our powers we then can determine how best to use our talents."

* * *

Four months later First Fleet was outside the third warp gate awaiting the message torpedo from their probe, which reported that there were three enemy formations of fifty ships each stationed about 200,000 miles from the gate. Clare was named by the other telepaths as their leader, who decided to test each telepath's ability by assigning each a different formation.

Hopefully, it would appear to the Xones that the Hulk fired three Laser blasts, one for each formation. Admiral Bloodworth approved the plan and the Flagship UES Hulk led the fleet through the gate.

Celena mentally simulated a Laser blast at the left formation, closely followed by Clare at the middle formation, and then Marie targeted the right formation. The goal was to make the enemy think they were watching an expanding Laser blast heading right at them at an incredible speed.

None of the Xones ships fired missiles at First Fleet because the enemy knew they would never survive going through the Laser blast. Ten minutes into the simulation all three formations broke apart trying to move away from the illusion of the expanding Laser blasts.

To the enemy it was as if the blasts had minds of their own as they followed the ships as they tried to flee. When the ships were finally engulfed by the blast the crews were made to experience extreme heat and think they were all melting. Most enemy crew immediately blew their ships up at this point, and those crews that didn't lost their minds leaving their ships to fly without guidance.

Clare told the others, "Stand down, we have done our jobs!"

Of the 150 ships, only ten remained and they were leaving the combat area at top speed. Unless they took action to reduce their speed, the ships would all eventually self-destruct.

Admiral Bloodworth continued looking at the scans for a few

moments before turning to his new human weapons. He came to attention and saluted the three telepaths, who quickly followed suit. "When we return to Earth, you three will receive medals and the thanks of all humans. Aqua may want to give their thanks before we leave for Earth, and Green when we return there will most certainly want to give them medals for their actions."

Before the fleet left the killing field inside the fourth gates solar system, they sent a probe into the fifth gates system and found no activity. Admiral Bloodworth decided to return to the Aqua system before returning to Earth and reporting their great victory over the Xones.

The Aqua citizens did want to honor the telepaths with their victory over the Xones without an actual shot being fired. Many didn't understand how such a victory was achieved, but with their pacifist background they were happy. All three members of the Psi Department received an achievement award, equivalent to an Earth Bronze Medal.

Later, after the fleet left the Aqua System for Earth, Admiral Bloodworth held several meetings with the three telepaths in an attempt to split the team into three fleet attack groups. However, since Earth only had two fleets, and neither Aqua nor Green had a fleet large enough to operate singly without support, they were at a quandary.

Erik, after his last session with the telepaths, asked his wife if she had any thoughts on the matter. "How far along are we on the Battleship earmarked for Third Fleet?"

"Admiral Cochran informed me when we were last on Earth that it should be ready for trials in six to nine months and when we get back to Earth it will have been almost a year their time. So you think its time for my Third Fleet?"

"Yes, but how are you going to use it? If you send out First and Second Fleets out on an extended hunt from Aqua and Green, what's Third Fleets purpose?"

"Green has that second warp gate that hasn't been explored yet. We could maybe start a third front from there or maybe even find a short cut to the Xones home planet. If we carry enough supplies to last a year we can travel further than we've ever done before."

Hanna nodded her head in agreement, "Honey, do you think Adam and Karrie are experienced enough to handle Third Fleet?"

He nodded his head. "Yes, they have been on my mind for some time as being ready for Command responsibility. Do you think they want to take command of Third Fleet?"

"Well, let's find out. I'll ask Adam's family over for dinner tonight and find out. But first I'll ask Marie not to clue in her parents before they get here."

That's okay with me. I'll keep quiet, but if they go with Third Fleet, I want to go with them.

Hanna and Erik looked at each other and smiled. He replied, "It's going to take me some time before I'm going to get used to experiencing that kind of conversation."

* * *

Commander Marie Bloodworth smiled to herself as she read her grandfather's response to her intrusion into his thoughts. *I'm going to start looking for a husband now that I have at least some agreement with another person who's at risk encountering a man whose my opposite in a DNA match. Celena agrees that I'm probably safe from such an encounter, but who really knows. If I haven't met him by now then I figure, why wait any longer.*

Marie thought back over all the men aboard the Hulk whose thoughts she had heard after meeting them. There were only two or three whose thoughts were on a higher plane than what a nice ass she had. She decided to revisit those men and cull them down to one by close physical contact.

Her previous duty assignment was as Assistant Section Head of the port laser cannons. One of the men under her supervision at that post was a possibility. Previously, she didn't let herself think about him as a lover, let alone a husband.

Now, every officer aboard the ship was fair game for her now that she was with the Psi Department. She let her mind drift among the crew until she felt the marker she previously placed on men she liked. Lieutenant Tyler Bales was a tall lean physically attractive man, but what really drew her to him was his intelligence.

He was currently off-duty and was chatting with several of his fellow crew at the Midship Bar. It took her fifteen minutes to reach the bar where she stood just inside the room for a moment to gage whether she should approach him or let him come to her.

Tyler was over six foot and generally towered over his crewmates, so it was easy to find him. He was with three others, two women and a man, all members of her former laser crew. She decided to act coy and walk by the group, who were playing a game of darts.

Marie was even with the group when she caught the eye of Lt. Julie Shields and stopped to talk. Julie had a loud voice and her; "Hey, it's Commander Bloodworth!" caught everyone's attention.

Marie, while their leader, always had an easy relationship with members of her crew when not on duty - so it was natural for her to join with them in catching up on what's happened with them for the past six plus months.

Tyler held back as the others excitedly told her of their experiences until she asked, "Who took over my position?"

They all turned and pointed at Tyler, who was now wearing Lt. Commander stripes. Marie walked up to him and held out her hand, saying, "Congratulations Tyler, you deserve the position."

He took her hand and started to reply when they both felt a sharp jolt that froze them in place for a moment, but then they both felt an overpowering desire to embrace each other. He pulled her to him in a tight embrace. It was a little awkward, because her head only reached his chest, but they were both vested in their struggle to kiss each other and she pulled herself up by placing her arms around his neck and pulled herself up until their lips touched.

The instant their lips touched, there was a loud boom that only they heard and both collapsed to the floor in a dead faint. For several seconds nobody moved as they were all in shock over what happened.

Julie Shields recovered first and used her hand-held to call for a medic. While waiting, she then called the Captain, letting her know about her granddaughter.

The Captain and the corpsman arrived at the same time and both checked the unconscious pair. Hanna asked, "Lt. Shields, tell me what happened?"

"Ma'am, I'm not sure. Commander Bloodworth started to shake his hand on his promotion, when everything went south. When they touched, they both stiffened as if they were shocked and they stood there stiff as a board, when suddenly they both acted as if they couldn't get close enough to each other and she actually pulled herself up his body until they kissed. When that happened they both collapsed to the deck."

Captain Bloodworths eyes widened as she said, "Holly Crap!" Before turning to the corpsman and said, "Call for two gurneies and inform the doctor on duty that we have another Ancients incident involving Marie."

Julie asked, "Captain, is there anything we can do?"

Hanna looked at her thinking, "Who else saw what happened?"

"Just Lieutenant's Walker and Cantrell. We were playing darts when she joined us."

"Very well. When they take these two to the hospital, you three follow them and tell the doctor what you told me and anything else you can remember. Here they come now!"

Hanna watched as they carted off the two unconscious officers, before heading toward the cabin of Marie's parents - her son, Adam and his wife, Karrie Bloodworth. When she informed them of what had just occurred, they all immediately hurried to the hospital.

Commander Lucy Hendricks was the senior doctor aboard the Hulk and was called to attend the patients when the female patient was identified. When the Captain arrived with the parents of Marie Bloodworth, Lucy left the still unconscious patients to council the new arrivals.

She addressed Marie's parents, "Adam, Karrie all I can tell you at this time is that their physical readouts are normal except their EKG's. Something is going on mentally with these two that we don't understand."

Just then, the gurneys the two patients were strapped onto started to move together until they touched. Marie's hand reached across until she touched Tyler's hand and they both stiffened as if shocked by an electrical current, and then they both opened their eyes.

Lucy ran to Marie and asked, "Marie, its Lucy. How do you feel?"

Marie slowly smiled, "I guess I was wrong about being safe from my DNA opposite. My, he has such a deep personality and look at how attached I am to him."

Tyler responded, "I don't know what's happened to us, but I can't stand to be away from Marie. I need her touch, like now."

Their joined hands rose up from the gurney.

Hanna asked, "Which of you moved the gurneys together?"

Marie gave a little snicker of laughter. "That would be me. I must be stronger now than I was before."

Suddenly, the straps holding them both to the gurneys dropped away and the two sat up facing each other. Tyler smiled at Marie in wonder. "Marie, you were attracted to me before when you were my supervisor! You hid your attraction well, but I guess I did too."

"Oh Tyler, I love you so much. Mom! Our attraction to each other is growing so fast, maybe if I sat on his lap we can get some relief."

She immediately climbed onto his lap with her arms around him and sighed into his chest. "Oh, this is so much better, isn't it Tyler?"

"Yes dear. But I don't think we can do this the rest of our lives."

Lucy shook her head with a slight smile before saying, "Hanna, you better get the minister here so they can get married. Based upon the others they won't be able to function apart until they mate."

Marie whispered into Tyler's ear. "They mean we won't be able to function apart until we have sex."

"There have been others like us?"

"Yes dear, we're not alone in what's happened to us. I thought I was exempt, but apparently not. I'm a telepath, how about you? Can you hear the thoughts of others?"

"Not you, but the doctor just thought, "Oh shit, what now?""

"Mom, I guess my mate qualifies for the Psi Department too."

Clare entered the room unseen and replied, "Well, this complicates matters – but in a good way. Marie, you seem to have gained more powers as well. After your wedding and some time off to get to know your mate, we need to test both of you."

CHAPTER 27

Admiral James Cochran, the head of Earth's Star Fleet, upon reading of the great victory over the Xones in the Aqua War Zone wanted Fleet Admiral Bloodworth and his Psi Department to address the Star Fleet Board. The following day Fleet Admiral Bloodworth, his Flag Captain, and members of the Psi Department departed the Hulk for Star Fleet Headquarters.

Later, upon arrival at the shuttle landing field at Star Fleet Headquarters near Phoenix, Arizona, transport vehicles carried the Star Fleet Officers beneath the headquarters building. A military escort guided them to elevators that eventually ended twenty stories down.

Fleet Admiral Bloodworth led the group into a conference room dominated by a large table where the Board sat awaiting their arrival. When the Fleet Admiral entered the room, the Board as one stood and clapped its approval.

After everyone was in the room, the Board sat, leaving Admiral Cochran standing. He approached the Fleet Admiral and shook his hand, saying, "Well done! You and your people have done the Star Fleet proud. Please introduce your Psi Department that has done such an exceptional job defeating the Xones."

Bloodworth smiled at his team of telepaths before saying, "When I call your names, please hold up your right hand. First I want to introduce their leader, Commander Clare Eiberger, Commander Celena Eiberger, Commander Marie Bales, and their most recent addition, Commander Tyler Bales. I should mention that all members of the department are family members of my wife, Flag Captain Hanna Bloodworth and myself. Clare Eiberger is the older sister of Hanna, Celena Eiberger is the daughter of Clare's son, Marie is the daughter of our son, and Tyler has recently married Marie. You might say it's a family affair."

Director William Strafford asked, "As I understand this relationship, their background is even more murky. Can you try to explain their background?"

"I'll try. We believe it started with the marriage of Aqua's military leader Karrie Fieldspire to my former Chief of Staff Commander Robert Becker when they developed an extremely strong attraction to each other. I didn't at first recognize just how strong their attraction to each other was until later when others came under the same spell. I authorized his loan to Aqua as a military advisor that became permanent when he married Karrie and eventually became Commodore of the Aqua Fleet.

Their daughter and my son, Adam later met and had an even stronger attraction toward each other that resulted in their marriage and a daughter, Marie.

Commander Ian Eiberger met Commander Aundria Eoff of the Green Star Fleet when she arrived to learn our battle tactics. When they first met it was such a strong attraction between the two that they had to be forcibly separated and were married within the hour. Commander Ian Eiberger was lent to the Green Navy as an advisor, who later became Commodore of their Fleet.

Their union produced Celena who traveled to Earth to visit Clare, her grandmother who she had never seen. She risked the trip on an Earth ship because of an extremely strong inner compulsion to see her grandmother. When she met Clare there was some kind of transfer of energy between the two resulting in both having telepathic powers. In addition, Clare started to physically get younger. She is approaching 100 years old, but appears to be in her low forties now.

Marie Bloodworth, the issue of the marriage of Adam Bloodworth and Andria Eoff received her telepathic powers at about twelve, but hid it because she didn't want others to think she was an oddity. This changed when she met the others of the Psi Department. Recently she met her male DNA match and their encounter left him with telepathic powers as well."

Director Strafford looked at his colleagues before saying, "How or why do you think this has happened to the people of the three human Star Systems?"

Bloodworth shrugged his shoulders, "I can only give you an educated guess. The Katz tell of an even older species than themselves, that they call The Ancients. Nothing of their works has apparently survived except rumors and perhaps the Warp Gate System. It may be that they have seeded our three planets with the beginnings of humankind and if we should be threatened by an outside source and travel and meet people from these worlds, then perhaps something triggered a response. It appears Earthmen triggered something in the females of the other two worlds. This is only a WAG of what might have happened."

Strafford frowned, "A wild ass guess was not what I wanted to hear, but who knows. I would suggest that when we finally get around to exploring we keep this in mind. Now, I'd like to honor the members of the Psi Department who participated in the recent telepathic attacks upon the Xones Fleets in both the Green and Aqua War Zones. For those who participated in both zones you will receive two Silver Stars. Please step forward when I call your name."

Later, as they were returning to their shuttle Marie removed the Silver Star from around her neck and placed it back into its presentation box and then looked at it in pride. Before she could close its lid her husband asked mentally, *Marie may I look at your medal?*

She nodded her head and handed it to Tyler. *Honey, I've never seen one this close before. I wonder what our future holds for us?*

Tyler, I think we're going to be the tip of the spear, at least for the near future, in our fight with the Xones. Grandfather Bloodworth is planning to add a Third Fleet that is potentially going to add a third front against the Xones when it explores the second warp gate in the Green System. I don't think we're going to be bored when we join them.

When the Second Fleet joined them in Earth orbit from their tour in the Green War Zone, Commander Celena Eiberger joined them as their Psi Department representative. Admiral Vlad Pavlova was at first concerned because she was so young, but after meeting her and learning of her reason for leaving the Hulk and her DNA opposite behind, he agreed the accept the young officer.

Commander Clare Eiberger would remain aboard the Hulk as its Psi Department representative and when the newly commissioned Battleship, the UES Enterprise begins it duty as the Flagship of Third Fleet, both Commanders Marie and Tyler Bales would be its telepath crewmembers.

Before Second Fleet left Earth orbit for the Aqua War Zone, Fleet Admiral Bloodworth ordered four Heavy Battle Cruisers detached from both the First and Second Fleet to the newly created Third Fleet. Both Commanders Adam and Karrie Bloodworth were ordered to begin readying the Battleship for its shakedown cruise scheduled to depart in two weeks.

After Second Fleet broke Earth orbit for Aqua, it left at least 300 of its crewmembers behind as volunteers for positions aboard the new Battleship. First Fleet also lost about the same numbers, with the remaining 500 plus crew coming from fresh out of schools preparing them for positions aboard the Enterprise.

Temporary Captain Adam Bloodworth with the assistance of XO Karrie Bloodworth finally prepared the Battleships crew to respond during the last three days to achieve about eighty percent compliance to computer simulated running conditions. His goal was 100 percent before the ship left orbit. Next would be a Battle Stations drill. Adam placed his hand over the button, while Karrie crossed her fingers.

Suddenly, the ship's speakers screamed the loud sound of the Battle Stations Klaxon. Three minutes later the Bridge started getting the returns from the various departments that they were ready for action. Five minutes after the BS first sounded all departments had responded. His goal before leaving orbit was three minutes.

Drills continued throughout all three shifts for the first twenty-four hours before Adam gave them a break. All those crew not on duty immediately ate a meal and hit the sack, not knowing how long they had before the next drill. Every day for the next three days he had a BS drill during a different work shift until he was satisfied they could get to their Battle Stations in their sleep. The best time was now less than three minutes.

After ten days the Captain was gratified that the computer simulations showed the ship was operating at 100 percent efficiency and he decided it was time to take the ship out of orbit for a short trip around the moon and back for a true check of their efficiency. When he announced his plans to the crew, the only ones who smiled were the officers and the experienced crew.

Captain Bloodworth gave the orders to break orbit and take the ship at 1g acceleration to the moon for a close orbit of 2,000 miles and then return to its original Earth orbit position. After making the necessary calculations the Enterprise slowly maneuvered until it was headed toward a close orbit of the Moon.

Captain Bloodworth asked his duty officer, "How long would it take for the Enterprise to reach the moon?"

"Sir, at the present speed it will take one hour to reach the 2,000 mile orbit distance. If you want to impress the people on the Moon-1 Station, I can maneuver the ship to pass over them?"

"Very well, give them notice of our passing so that they may take any readings they may want to make."

"Yes Sir, …Sir, I've commed them with the information and they replied, Thanks for the experience and test of our equipment."

The UES Enterprise completed its turn around the Moon and returned to Earth orbit without incident. After making sure they had the proper separation from the other parked ships to be added to Third Fleet, Captain Bloodworth queried his department heads about any problems they encountered on this first short voyage.

He saved the ships engineering section for last. "Commander Jenkins, any problems with the ships power plant?"

"No Sir. But when we leave Earth for the shake down, let's start slow while I watch her get her running legs before we run her hard."

"Any problems with your crew?"

"No Sir! They give me problems I tell them to shape up or I'll space your Asses, then I have no more problems."

"Very good Mr. Jenkins. Maybe I'll send some of the more difficult crew your way for an attitude adjustment."

"Captain, don't do that, they might jump ship before they get down here!"

"Very well Commander, I intend taking her out in three days, do you see a problem with that?"

"No Sir. Just take her out slow at first, as I said."

"Very well, until then."

When Eric looked up he found his XO smiling at him. "What?"

"Commander Jenkins is quite a character, isn't he?"

"Yes, one of a kind. I wish every one of my department heads were just like him."

Karrie replied, "Well, it looks like we're in pretty good shape after that short moon trip. We have enough provisions aboard for our shakedown cruise, and have you made arrangements with the Home Fleet for our little surprise?"

"Yes, Admiral Laura Hiller thought it was a great idea. It would be a training tool for both our fleets."

The day of departure soon arrived and the UES Enterprise broke Earth orbit for its first extended shakedown cruise. Eight Heavy Battle Cruisers followed the Battleship, giving the future Admiral some experience leading a battle fleet.

Adam ordered the fleet to head for Jupiter at an initial sedate 1g, a speed they maintained for eight hours before increasing it to 1.5gs. After another eight hours the speed was increased to 2gs, a speed they maintained for twenty-four hours.

After consultation with Commander Jenkins, he recommended they jump to 3gs for six hours. Some additions had been made to the ships engine that they needed to test, so they continued to watch for any stresses the engine might display.

At the end of the six hours, they reduced speed to 2gs and continued to analyze the engines output. Captain Bloodworth ordered the fleet to continue its course to Jupiter at 3gs and wait for their arrival while refueling at the planet.

After six hours Commander Jenkins thought it was safe to continue and the Captain ordered the ship to accelerate at 4gs, a speed the Space Fleet only used in emergencies by previous ships. At this speed they were soon approaching their sister ships. Captain Bloodworth told them to decrease their speed to 2gs until they caught up with the Enterprise at Jupiter.

Commander Jenkins commed the Captain, "Sir, I believe it's

time to increase speed again, and I recommend we increase speed to 4.5gs."

"Make it so Commander. Let's see what she can do."

* * *

Jenkins watched the indicator slowly rise from 4gs without any hesitation or problems showing on any of the gages. They were now pushing upwards into speeds never attempted before as the gages showed 4.5gs.

The gage Jenkins was most concerned with was the ships artificial gravity indicator that didn't seem to be affected as it reflected a steady 1 gravity. If this equipment failed the crew and ships equipment would instantly experience 4.5gs, something nobody wanted – hence a failsafe devise that would immediately bring the ship back to 1g acceleration.

The ship maintained this speed for three hours until they passed the orbit of Mars, whereupon Jenkins commed the Captain. "Sir, it's time to cut power and turn the ship for deceleration toward a Jupiter orbit."

"Very well Commander Jenkins, make it so."

CHAPTER 28

The UES Enterprise arrived at Jupiter and refueled its reaction mass by a close orbit of the planet. The ship waited for the remainder of the fleet to arrive for two days and according to their instruments they would not arrive for another eighteen hours.

The record speed the Enterprise achieved didn't appear to have stressed any part of the ship and they now knew at least one of their ships had this ability. They continued to run drills to test the ships equipment and crew as they awaited the arrival of their escort ships.

Sensors also picked up ships of the Home Fleet near the systems two warp gates that were located at opposite ends of Jupiter's orbit swing. Both groups of ships had queried the Enterprise and after Captain Bloodworth reply, commed their acceptance of the training exercise.

XO Karrie Bloodworth shook her head at her husband, "Adam, I'm going to bet you that Lt. Commander Alecia Phillips discovers your surprise within an hour into her shift."

"You're on, what's the prize for the winner?"

"Whatever the winner wants from the loser."

"Whoa! That's pretty broad...but yes, the bet's on."

An hour later the 08:00 shift changes were made on the bridge and Lt. Commander Phillips took her place at the Tactical Station. She immediately reviewed current scans and then for a comparison she reviewed those taken two hours previously.

She straightened in her seat, reviewed the data again, and in half hour increments reviewed the scans again. *Crap, this can't be right, two Home Fleet ships don't just disappear! Unless?*

She reached for a clipboard that was positioned where she could see the Captain's Chair, and then turned her attention back to her station. *Yep! Something's up, because they're watching me like a hawk.*

She backed the scans up until she noticed the missing two ships start a fast withdrawal toward the Enterprise before their scans disappeared. She did a fast estimate of each ship's speed before vanishing from the scans and where they would be now.

"Captain, two Home Fleet ships are approaching the Enterprise without power with the apparent purpose of hiding from our scans. Bogy one is about 100,000 miles to our right, and bogy two is about 98,000 miles to our left. They are both approaching at a steady 30,000 mph."

The XO smiled as she caught her husbands' eyes, and he nodded his head in defeat.

Captain Bloodworth said, "Comm the Ajax and Nomad to give us their respective positions to the Enterprise and speed."

"Sir, the Ajax reports they are about 97,000 miles to our left and Nomad reports they are about 99,000 miles to our right, and both are travelling at 30,200 mph."

"Very good, Comm them that the exercise is over and it took our Tactical Officer eighteen minutes to find them. Thank you for your help in this exercise."

"Lt. Commander Phillips, congratulations on your successful completion of this exercise. You will receive my well done for your personnel records and a bonus. Pass this test on to your friends; however, no one will know when it's a test or the real thing."

The Enterprises scans showed the two ships previously dark, were restarting their engines and maneuvering to return to their former positions. "Sir, the Ajax and Nomad are returning to their former positions. I've made a record of the test exercise."

"Very good Lt. Commander."

After the fleets Heavy Battle Cruisers reached Jupiter and refueled, Captain Bloodworth ordered the fleet to follow the UES Enterprise back to Earth at 3gs. Two days later they were in Earth orbit where he conned Fleet Admiral Bloodworth, "Sir, the Enterprise has passed its trials as planned and is ready for duty."

Six hours later Captain Bloodworth received a message from Fleet Admiral Bloodworth that read, "The UES Enterprise is officially entered onto Star Fleets records and will be captained by Karrie Fieldspire Bloodworth. Third Fleet will be under the command of Rear Admiral Adam Bloodworth. Both changes in command will be accomplished tomorrow at 10:00 hours ship time, followed by a reception attended by the Fleet Admiral and his wife."

Adam showed the message to Karrie, who took a big breath and smiled her satisfaction. "We did it. You're the head of Third Fleet and I'm the Flag Captain."

"Who do you want as your XO?"

"Why, Lt. Commander Phillips of course. I'll let her know today, so she can prepare herself to handle Bridge duties while the Changes in Command ceremony takes place. She's a little young for the XO of a battleship, but I have confidence in her abilities."

Later, after the command ceremonies were over and everyone moved to the reception room, Admiral Adam Bloodworth and his Flag Captain shook the hands of the invited guests that included the eight Heavy Cruiser Captains of Third Fleet. Four of the captains were female and most have held their positions for over ten years. The least command experience was the new captain of the Enterprise, the most powerful ship of Third Star Fleet.

After the initial personal greetings were exchanged, their daughter Commander Marie Bales hugged her parents while mentally commenting, *don't be too concerned about your fleet captains. I'm sure they'll measure you against Grandfather and Grandmother, but Tyler and I think everyone's going to be too busy with the enemy to worry about your command skills.*

The two watched their daughter and son-in-law walk toward Commander Clare Eiberger, Adam's Grandmother and the head of the Psi Department of Star Fleet.

Karrie squeezed Adams hand saying softly, "Is that a guess or a premonition?"

"Remember who she is. I'm going to make sure we're properly supplied before leaving Earth. I plan on taking with us two cargo ships, each carrying food consumables and replacement missiles."

Three weeks later First and Third Fleet left Earth for the Green War Zone. When the combined fleets approached the warp gate, Fleet Admiral Bloodworth decided that First Fleet would go first and go directly to the Third gate without first stopping at the Green system. Third Fleet would stop at Green for a port call before leaving through the systems second gate.

After entering the Green System the UES Enterprise ordered its escorts to await their arrival at the second warp gate while they were escorted to Green orbit by the Flagship of Green's Star Fleet, the UGS Tiagerfish. Admiral Ian Eiberger and his Flag Captain Aundria Eiberger were invited aboard the Enterprise for a conference.

After arriving by shuttle the Green Star Fleet dignitaries were piped aboard the Enterprise with honors and escorted to the Admirals/Captains suite. Once everyone was seated, Admiral Adam Bloodworth made introductions, ending with the two youngest members in the room, Commander's Marie and Tyler Bales.

"They are two new members of Star Fleet's Psi Department and are both telepaths, as is your daughter Celena."

Aundria asked, "Did you know of your daughters abilities when you were last here?"

"No, she was hiding her abilities at that time, but has since taken her place in the department. A short time later she and Tyler discovered they were a DNA match for each other, much like you and Ian. After their mating bond they discovered she had passed the talent of telepathy to him. That's why we have the honor of having two telepaths aboard the Enterprise."

"Where is Celena assigned?"

"She's aboard the Second Fleet's Flagship, the Tiger, and is currently in the Aqua War Zone. Her DNA match is aboard the

Hulk and she's still hoping to avoid their mating bond until she's at least twenty. As you well know, she's a very strong willed person."

Aundria looked at her husband with a crooked smile, "Yes, we're quite aware of her personality. What's Third Fleets purpose here?"

Adam smiled as he answered, "We're going to explore where your second gate goes and hopefully find a short cut to the Xones Home System, or at least open up a third front against the enemy."

Admiral Bloodworths personal comm beeped and after receiving its message, said, "There's a small Katz formation of ship's arriving in-system that wishes to speak to the current Earth Battle Fleet in the Green System. I've ordered the Enterprise to comm that we would await their arrival in Green orbit, and based upon their past capabilities they should be here in three days."

Three days later Katz Admiral Gamma Killa arrived aboard the Enterprise with the normal pomp of a visiting foreign military dignitary. Admiral Adam Bloodworth introduced himself, his wife, and the Green Star Fleet officers before leading everyone to their personal stateroom.

Admiral Killa stopped just inside the stateroom and looked around in amazement for a moment before following her host's motion to sit at a small conference table. Captain Karrie Bloodworth asked. "Do you desire any refreshment you liked from the last time you were in Human Territory?"

"Yes! Coffee, yes that's what I think it's called, a black, bitter tasting drink that sets my body on fire."

The Captains Steward quickly set a steamy hot cup of coffee before her, which she picked up gingerly and smelled the slight aroma coming from the cup. "Yes, this is as I remembered. I took coffee beans back to my home planet, but the plants grown there didn't have the same reaction for me. It still was a great delight for others and was an economic prize for me – but this is what I wanted."

After finishing her cup she placed it back on its saucer and gave a satisfied sigh. "Admiral Bloodworth, you and your mate remind me of your parents. Are they well?"

"Yes, they are in their late fifties and he now commands three Battle Fleets; however, to me he is the same man as when I was a child. We have recently added a new weapon that has proven devastating to the Xones."

"Yes, that is the reason for my visit. Is it a weapon that the Katz can weld as well?"

"Do any of the Katz have telepathic powers?"

"Telepathic powers, do you mean people who can read the minds of others?"

"Yes, it also may mean the ability to influence what they think they are seeing."

"No, I don't think that it's possible. At least we haven't encountered any race with that power."

"Marie, can you influence the Admiral to see something unexpected?"

Marie thought a moment before asking, "Admiral Killa do you know what a dragon is?"

"I don't think so?"

"It's from an ancient Earth legend that had creatures that could fly and breath fire that were called dragons. Please look at that open space before the bedroom and try to empty your mind of any thought."

The Katz Admiral did as Marie asked and suddenly a creature much like she described suddenly appeared and turned its head toward her and bellowed a loud roar before unfolding its wings and extended it's long neck and head in her direction and shot flames at her, causing Killa to jump out of her chair to avoid the flames. Suddenly, the vision vanished before her.

The Katz Admiral looked at the young woman in surprise for a few moments before smiling. "This is your weapon! No, we can't use it. How did you suddenly become a people with these powers?"

Marie shrugged her shoulders as she answered, "My father thinks it's a gift from the Ancients. He thinks it's the end result of the strange mating's between the three human worlds that we have experienced. We initially placed a vision of a huge Laser blast from a battleship toward three formations of Xones ships. It was so real for them that they broke formation trying to avoid the blast and when it followed them and started burning their ships, many lost their minds and/or destroyed their own ships."

"You didn't have to use any actual weapons?"

Adam answered, "Marie's weapon is her mind. It's much more

powerful than any laser or missile we have available."

"May I travel with you in this beautiful battleship and observe your actions?"

"Yes, of course we would be happy to host you aboard the UES Enterprise; however, we may be gone for as long as two years."

"That will not be a determent aboard such a fine ship."

"Very good. Green Star Fleet is also sending a ship with us to observe what we encounter, and we expect to leave in three days. Is that sufficient time for you to bring aboard what you may need for that length of trip?"

"Yes, that will not be a problem as long as I have my personal Steward. Will my stateroom be comparable to that aboard the Hulk?"

"It will be slightly larger and I'm sure you will be satisfied."

Admiral Killa nodded her acceptance with a smile. "Thank you for your consideration."

Three days later the Enterprise and a Green Heavy Battle Cruiser broke away from Green orbit and headed toward the systems second warp gate where the remainder of Third Fleet was awaiting their arrival.

Admiral Bloodworth commed every ship to go to Battle Stations before the Enterprise sent a sensor probe through the gate at 2gs speed and then they all awaited the return of a message torpedo. Fifteen minutes passed before they received a message showing an all-clear system.

Since this was their first attempt through this gate, the admiral decided to experiment by sending another probe at 1g, and then at 3gs, followed by 4gs if the previous attempts failed to produce results.

When the last attempt at 4gs was attempted, a message returned showing a small fleet of six ships 622,000 miles away heading toward this gate at a speed of 3gs. Admiral Bloodworth ordered the fleet to proceed through the gate at 4gs, following the Enterprise in alpha order every ten minutes.

Admiral Bloodworth told his daughter to try and determine who these ships were by using her powers as soon as they cleared the gate. Once clear of the gate the Enterprises sensors immediately indicated that the ships were not Xones by their size and engine signatures.

Marie said, "Admiral these are people like us. I can't understand their language but I can see how they appear by looking through their eyes. They are very excited by our sudden appearance through the gate. I can make myself appear before them on their bridge and try to calm things down if you think this is wise."

"Yes, try it before they start shooting at us."

* * *

Marie pictured herself on the bridge of the largest ship of the approaching fleet. She was dressed as herself in the military uniform of a Commander, wearing her red beret. When she appeared on their bridge, she turned toward who she thought was their leader and held up her right hand, hoping they wouldn't panic.

The female officer yelled at the others, probably to be calm, before stepping down from her command chair and slowly approaching her. Marie pointed at her cuff markings to indicate her rank, and then at the officer.

The officer raised her own arm comparing the two different markings and then nodded in head in understanding by holding up one finger and then pointing at herself. Marie pointed at her beret and then shook her head before moving her hand in a rocking motion trying to show she wasn't in a command role.

The officer looked at her questioning for a moment before smiling her understanding. Marie looked around trying to find something to write on before using a finger to write in the air. The officer caught on immediately and apparently asked someone to bring Marie pen and paper.

Marie drew a stick figure and then pointed to herself several times before the officer nodded her head. Marie then drew two ships, one larger than the other, before pointing at the large ship and then herself. She then pointed at her head and then the small ship, before pointing at the officer.

Marie waited until she was sure the officer understood as she watched the expression on her face change. Marie placed the pen in the air and slowly moved it toward the officer watching her eyes widen in understanding. The officer took the pen out of the air and brought it back to Marie, who then pointed at the officer and then at the large ship drawn on the paper and raised her eyebrows waiting on a response.

While waiting on her to make up her mind Marie drew eleven smaller ships beside the large ship and winked at her. The officer immediately shouted a question to her TO, who was watching them rather than her job. She quickly replied after checking her instruments. The officer turned back to Marie and showed five fingers, one at a time. Marie counted off her fingers one at a time until she showed eleven.

The officer looked at Marie for a moment before pointing at herself and then the large ship before shrugging her shoulders. Marie pointed at the officer and then drew a box on the paper and tapped it and then the officer. She then pointed at her own mouth and then the officers. The officer quirked her own mouth and stared at Marie.

Hoping to dispel any misunderstanding, Marie produced a replica of a learning machine before them, opening it up and climbing inside before making it disappear. The officer nodded her head at Marie and slowly smiled her understanding.

After making an agreement to meet 400,000 miles from the gate, Marie withdrew from the bridge of the alien ship and reported what she learned from the encounter to her father.

CHAPTER 29

Ten hours later both formations of space ships reached their rendezvous point and a shuttle from the Enterprise traveled to the lead ship of the aliens. Commander Marie Bloodworth Bales was its only passenger as it settled into the open shuttle bay. Marie noted that there was a small greeting party outside the shuttle, so she ordered the shuttle door to be opened.

There was some risk to her health, which was the reason she was alone. She used herself, as a test of whether the air she breathed was fatal. She slowly stepped down to the deck and walked toward the Captain and five other crewmembers standing nearby.

Marie clicked her heels together and gave a small bow to the officer she interacted with previously. The two women were similar in height and weight, both wore their hair short for easy maintenance and while the alien was of fair complexion and had blond hair, Marie's skin color was darker and she had dark brown hair.

The two finished examining each other and Marie stepped forward with an outstretched hand, hoping she was not offending the other. After a slight hesitation the alien officer took Marie's hand in both hers and squeezed while smiling.

Marie then turned and used her arms to indicate they should enter the shuttle. The shuttle nearly filled the bay it occupied indicating it was designed for a much smaller craft. Marie turned to the shuttle's door and led the others aboard. She stood just inside the door and pointed to the seats they should occupy and then helped the shuttles crew secure the passengers.

Marie returned and sat next to the Captain and tried to give her a reassuring smile as the door shut and the shuttle immediately left the ship heading toward the Enterprise. She pointed to the various screens that showed the surrounding space and then the approaching view of the Enterprise that quickly grew larger as they approached the Battleship. Soon it took up the entire screen and as they approached the side of the ship a shuttle door opened before them and the shuttle quickly slid inside and dropped to the deck with hardly a bump.

When the shuttle door opened it was to the eerie sound of pipes welcoming them aboard. Marie stood and motioned for everyone to stand and leave the shuttle. When Marie stood on the shuttle bay deck she gathered the six aliens into three ranks of twos and led them down the two rows of the ships Marine Honor Guard, where at its end stood the Admiral and Captain.

Marie saluted the Admiral, then the Captain before asking permission to board. Receiving permission, Marie took the alien captain's hand and told her parents that this was the ships' Captain. They both saluted the Captain and then Karrie told Marie, "Take them to the Learning Machines so that we can converse with them."

Marie quickly led the group to the first set of machines, where she started the Captain and her selected next officer. After making sure the machines were operating as designed, she led the others to another set of machines a fifteen minute walk away, where she left the next two aliens. Another short walk brought them to the final set of machines where the last two aliens were taught the Universal language.

Two hours later, Marie started recovering the aliens from the Learning machines beginning with the Captain until they all were together again. She smiled at the Captain, "I'm sorry for this procedure, but it was necessary that you learn the Universal Language all Star Fleet personnel use. Each of our three worlds has their own languages, but with our use of the Universal Language we can all communicate with each other. Please follow me and you will meet the Third Fleet's Admiral and his Flag Captain, my father and mother."

The two senior members of the alien group quickly looked at each other before following Marie. Twenty minutes later the aliens were escorted into a small conference room where they were seated facing members of the Third Fleet.

Admiral Bloodworth introduced himself and his Flag Captain, and then Commander Marie Bloodworth Bales, and her husband Commander Tyler Bales before addressing the aliens. "I see your command structure is of mixed gender as we are. What race do you call yourselves?"

"My name Captain Karisse Totty and we are from the planet Paradise. I guess we are humans since we appear to look alike."

"How did you achieve Star Travel and how long ago?"

"We first left our star system almost 600 years ago. Our system was settled by an old civilization more than two thousand years ago and we eventually reengineered their ships to achieve space again. We were on an exploration trip when we found you."

"That's interesting because we have a story that may be a tie-in with your past. However, the reason we are here is because we are fighting a space war with a enemy called the Xones who destroy every intelligent life form they encounter."

Captain Totty quickly stood saying, "What! We were searching for a group of ships that are slightly smaller in size than your main force ships, which attacked our force without provocation. We destroyed six of their ships before they broke off and disappeared through a warp gate."

Admiral Bloodworth asked, "Do any of your ships have battle damage?"

"No, the ships that sustained damage have returned to our home base under escort."

"How large a force attacked you?"

"Our force of ten ships came into a new system through a warp gate and encountered the enemy force of sixteen ships who immediately launched missiles at us. We counter launched and moved away from their missiles, but sustained damage to two of ours while destroying three of theirs. The sustained battle that ensued destroyed three more of the enemy before they withdrew."

Captain Bloodworth said, "The Xones generally immediately attack if they believe they have a numeric advantage. Your success in battle was sufficient to make them withdraw. Our past experience with them is that we've found that they are reluctant to change tactics."

"Admiral, how many battles have your fleets fought?"

"This is the first voyage of Third Fleet and we haven't yet encountered the Xones. Since my home planet has joined the fight against the Xones we have fought hundred's of battles, destroying thousands of their ships with minimal losses ourselves. Our current mission is to either find the home planet of the Xones or start a third front against them. My parents started this war with the Xones using ships similar to the enemy. Those ships were captured by the Xones from another old race called the Katz."

"The Katz realized they needed fresh blood in their fight with the Xones and convinced our race to help in their fight. Since we were not yet a space capable race, they provided ships, a shipyard, and teaching machines so that we quickly got into the fight. By happenstance we have aboard the Katz Admiral who convinced us to fight with them against the Xones. Would you like to meet her?"

Captain Totty said, "Yes, of course."

Commander Marie Bales quickly went to the door and opened it wide to admit the tall alien, who followed her back into the room. The Katz were truly an alien race as she stood almost seven feet tall, thin of body, arms and legs similar to a human, and a head resembling an earth cat with large eyes, and ears rising from the top of her head. She was dressed in layers of a thin material resembling silk revealing glimpses of her body as she moved.

Marie said, "People of Paradise, I give you Admiral Gamma Killa."

Admiral Killa gave the others a small head bow and smiled. "This is a great honor for me to meet another human race apparently not directly connected to the three my race is involved with in fighting the Xones."

Captain Totty nodded her own head in greeting. "Admiral Killa, our new friends stated that you are an old race. How many years have you been a space force?"

"At least 5,000 years, but you are only the fourth human species we have discovered. There are rumors of another ancient race responsible for developing the warp gate system that has been gone longer than our own history."

Totty replied, "Our own history is somewhat vague. We are apparently the descendants of a race that colonized our world because of some unknown problem. It may have been overcrowding or something worse, like fleeing a race like the Xones. In any case, because of the Xones actions they have earned themselves another enemy. I'm sure my world would be anxious to join the other human worlds in fighting this evil cancer."

Admiral Bloodworth asked, "Do you think your leaders would be interested in formalizing a written agreement between our alliance and your world. It would come with sharing battle tactics and hardware advances. Our current greatest weapon is our newly created Psi Department. Do any of your people have the ability to read others thoughts?"

Captain Totty nodded her head, "Yes, but it is quite rare and I don't believe any has the ability your daughter has demonstrated. When she appeared on my bridge it was quite disconcerting for everyone there."

Captain Bloodworth asked, "Captain, without her appearance, what would have been your response to our arrival?"

"Well, I wouldn't have launched a first strike – not against this humongous sized ship. I would have tried to get out of her range and attempt to communicate with you. What are those two odd shaped ships that came through the gate last?"

"Supply ships, we thought this might be a long hard voyage and we brought extra missiles and consumable food."

"Sir, I'm curious about the range of your missiles and laser weapons?"

"We have the ability to turn off the missiles engines and later restart them when in attack range – so basically their range is unlimited. Our lasers are effective in excess of 100,000 miles. However, our new psi weapons have completely wiped out six formations Xones ships without use of any conventional weapons from our ships."

Captain Totty quickly looked at the two red bereted officers in surprise. "It's really possible then, to use your minds to influence what the enemy thinks they are seeing?"

Marie nodded her head, "I made them think a huge Laser blast came from this battleship heading right at each enemy ship, and then when the blast engulfed their ships they felt the heat and heard their ships coming apart. They either self-destroyed their ships or went insane leaving their ships speeding off until they came apart from the g's they were under."

"My, that is a great weapon to have at your disposal. Your other two fleets have this same type telepaths?"

"Yes, they are actually a family of telepaths that came into being from a series of events that originated from women from each of our three allied human worlds and men from Earth. It's a long story that appears wildly improbable, especially when we try to place the Ancients behind what happened."

Captain Totty replied, "I don't understand what you are saying and who were the Ancients you mentioned?"

Marie smiled and shook her head at her parents, "I'll give you a more detailed history of how we gained our powers later. The Ancients are a myth about who created the warp gates and maybe seeded our three planets with humanity. We think that they left something in our DNA that activated when Earthmen encountered certain women from the other two planets. Perhaps an alarm when we became a star traveler, or a way to protect ourselves against enemies."

Totty frowned in disbelieve, "Sounds to me like you are grasping at straws in an effort to understand what has occurred. I don't think my ancestors were your Ancients, but you probably are thinking they are a much older race that predates even them?"

"Yes, perhaps even thousands of millenniums ago. It would have taken them a long time to build the warp gate system and that seems the only concrete evidence of their existence."

Admiral Bloodworth interrupted, "When we left the Green system we travelled over four times the distance we normally travel to reach another star system when we entered the gate at a speed of 4gs, instead of our normal 2g or 3g speed. What speed did you enter this system?"

"We entered at 2gs and we are two systems away from this system."

"Yet, this was your first time encountering the Xones. A strategy warning, you should send a probe through the gate and wait for a return before entering. Sometimes the Xones await in ambush near a gate hoping to catch us in an ambush, especially any gates where a battle was previously fought."

"So you knew we were approaching the gate you entered from, yet your battleship came through first. Let me try to figure out your reasoning. Our six ships didn't represent a large force if we were Xones and a potential easy target for you; however, when your sensors showed we weren't Xones, you immediately wanted to communicate with us. Whose idea was it to send Commander Bales to us?"

"It was her idea. We needed to do something quickly before you panicked and did something we would have regretted."

"Yes, and since she wasn't actually on my bridge there was no physical risk to her. But still, it was something she hadn't done before. Admiral, have you ever tried to communicate with someone without words in a stressful situation? Well, she did very well. She tried to indicate she was not part of your normal chain of command, and now I understand why. It's good that she is family or you would need to worry about her wanting to take command of your ship."

The admiral nodded, "Normally you might have a point. But the only one in the Psi Department not family is Marie's husband, and they are so tied together emotionally that couldn't happen. How far away was this battle with the Xones?"

Totty thought a moment, "This is the third system from where it took place. You think there's a chance that they may have come back to set an ambush?"

"Yes, and if so they may be watching the wrong gate for your return. Are you game for some payback?"

Ten days later they were at the warp gate leading to the system of the Paradise's ship's last battle. Admiral Bloodworth ordered a probe sent through the gate and they awaited its result. Depending upon where the enemy ships were located and the size of their fleet, it was agreed that the Paradise ships would act as a decoy to draw the Xones toward this gate. Once they were far enough into the system, the Enterprise would show herself and Marie and Tyler would attack with their special talents.

Soon they received their reply from the probe and discovered three large groups of ships near the system's other gate. Admiral

Bloodworth commed Captain Totty, saying it was now her turn in their plan. She replied, "Aye, aye Admiral."

The six Paradise ships quickly transited through the gate and headed toward the thirty enemy ships at 2gs. The Xones initially took no action as if surprised that their quarry didn't immediately flee back through the gate they entered, but then they started a 3g advance (their normal top speed) toward what they obviously thought would be an easy victory.

After two hours the Enterprise and all her consorts entered the system finding the Xones ships still grouped together in three, now loose formations. The enemy ships were 800,000 miles from the Enterprise. However, when the Paradise ships reversed thrust to stop their forward motion, it seemed to awaken the awareness of the Xones to the danger they were in and they immediately copied the Paradise ships maneuver to bring their formations to a stop.

The Xones may not have heard about their enemy's battleships or their capabilities, but its sheer size must have given them pause to reconsider. The Paradise ships then maneuvered to give the Enterprise a clear shot at the Xones ships.

Suddenly, from the Xones' viewpoint, the Enterprise shot two Laser blasts at their ships from an impossibly long range. When the blast continued past the halfway point toward them without dissipating, the Xones formations started to break down as individual ships tried to maneuver away from the path of the Laser blasts heading in their direction. As the blasts drew closer, the Xone maneuvers became more frantic until there were collisions, causing even more panic as the ships tried to avoid the fiery embrace of the Lasers.

When the enemy ships were engulfed by the Laser blast, the two telepaths made the Xones crews think their ships were coming apart as the fiery death engulfed them. Those not going insane decided to destroy themselves rather than be burned alive. Ten ships left the scene at a speed that soon resulted in their destruction, while the remainder self-destructed.

The Paradise ships slowly approached the debris field and used their shuttles to take a sample of the ships and their crewmembers, while the Third Fleet approached their location. Captain Totty commed the Admiral and requested another meeting aboard the Enterprise.

The meeting included members of the Paradise, Enterprise, and the Captain of the Green Heavy Battle Cruiser. Admiral Gamma Killa asked to be present as an observer. Captain Totty introduced another member of her crew previously present, but who had remained silent. "This is our Science Officer, Commander Kali Tebo, a crewmember whose position is present on all exploring fleets. She is extremely interested in your Psi Department, especially after witnessing Commander Bales initial appearance on my bridge and later, the destruction of the Xones fleet. I'll let her ask her questions."

Commander Tebo slowly stood and looked at all those present. "I understand we have a representative of all three human planets party to your alliance. With us that brings the total to four known human planets. Personally, I'm now sure we'll eventually find others. I, like Admiral Bloodworth, think some intelligence long ago seeded this spiral of our Galaxy. After observing the remains of the Xones, it's quite obvious they are not part of our DNA. Based upon what's been relayed from Admiral Bloodworths and Katz Admiral Killa's direct observations and our own experience, we must join you in your fight to either isolate or eliminate the Xones. I recommend that our fleets return to Paradise to formalize a treaty to that effect."

Admiral Bloodworth stood and gave her a slight bow. Commander Tebo appeared to be middle-aged, slightly taller than her captain who stood as tall as Marie, who was six foot. Her hair was a dark frizz around her head, and while attractive, her frame was quite lean.

Tebo flushed at Adam's scrutiny, but met his eyes without flinching. He asked, "In your explorations have you met any other human worlds?"

"No! Your alliance is our first."

"In your explorations, did you vary the speed through the gates? We've found that different speeds resulted in different locations, the higher the speed, the further the distance travelled. My planet Earth is located three gates distance between Aqua and Green. Green was found by lowering the speed we normally used at this gate."

Tebo looked at Adam closely. "You've been travelling the gates for how long?"

"My father started about fifty years ago, ship time. I've been at it for about fifteen years as a ship officer."

"We've been doing it for hundreds of years and didn't know this. We've only used 2gs as our standard."

Captain Karrie Bloodworth said, "We used 4gs to get into the system where we found you; however, that was the first time we ever used that speed in a transit. Our probe spotted your ships and we investigated."

Tebo asked, "While we travel to my home planet, may I remain aboard and mine your knowledge and battle strategy of the Xones?"

Admiral Bloodworth smiled as he replied, "Yes, I think that would be helpful for both our races. We know nothing of your culture or your military hardware and you seemed surprised that we refueled our reaction mass by skimming the outer atmosphere of a systems gas giant. What fuel do your ships use?"

"Our ships absorb radiation from each systems sun. We both refuel as we travel through the systems we explore."

CHAPTER 30

When the combined fleets reached the warp gate into the Paradise System, the Paradise fleet preceded the others through the gate to pave the way for the Third Fleet's entrance into their system. About an hour later the Paradise's Flagship Discovery returned and commed, "Please have the fleet stop 1,000 miles inside the system while our government analyzes Captain Totty's dispatches."

The Third Fleet went to Battle Stations before following the Discovery through the gate led by the Enterprise. The systems Home Fleet consisted of twenty Heavy Cruiser type ships that were dwarfed by the UES Enterprise, her escorted nine Heavy Battle Cruisers, and two support ships.

Bloodworth lowered their readiness from Battle Stations to Battle Ready and waited through the long distance communication lag. Anticipating that they had at least an eight-hour wait, Adam and Karrie decided to take their sleep break.

They were eating breakfast when they received a comm from the Discovery that the fleet could proceed to the second planet where they should take station 1,000 miles from their space station Echo, which was in orbit around the planet Paradise, but was not capable of accommodating ships of their size.

They followed the Discovery at 3gs and were in orbit three days later. The Discovery and her five consorts were their designated babysitters while Paradise's government decided what to make of their guests. The Admiral noted that a shuttle left the Discovery soon after the ships were parked in orbit.

Third Fleet kept busy doing maintenance for three days until the Enterprise received a comm that a delegation from the planet's government wished to have a conference aboard the Enterprise tomorrow at 10:00 hours ship time.

At the appointed time a shuttle arrived aboard the UES Enterprise where ten individuals, four in uniform, stepped down to Enterprises deck and were greeted by the sound of the welcoming ceremonial pipes. At its end, the double row of Marine Guards came to attention and Captain Totty led the way to where Admiral Bloodworth and his Flag Captain awaited.

Captain Totty saluted the Flag and asked for permission to board, whereupon the two Enterprise Officers returned her salute and the Flag Captain granted permission. Captain Totty introduced her senior officer, Admiral Seth Speer and his adjutant, Commander Skyler Vang. The last military officer was Totty's Science Officer.

Totty then introduced the remaining six civilians of mixed genders representing the planet's government leaders. Captain Totty said, "Admiral, since most of my people don't understand Universal I've taken the liberty of bringing along a device that will interpret what we each say into a language we understand. Is this satisfactory with you?"

"Captain, this is wonderful. It will solve the language problem and speed up our talks, was this your idea?"

"Yes, your learning machine was great for a permanent solution, but for our talks we needed something we could use now. We are ready to begin our talks, if you are.

A fifteen-minute walk brought them to the conference room where Captain Karrie Bloodworth pointed at a buffet of snacks and drinks displayed on a side table. "Science Officer Tebo you've had the opportunity to sample our foods and beverages, would you offer recommendations to your people?"

Tebo quickly began to offer her recommendations and after everyone brought their choices to the table and the translation devices were set up, Admiral Bloodworth begin introductions.

"People of Paradise sitting with me are representatives of the alliance of three human planets, Aqua, Earth, and Green as well as Admiral Killa, our original benefactor, from another friendly race, the Katz. My ship and I are from Earth, while my wife is originally from Aqua. She is the result of a marriage between a male from Earth and female from Aqua whose parents are the head of Aqua's Star Fleet."

"Our daughter, Commander Marie Bales and her husband Tyler are both members of our Psi Department which have members in all Earth Fleets. I'll answer questions about these individuals later."

"Captain Thater of the Green Star Fleet joined Earth's Third Fleet as an observer. Admiral Killa first persuaded Earth to join them in their fight against the Xones and since we had not yet advanced in Space Flight beyond our own moon, they provided us with space cruisers and learning tools to operate them. They also gave us a portable yard to build our own ships. They did the same with both the Aqua and Green Systems. Without them, the Xones would have destroyed us when they discovered our systems. I'm now ready for your questions."

Admiral Speer stood and Bloodworth returned to his chair. "Admiral Bloodworth, from what Captain Totty has told me, Earth Star Fleets took the lead in your combined fight against the Xones, is that correct?"

"Yes, since we were the first human ships to fight the Xones my father developed strategies to fight the Xones. Initially our ships were similar to those of the Xones, who reportedly copied captured Katz ships. Since then we have developed our own designs and we now have much better ships than the Xones."

Admiral Speer smiled as he replied, "Like this huge ship you call a Battleship?"

"Yes, this type of ship is the spear point of our fleets. However, our Heavy Battle Cruisers have demonstrated they can hold their own against a Xones fleet two or three times their number."

Speer continued, "Even so, it now appears that you have an even more powerful weapon at your disposal. I'm referring to your Psi Department?"

"Yes, Captain Totty and her fleet were present when we

disposed of over forty-five Xones ships without using any of our powered weapons."

"Yes that! Can you explain how that happened?"

"Really, it's quite simple. Both my daughter and her husband have the ability to make others see objects that are not real. Captain Totty saw this when a projection of my daughter appeared on her Bridge when we first encountered each other."

"Yes, so she said. But I can't get my mind to accept that could happen. Would she give me an example of her ability?"

"Marie, can you think of something that will convince him?"

Marie quickly found a thought of a young woman from the Admiral's mind and projected a small image of her on the table in front of him. Marie influenced everyone's mind to see the two-foot tall image as well as it walked back and forth and then waved at the admiral before disappearing.

Admiral Speer's face turned white as his daughter's image disappeared. He took a deep breath before turning to Marie. "That's disconcerting! You used your own image when you appeared before Captain Totty, but you couldn't talk?"

"Actually, I could have made you think I was talking, but I didn't know your language."

Admiral Speer looked at Marie with a new understanding and a little fear. "There are more like you? How is this possible?"

Admiral Bloodworth interrupted, "We're not certain, but we think women from Aqua and Green mating with men from Earth created a series of events that ultimately resulted in children with telepathy and telekinesis powers that you saw Marie exhibit. It may also be possible for any future pairings between our races to repeat this same result, but that's pure speculation on my part."

Admiral Speer asked Science Officer Tebo, "What do you think about the powers demonstrated here today and previously?"

"Sir, It boggles the mind. They are not making magic and the telepaths are obviously using their minds to do these amazing feats. We need to be part of this effort to defeat the Xones and even if we don't fully understand what their telepaths are doing, we should support them in any way we can."

Admiral Speer turned to his civilian leaders and said, "Gentlemen, this alliance between Paradise and these talented military officers who represent three new human systems is strongly recommended without reservation. We need to be part of this combined effort to defeat the Xones."

An older woman stood and gave Admiral Bloodworth a short bow, which he returned. "Admiral Bloodworth, my name is Kristina Lor. I'm the elected President of Paradise and I wish to ask some questions about the society on your native planet Earth before giving you my approval?"

"We have a representative from each of our planets here and we are open to any question you may make."

"At present I'm only interested in Earth. You appear to have a family dominated command structure. Your mother and father command your First Fleet, you the Third Fleet. Who commands Second Fleet, another family member?"

Adam smiled, as he replied, "No, my father selected his best captain for that position. On Earth the land mass is divided among many different countries, many with different languages. Our early history is full of wars among the various countries that eventually resulted in two world wars where many died. The last world war ended with the explosion of nuclear weapons. Many believed we would have eventually destroyed ourselves if not for the arrival of the Katz. To fight the Xones, Earth joined together under a common flag of a United Earth, the same flag that Captain Totty saluted when she came aboard the Enterprise. My father came from the United States, my mother from Germany, and the Admiral for Second Fleet is from Russia."

"What criterion was used to select you and your wife for Third Fleet?"

"My wife is the daughter of the Star Fleet leaders of Aqua. They were the first to experience the unusual mating experience. When I first met my wife we too went through the same experience, although it was more severe. Our daughter apparently received her powers through this mating. My wife and I trained very hard to achieve command of a vessel together because we can't be separated without severe distress, perhaps even death."

"I see. Do the parents of the other Psi children have similar stories?"

"There is only one other child, and yes the situation is the same. The last Psi member is over ninety years old, but she is regressing in age and now appears to be in her mid forties. She is the grandmother of the last child mentioned and the older sister of my mother. So in this regard we are indeed a family organization."

President Lor slowly smiled at Adam. "I think I'm finally beginning to understand why you believe your obtaining these powers was brought about through someone's plan. Maybe even the so-called Ancients. I vote for Paradise joining this alliance, but there should be a clause for the sharing of technical knowledge. I'm sure we can both benefit from such a agreement."

* * *

When the Third Fleet left the Paradise system it included three Paradise Cruisers as they retraced their way back to the Green System, and after a short conference stop they continued on to the Earth system.

Paradise Admiral Seth Speer traveled aboard the Enterprise because his own ships didn't have quarters for one of his rank and he didn't want to displace one of his captains. He was particularly interested in the design of the fleets Heavy Battle Cruisers and the ease of converting their ships construction to build them. Basically, all they needed to do was swap out the engine designs.

When the fleets arrived in Earth orbit, Admiral Speer was struck by how much the beautiful water planet below them resembled his own planet.

Admiral Bloodworth commed Star Fleet headquarters immediately upon entering Earth's system informing them of finding another human planet system that wished to join their alliance with the three planets.

* * *

After their arrival in orbit above Earth the Star Fleet Council asked Admiral Bloodworth to return to Star Fleet Headquarters with the Paradise officials for discussions involving their Star Systems. Admiral Bloodworth and his Fleet Captain, escorted Paradise Admiral Speer aboard one of Enterprises shuttles to the Paradise Cruiser Discovery to add Captain Totty and her Science Officer Tebo to the delegation to meet with the Star Fleet Board of Directors.

The Board included twelve elected members from the major countries of Earth where three members rotated every three years. The Speaker was reelected or changed every third year, but could not stay in this position longer than six years. Generally, the countries selection was their President.

Paradise officers were not adversely affected by Earth's gravity, as it was only slightly different than their own planet. As they left the shuttle, the dry air of the Arizona desert struck them as they made their way to their transportation to fleet headquarters.

When they arrived at the Board Room Admiral Bloodworth introduced his guests to the assembled Board in the Universal language everyone now understood. The Speaker stood and introduced himself and the other members of the Board.

He then gazed at the military officers from yet another human type that was allied with them in the fight against the Xones. "Admiral Speer, your uniform is slightly different from what I'm accustomed, but otherwise we are the same, human's fighting against an alien race bent on destroying us. Our fleets have destroyed thousands of their ships, yet they continue to pursue us like a moth to a flame. From the reports sent by Admiral Bloodworth, your first engagement with them left them with such losses that they withdrew. We would be happy to share with your race anything that you may desire to help you fight our common enemy."

Admiral Speer smiled as he stepped forward and motioned toward his other officers present. "Captain Totty and her Science Officer where present at our first battle with the Xones, but later they were even more impressed when they encountered your battleship, the UES Enterprise when it came through a warp gate in front of them. A ship like they had never seen before, a ship almost twice the size of their own ships. Yet, what happened next was almost unbelievable when an alien human military officer suddenly appeared on her bridge without any warning and stood silently with a hand held up in an apparent sign of peace. Using hand gestures and drawings she convinced Captain Totty that they were friendly and wanted to talk. This led to where we are now."

The Speaker looked at Bloodworth with a raised brow, "We were not told how this first meeting was arranged, but we are aware of our Psi Departments abilities. I would have liked to see how this first contact happened."

"It all occurred in the minds of those present on the Bridge of the Discovery. Recordings didn't see anything except how our people reacted. I was reluctant to believe what was reported until Commander Bales gave me a personal demonstration of her abilities."

"Admiral Speer, is there anything specific that our Star System can provide before you return to your system?"

"Yes, I would like to leave Captain Karisse Totty with your Third Fleet so that she could observe your military battle strategy's when not using Commander Bales abilities."

Admiral Bloodworth replied, "I foresee no problem with that request. Does she come with her three cruisers?"

Totty replied, "Yes, maybe we can provide additional help as well."

"Yes, I'm curious how your ships were able to destroy so many of the Xones in your first encounter with them."

Later, while aboard their shuttle returning to their respective ships, Karrie asked Karisse, "Are you planning on taking shore leave on Earth before returning to the war zone?"

"I would like to try your island resorts to see how they compare with our own, but what about the language barrier?"

"They all speak Universal now because of the large number of space crews taking shore leaves, so that shouldn't be a problem. I'll also arrange a credit card for any who take leave from your ships, which you can reimburse us when we are next in Paradise."

CHAPTER 31

Third Fleet approached the warp gate where they previously encountered the Xones and sent a probe through to check for any activity. Admiral Bloodworth commed the Paradise ships to follow the Enterprise through the gate if he decided to enter the next system. When the probes message torpedo returned, six missiles immediately followed it through the gate.

The Enterprises lasers soon made short work of the enemy missiles. The probe's sensors found a enemy ship posted near each gate and three loose formations totaling 120 ships located near the half way point from each gate.

Bloodworth sent six missiles through the gate at the departing Xones ship before ordering the Enterprise through the gate. The only thing remaining of the ship that fired at them through the gate was an expanding debris field.

When the Discovery arrived, he commed Captain Totty asking, "Do you have any ideas on handling the large Xones fleets?"

"My three ships each have a broadside of twelve missiles, while your battleship can fire forty. Your nine Heavy Battle Cruisers each have a broadside of 20 missiles for a total of 256 missiles, that's more than two missiles for each enemy ship. If we staggered our fire and programmed the missiles to turn-off after 60,000 miles and turn back on when they are 30,000 from the target, then by the time the last missiles reach them there might not be any Xones ships left."

"Captain Totty I didn't know that your missiles were programmable?"

"After my discussions with you I had all our missiles adapted to conform with yours."

"Very good, after all my fleet is through the gate I'll comm them to conform to your plan. You have the honor of firing first, my escort next, and the Enterprise will fire last."

Later, when all ships were in firing position, Admiral Bloodworth ordered the Paradises three ships to fire their broadsides, followed after a three-minute break the nine ship escort fired their broadsides, and finally after another similar break, the Enterprise fired its broadside.

The Enterprises tech officer calculated that the first missiles would arrive on target in six hours and 22 minutes if the target failed to move. However, the missile's proximity sensors would turn their engines back on if the missiles came within 5,000 miles of the enemy.

Three hours later the Xones fleets started moving toward them at 2gs, while the computers calculated where they would now meet. Bloodworth commed his supporting ships with the new on target time of two hours and twenty-eight minutes.

When the clock was down to ten minutes sensors picked up their first explosion, followed quickly by several more, and then another pause for the largest volley of 180 missiles to arrive. Suddenly, the Xones ships seemed to explode with a seemingly continuous flare.

Sensors showed only twenty Xones ships staggering past the killing field behind them when the final forty missiles arrived among them and then they vanished from the fleet's sensors.

Admiral Bloodworth commed his fleet with a "Well done!"

He then ordered Third Fleet to continue on toward the Paradise System. Admiral Speer transferred to one of his Home Fleet ships before the combined fleet continued on through the second gate.

Before transiting the gate at the normal 2gs, Bloodworth sent probes through and awaited the results. The messages returned with no activity for 2gs or 3gs, but 4gs showed substantial activity within the system. A large group totaling at least 500 ships was apparently taking on reaction mass from a Gas Giant Planet, which would make them Xones. Other ships were massed around both warp gates in either an ambush tactic or making preparations to leave the system. The enemy presence in the system totaled over 1,000 ships.

Bloodworth commed all ships Captains to meet aboard the Enterprise to plan their response. Once everyone was aboard in the conference room and the graphics of the activity within the system displayed, Bloodworth asked for comments.

Paradise Captain Totty said, "Obviously, with over 1,000 ships disbursed throughout the system we couldn't insert enough ships into the system to effectively fight them before our ships would be overwhelmed. Are your two telepaths strong enough to handle all those ships?"

"Marie, you know your limits better than anyone. Can you do it?"

"I don't know, let me think on it. How many ships are near this gate and how far away are they?"

The tech officer replied, "Sir, I count at least 200 ships near this gate at various distances from 2,000 to 10,000 miles."

"How many are within Laser range of this gate?"

"Sir, there are six ships within their Laser range." She then marked the graphic display red for those ships.

"Captain, can you kill those six as we come through the gate?"

Captain Karrie Bloodworth walked up to the display judging the angles the Enterprises Laser Cannons had to make the shots. "We'll only have four cannons initially available for the shots as we come through the gate, maybe two more if we have the time before they fire. I'm eighty percent sure we can kill them before they fire at us."

"Okay, that gives me a little time to acquire the minds of those near this gate, hopefully before they launch missiles. Captain, can your Lasers take out any they may launch before I can work on their minds?"

"At this range I'm going to use all my Lasers to fire at everyone close to the Enterprise, this should include any stray missiles heading in my direction."

"Good, that will play into the illusion I'm going implant in their minds. If this works, Tyler and I will slowly start to expand the Laser blast, but once all the ships here are destroyed we'll quickly expand the illusion of the blast to all of the other ships in the system."

Admiral Bloodworth asked, "Marie how sure are you that this is going to work?"

She gave her father a faint smile. "100 percent, if we survive the first ten minutes."

"Captains, if you don't get word from me within an hour, send through a probe to determine what's going on. If the worst happens, spread the alarm here to kill any Xones ships that attempt to enter through this gate."

* * *

Forty-five minutes later a message torpedo appeared through the warp gate notifying everyone that it was now safe to enter the next system. The Paradise cruiser Discovery was the first to make the transit where Captain Totty's sensors first noted the huge battleship Enterprise stopped about 10,000 miles from the gate, surrounded by the debris of what appeared to be hundreds of Xones ships.

Totty received a comm from Admiral Bloodworth, "Welcome to my battlefield. The battle still continues around the system's gas giant and the area around the next gate, but for the moment this is a safe area. Sensors show that some of the Xones ships strayed too close to the gravity well of the giant planet in their efforts to escape the huge laser blast they see heading in their direction. My Tech Officer estimates that the battle will be over in about 1.5 hours. The only survivors will be some of the Xones ships near the next warp gate that may be able to transit before this ends."

The Green Home Fleet messaged their Admiral about the big battle the Enterprise fought against the Xones in the adjacent system, who quickly notified his government before bringing a delegation to study the after effects of the battle.

After reaching the site of the battle the delegation transferred to the Enterprise for a first hand report about the battle. Captain Karrie Bloodworth arranged for a graphic display of the action from the moment the Enterprise entered the system until thirty hours later when all activity ceased.

Admiral Speer of the Paradise system asked, "Admiral Bloodworth, I understand that you initially estimated the system contained over a thousand Xones ships including about 200 ships near this gate. Those are odds that most military men would think staggering, yet you persevered."

Bloodworth answered, "Yes, but I was more concerned with the number of Xones ships within Laser range of the gate. That was the key factor in my decision to do battle with the Xones. Normally, I would have backed off and observed the activity, which was very unusual for the Xones. However, they were inside this system for a reason – probably a staging spot for dispersal to systems where we have fought battles before."

"So, you deemed breaking up this concentration was worth the risk?"

"Yes, there were only six enemy ships within laser range of the gate and after carefully judging how many Laser Cannons the Enterprise would be able to fire at the six Xones ships within thirty seconds after emerging from the gate, I believed the risk was justified."

Admiral Speer asked, "I'm curious, did any of those six get off a shot?"

"Yes, one did; however, it was hurried and missed the Enterprise entirely before his ship was destroyed. All six ships were destroyed within thirty-five seconds of the Enterprise entering the system. It took forty seconds for the Enterprise to fully emerge into the system and by that time we were fully engaged with the nearby enemy ships with lasers and missiles."

"Unbelievable! When did your Psi people engage?"

"Immediately after they were physically inside the system. Without their help we could not have defeated the enemy forces at the gate and later within the system."

"Did any Xones survive?"

"Yes, not many – maybe less than ten ships. They may spread helpful rumors about this battle throughout their ranks. We will have to wait until we meet them again to judge just how much."

Speer shook his head in disbelief before asking, "Did you ever get a true count on the number of enemy ships in the system?"

"Not really. I think the original estimate of 1,000 ships is close. I've got three of my Heavy Battle Cruisers standing guard at each of the gates to prevent any more Xones from entering this solar system. After we leave you should continue this for at least a year."

"How about our own system, what should we guard against?"

"The Xones only use the original Katz design, but the Katz have now adopted our Heavy Battle Cruiser design as their standard, so you can be certain any ships you find of the original design are going to be Xones. Another item of interest is that the Xones ships have a top speed of 3gs, but they use it sparingly."

"Admiral Bloodworth, what are your plans now?"

"I'm going to sample the far gates destinations and try to determine the Xones home planet."

"I wish you well and if you're willing I'd like Captain Totty's squadron to continue with you until you return to Paradise's system."

"She's been an asset to Third Fleet and I welcome her addition to our efforts against the Xones."

The Paradise Admiral and delegation left the Enterprise and the Third Fleet sailed toward the system's other warp gate. After sampling the gate at speeds 2g through 4g, the only system with any activity was at 2gs, and that was one small fleet of eight ships heading toward their gate at a distance of 320,000 miles.

Admiral Bloodworth commed the fleets, informing them that the Enterprise would transit the gate and provide cover for them when they followed. After the Enterprise emerged into the occupied system its sensors verified that the approaching ships were Xones.

There was no reaction from the approaching ships for another five minutes until one of Third Fleets escorts entered behind the Enterprise, at which time they immediately turned ship trying to reverse course to avoid battle.

Adam turned to his daughter and asked, "Marie, what reactions from the Xones crew are you getting?"

"There is much fear now that they recognize that we are a battleship with an escort. I also get something else…still fear, but I believe they are planning an ambush at the next gate, but now think they may have made a mistake with the appearance of escorts adding to our force."

"Comm, relay a message to the fleet to expect an ambush as we near the next gate."

"Marie, would you prefer to attack now or later when the larger force appears?"

"Let's delay for a few hours, we may have an opportunity to learn something from the crew here."

Admiral Bloodworth was happy that he replenished his missiles used in the last battle now that he was about to face another battle against unknown odds. He commed the Paradise ship Discovery and gave her what information they had gathered from the minds of the Xones and his plan, before asking if she had any thoughts regarding the coming battle?

Captain Totty commed her reply, "Sir, is this the normal behavior from the Xones? An ambush from a warp gate where it would take considerable time for their fleet to assemble?"

Bloodworth commed his reply, "Very good Captain. I now believe they must have set their trap with mines. I'll see if I can use their ships to clear the way through the mines."

"Commander Bales, you may now begin your attack. I hope to drive them through their own mines if possible."

* * *

Marie looked at her husband, *Tyler let's start with a large laser blast from this ship. They are about 260,000 miles ahead of us so we have room for it to expand somewhat before it gets there. On the count of three...one, two, three!*

The six enemy ships immediately tried to shift their positions and increased their speed to 3gs, but there was no place they could go as the Laser blast quickly gained on their position. Thirty minutes later the blast appeared to the enemy as about to catch and engulf their ships 100,000 miles from the warp gate. This was apparently where they set their minefield as the Xones ships started to explode.

Captain Bloodworth said to her tactical officer, "Mark that minefield on the chart and when we get close enough, use our lasers to clear out any remaining mines."

Later, when the fleet reached the next warp gate, Admiral

Bloodworth sampled the systems available for entry speeds of 2gs through 4gs. Again, the only system with activity was at 2gs speed, that showed two large fleets totaling twenty ships each who were 310,000 miles away and heading in their direction at 2gs speed.

Admiral Bloodworth commed his fleet and informed them he was going to try a new tactic. He was going to position the Enterprise and two Heavy Battle Cruisers 5,000 miles from the gate and have the cruisers alternate destroying the Xones ships as they enter the system through the gate. After the first two Heavy's kill five ships they will be replaced by other HCs. While the transfer is being completed the Enterprise will assume sentry duties and the clearing of the debris field. He estimated their arrival time to be about eleven hours to reach this gate.

CHAPTER 32

The Third Fleet was back in orbit above its home planet Earth. Admiral Adam Bloodworth and his wife, Captain Karrie Bloodworth were ordered to appear before the Star Fleet Board after an absence of over three years from Earth. Their comm report generated such an uproar that the Board wanted to hear from them directly.

When they arrived at the headquarters building they brought with them an independent witness, Katz Admiral Gamma Killa. Board Speaker Joseph McLarry from Great Britain brought the meeting to order.

"Admiral Bloodworth you've brought exceptionally good news back from your first battle cruise. Not only has your fleet destroyed over 10,000 Xones ships, but you also have found the long sought after home planet of the Xones. Admiral Killa, you were a witness to these extraordinary events. Did you think you would live to see this great victory?"

Admiral Killa bowed her head slightly before speaking, "I suspected that the Third Fleet under the leadership of Admiral Bloodworth would accomplish much when they encountered a system that held over 1,000 Xones ships and using only the

Battleship Enterprise they eradicated most of the ships inside the system. Those few who survived escaped through the other systems warp gate."

Speaker McLarrys' mouth was open in surprise before he blurted out, "How was this possible?"

"I'll let Admiral Bloodworth tell you this story. Even though I witnessed this great victory it still boggles my mind."

Adam began his story of the Star Fleets most epic battle to date. "Speaker, there were over 200 enemy ships guarding the gate I was going to enter, but only six Xones ships were within laser cannon range. After analysis of their positions we thought that enough of the Enterprises Laser Cannons would be available to destroy these ships as we emerged from the gate. We brought along video graphic of the battle if you would like to see how the battle progressed?"

"Yes, that would be helpful. How long will it take to setup?"

"It's ready now, please start the program!"

Admiral Bloodworth watched this replay several times in the past, so he now watched the faces of the Board as the Enterprise moved into the system firing its Laser Cannons as each cannon came through the gate, catching the Xones completely by surprise except for one hurried laser shot that missed the Enterprise completely.

"My Psi Department personnel started their attack as soon as they emerged into the system. The Xones reactions are mainly because of the illusion created by their attack coupled with the Enterprises actual Laser attack."

The Speaker asked, "Admiral, how long did it take to clear all the Xones ships from your gate area?"

"Not long, maybe twenty minutes. The Psi Department's efforts caused at least half the ships to leave the gate area to try to avoid the illusion of a huge Laser Blast heading toward them."

"I see from your display that these ships appear to be heading for the group around the systems other gate. The illusion must have been terrifying because those around that gate seem to be preparing for an exit through that gate."

"Yes, you may even see that in their rush to leave some collisions are occurring, which is bottling up their efforts to transit through the gate."

"Admiral, how many enemy ships actually escaped through the gate?"

"Not many, but at least six, because we encountered that many later when we followed them through the gate. They attempted to lead us into an ambush near the system's next gate by laying a minefield in our path to the gate. I'm guessing at least one other ship was sent ahead to warn others of our coming."

"Admiral, what happened next?"

"Third Fleet passed through four star systems before reaching a system that we later learned was the Xones home. At every system we passed through we were met with a larger defense force in an attempt to stop our progress, until we passed through the third system. Only one Xones ship stood before the gate into their home system. Commander Marie Bales informed me that someone of importance was aboard this ship, perhaps their leader based on the awe they gave him."

"I asked Marie if it was possible to project her and my image aboard their ship in an attempt to discuss their surrender. She agreed and suddenly we were aboard their ship facing their leader/negotiator. At our arrival he cowered back from our images in fear, and before we could even attempt to communicate, he killed himself with a blade. His crew followed his example and soon everyone aboard the ship was dead."

"When we sent a probe through the gate there were no ships near the gate, but expecting some kind of defense the Enterprise was ready to use its Laser Cannons to clear an expected minefield when it entered the system. However, no defensive actions had been taken to impede our arrival. Sensors discovered only sporadic ship traffic in the system that showed no reaction to our arrival. Later, we found no live Xones within the system and speculated that they all died by suicide."

"So, the Xones destroyed themselves rather than surrender to their victors?"

"Yes Sir. Have you heard anything from the other two fleets? It's been almost six months since we left the Xones System."

"Both fleets recently entered our system and commed a request to meet with the Board. I assume they bring news about the deaths of the Xones. Admiral, I congratulate you and your fleet on this great victory against the Xones. Please return to your ship and await further instructions until after I meet with the Fleet Admiral."

Upon their return to the Enterprise, Admiral Bloodworth commed his ships "First and Second Fleets are now in-system and we are ordered to stand down until we receive instructions from the Fleet Admiral. Normal maintenance and orbit supplies may be conducted, anything else will need my prior approval."

When Fleet Admiral Eric Bloodworth arrived in Earth orbit he commed all ships of Star Fleets Battle Groups to send their Admirals and Captains to meet with him aboard the UES Hulk the next morning at 09:00 hours.

Later, at the appointed time Fleet Admiral Eric Bloodworth stood before the assembled heads of the victorious Earth based Battle Groups. "Ladies and Gentlemen, I'm sure you are now aware of the tremendous victory Third Fleet has achieved under the leadership of Admiral Adam Bloodworth. This was achieved largely with the assistance of members of our new Psi Department. Third Fleet also discovered another human civilization in the Paradise System, which aided him in defeating the Xones. Admiral Adam Bloodworth, please come forward and receive the accolades you richly deserve."

Adam Bloodworth stood and walked to where his father stood and they embraced each other, to the loud applause from the Captains of the battle fleet ships. Fleet Admiral Eric Bloodworth then turned to his audience. "My fellow officers, we now face the prospect of peace. Peace is something new to our way of thinking, but still it's a challenging prospect. We must face it and learn how to make it work for us. Trade between our four systems is now possible without worrying about the Xones presence. We still must guard our systems against another possible threat, but until we discover such a possibility we no longer need a battle fleet. Those ships not needed for a Home Fleet should be saved for just such a contingency."

"I've talked to our Star Fleet Board and until they make their final decisions all ship's will start making normal shore leave assignments. I expect some transfers to other Star Systems Home Fleets as assessments of need occur. I also expect convoy duty for some Cruisers between Star Systems; however, for many there will no longer be a ship for you to serve on. Those with seniority will have first pick for those ships still in service. Captain's, please make appointments with me to make your needs heard."

EPILOGUE

A year later the Earth's Star Fleet was finally settling into a peacetime Fleet. All the battleships were kept on duty as Home Fleet, as either active or reserve. The reserve BS's will replace the active ships every five years to maintain their current status. The twenty-two Heavy Battle Cruisers were divided up into eight to active Earth's Home Fleet, and seven each to the Home Fleets of Aqua and Green Systems. Those ships sent to other systems included some crew by Earth volunteers who wanted to remain aboard a star ship.

The Psi Department was split up according to the Star System they were from. Celena Eiberger and her fated mate were finally married and were now part of the Green Star Fleet.

Former Fleet Admiral Bloodworth and his wife, Hanna, retired from Star Fleet to their new home in Hawaii. Their famed son Adam was named Fleet Admiral, but since there was now only a Home Fleet it was largely a title position overseeing the disposition of Earth's Star Ships.

THE END

ABOUT THE AUTHOR

Hugh A. Flowers retired after almost thirty years with the Federal Deposit Insurance Corporation as a bank examiner. He now spends his time reading and writing novels and short stories and traveling the world.

OTHER PUBLICATIONS BY FLOWERS

The Salvation Trilogy
Salvation
Angel's Triumph
In Perpetuity

Other
The Adam Project
Emergence
Reclamation
Oklahoma Tomboy

Katz Series
The Katz Solution